THE LADY JEWEL DIVINER

BOOK 1 IN THE LADY DIVINER SERIES

ROSALIE OAKS

Parkerville
PRESS

CONTENTS

IN WHICH A SPINSTER VAMPIRE INTRODUCES HERSELF TO ELINOR

*D*iamonds or cream tea? Miss Elinor Avely contemplated this difficult choice in the abstract as she stood in her new sitting room, holding two invitations in her hands. She concluded (rather quickly) that, in her case, fresh clotted cream would theoretically trump diamonds. Cream was *always* enjoyable, whereas diamonds were simply distracting for one such as she.

Cream tea, then.

Elinor pursed her lips. However, in this instance the invitation was issued by the Countess of Beresford, which made the matter more complicated.

Placing the thick paper on the dresser, Elinor eyed the red sealing wax. Tea with the Countess of Beresford would be … fraught. The countess was the earl's mother, after all, and it wasn't good etiquette to receive comestibles from a family when you had blackened their name with scandal.

Elinor sighed. That left her the diamond hunt.

The other letter, with its provocative proposition, was still in her other hand. She considered the foolscap with its scrawled handwriting, knowing what her answer *ought* to be. She certainly had not exiled herself, her brother, and her mother to the wilds of remote Devon so she could use her special gift to search for lost diamonds. That was the kind of thing that had landed Elinor in trouble in the first place.

So, no diamonds either. It was going to be a sorry existence, out here in Devon. Unless Napoleon invaded; that might make things more interesting.

She put the letter down next to the countess's invitation. Then she paused. Better to keep the letter about diamonds out of sight, especially from her mother, who was always so anxious to keep Elinor's gift a secret. Opening a Radcliffe novel, she slipped the letter between the pages – Mother wouldn't dare be seen opening *The Mysteries of Udolpho* – and closed the book with a snap.

Unfortunately, out of sight was not out of mind.

Elinor looked around the sitting room of their cottage, trying to be grateful for the refuge. It was on the edge of known civilisation, but at least their new residence was cosy and warm. She sank onto an armchair and looked out the window. Outside, the view was barren: the lonesome horizon of the Devon coastline, with hills hunched against ocean gales.

Out of habit, she was dressed for dinner in a high-waisted pale sage gown, one which she had purchased in London because it suited her honey-blonde hair and hazel eyes. Of course, they wouldn't receive any callers here at Casserly Cottage. In a way, Elinor was glad, for it gave her time to recover from the London debacle. Regrettably, it also gave her too much time to think about the earl.

The Earl of Beresford wasn't the handsomest man she'd ever met, she reflected, but he had the broadest shoulders and the most striking grey eyes. Was that the sum of his attraction? There was, of course, his nicely tapered waist to consider, his intelligent sense of humour, and his utter disregard for debutantes. All of which, somehow, made him irresistible. A pity she had managed to drag his name through the mud – though she was sure the Earl of Beresford would recover his reputation more quickly than she would.

Pressing her lips together, Elinor decided that a divination *would* be a good distraction. Would it do any harm to see, for curiosity's sake, if there were any diamonds hidden nearby? Mother need not know she had used her gift only briefly. Elinor's brother, Peregrine, was out walking, and the two servants – a housemaid and a cook – were busy cleaning up after dinner, while Mother read upstairs.

Elinor crossed to the window and peered outside. Between two hills was a stretch of rough sea on which a distant ship battled the waves. The sky, however, was glorious: piles and swirls of clouds, reflecting the last of the sun. Momentarily, she swept her inner sense over the scene below, as far as she could reach. No diamonds. With a shrug, she closed off that part of her mind and leaned desultorily against the edge of the window.

A shadow of a bat flitted across the garden. Elinor raised her hand to pull the curtains shut and saw a white, swooping barn owl hurtle out of the blackness. Catching her breath, she watched the owl's lethal power as it hunted the bat.

The white shape of the owl veered suddenly upwards. Then, as she watched, a small black shape shot out of the gloom and thudded into the window.

There was a horrible *thwack* and it dropped like a stone.

Elinor murmured in distress and bent to look at the creature that lay sprawled on the wooden sill. She blinked. It appeared to be pale white, not black as she had thought, and more like a tangle of limbs than a tangle of wings. She paused, and quickly snatched the iron key out of the dresser door. Her brother would laugh, but now Elinor was armed to her satisfaction. Slowly, she opened the window.

A tiny, white face lay against the wood, partially obscured by an upflung arm and a swirl of black hair. Elinor drew a breath. The creature was a girl, or woman, no larger than Elinor's hand. Furthermore, the woman was completely naked. Elinor shivered. The evening was cool, so she hastily pulled out a linen handkerchief to throw over the little person. As Elinor did so, the creature's eyes fluttered open.

"Arrggh. Cursed owls." She blinked at Elinor with deep blue eyes and tried to sit up. "Good evening."

"Good evening." Elinor was glad to hear her own voice was firm.

"I apologise for this irregular visit." The creature glanced down and pulled the linen closer around herself. "And for my lack of accoutrement."

Elinor gathered herself, though her heart was beating rapidly. At least this was a distraction from jewel divining. "Do you require some help?"

"I am a little indisposed," admitted the miniature lady. Her accent was odd, with a faint trace of French, but it spoke of noble breeding. "I will recover if I rest a while."

"Would you like to come inside? It will be warmer."

The lady spotted the iron key in Elinor's hand and her expression suddenly sharpened. "What is that? Do you mistake me for the fae?"

Embarrassed, Elinor hastily hid the key in the folds of her skirt.

"I tell you I am no such thing," snapped the lady.

"I apologise. I was not sure what kind of – er – personage was – er – calling upon me, and I thought it best to be cautious." Elinor paused, hoping the creature would enlighten her.

"Well, I am not fae. If you don't believe me, put that key against me. I won't shriek and die."

"I am sure that is not necessary," said Elinor, though she hesitated. Everyone knew the fae were notoriously given to trickery. That is, if they even existed.

The linen handkerchief rustled in indignation. "It is necessary, because you think I am trying to fool you."

Elinor narrowed her eyes. "If putting the key upon you will calm your nerves, I will do it." She held the iron up and moved it towards the little woman, who glared at her but showed no other signs of distress. Reluctantly, Elinor placed the key against her tiny hand.

The woman raised her brows and pursed her lips.

"Very well," said Elinor. "I am satisfied you are not fae. However, I might as well tell you – I don't believe in the fae."

"Oh, is that so? Lucky you. They are nasty creatures, rude and ill-bred."

"Will you tell me your name?"

"I am Miss Aldreda Zooth. I do apologise for the lack of proper introduction. Normally I would obtain one via my queen, but she is in France. I hope." A frown crossed the pale face.

"I am Miss Elinor Avely."

They stared at each other in the twilight. Eventually Miss Zooth smiled. "You seem singularly calm for someone who does not believe in the fae."

5

"You have just assured me that you are not fae."

"No, but I am a vampiri."

"I am afraid I do not know what that is."

Miss Zooth looked cross again. "Hmph. We are magical and useful. And polite, even if my current state of dress indicates otherwise."

Elinor cleared her throat. "Please do come in, Miss Zooth. May I assist you?"

The miniature lady tried to stand, clutching the handkerchief around her, but her legs were too weak. She collapsed in a heap again. "Perhaps if you carry me? I promise not to bite."

The little face turned away, eyes closed. Elinor felt a stab of pity. "Shall I gather you up?"

Miss Zooth nodded, and Elinor carefully scooped her up. She was light as a bird and seemed oddly frail. Elinor bore her into the house and placed her on a settee, pulling the primrose coloured shawl from her shoulders to tuck around her visitor. Miss Zooth tried to sit but struggled to hold herself up.

"Can I fetch you some tea? Some food?"

"Please."

Elinor strode quickly to the kitchen, where she fetched the teapot and cups herself rather than disturb the servants – who would be doubly disturbed if they saw the impossible Miss Zooth. She snatched up a bread roll and a chunk of cheese. What cup would serve? After a moment's thought she detoured to her sewing basket to obtain a thimble.

Miss Zooth accepted it gratefully, though it was more like a large mug in her hands. She took dainty sips and eyed the bread and cheese.

"I don't suppose you have any meat?" she asked. "I

know it is rude to request it, but when I am this weak it is the best thing for me."

"I can find some corned beef. I believe we have some in the kitchen." Elinor stood again.

Miss Zooth shook her head, looking embarrassed. "Do you have any ... raw meat?"

"I am not sure," said Elinor. She looked at her curiously. "I don't know what the cook has in store. Her shopping day is tomorrow, so I fear we may be out of fresh meat."

Her visitor's shoulders sank a little. "I may have to leave soon, to find some."

"You are not fit to go anywhere." Elinor paused. "I am curious as to what sort of creature requires raw meat."

Miss Zooth lifted her head and looked Elinor squarely in the eye. "I require the blood of others to live. It is an unfortunate aspect of my nature."

Elinor considered this. "You practice ... dark arts?"

"No doubt you eat meat," said the vampiri sharply. "It is not so different. I merely need it fresh. With – er – blood."

"What kind of blood?" Elinor had an uneasy feeling that humans were not excluded. She had vague recollections of such beings from old stories. In fact, she had recently seen a stone depiction of something similar: a small woman with bat wings.

Miss Zooth currently had no wings, however, and Elinor had not imagined that a dark creature would have deep blue eyes, a pert nose, and finely shaped hands. The vampiri's black hair curled softly over her shoulders, and her skin was a delicate white, almost translucent. She seemed rather more vulnerable than terrifying.

"I can make do with sheep," said Miss Zooth. "There are

plenty of those around here. Or cows, if I have to. I don't like to take from small creatures, as it leaves them weak." She brightened. "I don't suppose you have a large dog, do you?"

Elinor blinked. "No, I'm afraid I cannot offer you a dog."

Miss Zooth looked disappointed.

"What about a cat?" suggested Elinor. "There is a cat who lives here." The large cream-coloured tom – named Samuel – lazed around the garden during the day and conducted mysterious business at night. He and Elinor were becoming friends, so she hesitated to offer him as Miss Zooth's snack. But the health of a small lady surely warranted more than a cat's dignity.

"I am afraid I would leave a cat somewhat incommoded," said Miss Zooth. "Besides, cats generally don't like me, and they are hard to catch." She swallowed and sank back into the shawl. "I fear I am at rather a low ebb. I must leave soon and find something."

Elinor regarded her thoughtfully. Then the front door opened, and Peregrine's voice floated through the house.

"Elinor? You'll never guess what I just saw."

She moved quickly to the sitting room door, blocking the entrance. "What, brother?"

2

IN WHICH A FAVOUR IS GRANTED

*P*erry came up to her, his blond hair dishevelled from the sea winds, his cheeks aglow. He was two years younger than Elinor but sometimes it seemed more.

"A little schooner, battling the waves. Did you see it? I am sure it is a smuggling boat. Who else would brave this weather?"

"You think every boat is a smuggling boat. They would not be so obvious."

"Why not? There is no one here to stop them, really." Perry pushed past her into the sitting room, and Elinor turned, her heart in her mouth. The shawl on the settee was rearranged slightly, with no vampiri in sight. Elinor hastened over and perched next to it, to prevent Perry from sitting on her visitor.

He walked over to the dresser and picked up the invitation. She cursed herself for leaving it out. She had thought to hide Lord Treffler's letter from her mother, but had forgotten to hide the countess's invitation from her brother.

"Ho, what is this?" Perry perused it and looked up.

"Tea with the countess? Does Lord Beresford know about this, do you think?

"I imagine not," said Elinor repressively.

There was no chance the Earl of Beresford would be at his mother's house. He would still be in London with everyone else, finishing off the Season, going to balls, routs, and masquerades. He was looking for a bride – at his mother's appeal – and his tall figure, title, and money meant he would easily succeed. Beresford was probably at that very moment courting some beauty who would receive his attentions with due reverence. Elinor ignored the twist in her heart at the thought.

Perry shook Lady Beresford's invitation teasingly. "Shall we accept?"

"No."

"Maybe we should."

"No." The countess, Elinor reflected, might not yet have heard the gossip rife in London, and so unknowingly had invited a pariah into her house.

Perry quirked his eyebrow. "You are too proud, Elinor. You don't want to embarrass her ladyship, do you? Maybe she can help us squelch the rumours. All very proper, an invitation to tea with the Countess of Beresford. Might make things a little less ... awkward."

"Awkward is an understatement, Perry. I don't want to ask for her help."

"Maybe she wants to give it."

"The countess has not even met us! She might not even know about what happened in London." Elinor was uncomfortably aware of her invisible listener.

"Oh, she most certainly does know," said Perry. "I'll wager she has received a dozen letters describing it all. She is consumed with curiosity. Poor countess – you should have pity on her."

Elinor smiled. "What is it to be, Perry? Is she to have pity on us, or are we to have pity on her?"

"Both, of course. Also, the missing jewels might be somewhere about there. Good excuse to look around."

"Perry!" Elinor stiffened. "Let us not go into that again. I've told you I won't do it." No need to mention her cursory divination for diamonds that very evening.

Perry raised his eyes heavenwards. "Yes, sister. Though we don't have to look very hard, with you –"

Elinor interrupted to stop him revealing any more. "I don't want to talk about it. This is meant to be a quiet retreat, not an opportunity to become enmeshed in further larks."

Perry shrugged and put the letter down. "Well, tea with the countess won't really be a lark, will it? You never know, Beresford might be there after all." He waggled his eyebrows at Elinor.

Elinor frowned. Beresford did not know where Elinor had gone, and if he did, he certainly would not follow her out to Devon. Nor would he want to have cream tea with her and his mother.

"If he *was* there, it would be even more reason not to go," she said coldly.

"Come now, you're longing to see him again."

"Only to apologise."

"Maybe this will be your chance."

"I am not going to turn up on his country estate unless I am assured he condones it."

Perry shrugged again. "Have it your way. We can stay here in self-imposed exile and be bored to death."

"Not entirely self-imposed," Elinor pointed out. "Now, why don't you fetch a book to read? You can use this time to enrich your mind."

She was being deliberately provocative, and it

worked. "Ha," he scoffed. "My mind doesn't need enriching. I'm destined for the sea, I tell you, and there are no books on a ship."

"Then you should make the most of this time to peruse some educative material," she said, ushering him to the door. Perry grumbled that he wasn't a child anymore but went upstairs to change out of his walking clothes.

Elinor turned back to the settee and spoke to the shawl. "It is clear now. He is gone."

There was no response. With a flash of worry, Elinor stepped closer and gently lifted the yellow cloth. Miss Zooth lay with her eyes closed, very still and white.

"Are you awake? Are you well?"

The dark blue eyes fluttered open. "What year is it?"

Elinor raised her brows. "1804, of course."

Miss Zooth sighed and spoke softly. "I have not eaten for eighty years."

Her voice was so weak Elinor thought she must have misheard. "Pardon me?"

"I have been sleeping. Hibernating." Her head dropped. "I may need to ask a large favour."

Elinor had a sinking feeling. "What is that?"

"Can you fetch me a sheep?"

Elinor laughed. "I'm not bringing a sheep into my sitting room!"

"You could carry me to the sheep."

Elinor examined the tiny face, wondering how much she could trust her. "Did you hear what my brother said?"

Miss Zooth's eyes lifted and held Elinor's own, calm and curious. "About tea with the countess? Or do you mean the jewels? I hope you will tell me all. I think such intrigues are always better shared."

Elinor smiled. "You show vast acumen. Tea with the countess is most certainly an intrigue."

"Sheep first, however. Then we may exchange confidences." The vampiri blinked slowly, her little hands tightening by her side, as if in pain.

Elinor felt sympathy stir within her. Miss Zooth's determined dignity reminded her of her own self. She made a decision. "You could drink from me. I believe that may be customary? You are only small and I imagine you will not take much."

There was a long silence. Worried she had offended, Elinor added, "I hope I have not misspoken."

"No," said Miss Zooth at last. "I am surprised at your offer, so soon. It is very kind. I may have to accept."

"Very well then," said Elinor, rolling up her sleeve. "How do we go about such a thing?"

Still her visitor seemed reluctant. "You do realise this will bond us?"

Elinor dropped her arm. "What do you mean?"

"It is traditional for vampiri to bond with humans in this fashion. I was hoping we could form such an alliance –" Miss Zooth's voice stumbled. "Of course, one exchange will only make a weak bond. You need not fear it. I just want you to be aware of what you are about to do."

Her soft tones trailed away into nothing. Even as Elinor stared, the vampiri seemed to shrink a little, folding in on herself.

"What sort of bond?" Elinor asked warily.

"Merely to help each other; protect one another. You are doing so already, with your kind offer." The vampiri's shoulders hunched. "I offer my assistance to you also, but as I said, the obligation will not last very long."

Elinor swallowed, considered, and finally spoke.

"Very well. You seem to be polite, honest, and in dire need of sustenance. I am not averse to – er – forming an alliance with you." She smiled. "You may find, in fact, that *you* have the worse end of the bargain."

Miss Zooth barely seemed to hear her. "Please, if you will." She gave a weak gesture to Elinor's arm.

Elinor quaked inwardly, in spite of her calm exterior, and held up her wrist to Miss Zooth's mouth. Two tiny pricks stung her skin, and she felt a pulling sensation. Elinor cast her eyes away, not wanting to embarrass her guest. The grip on her wrist grew a bit stronger.

Five minutes passed. Elinor felt a little dreamy, as if she could sit there all day. Her mind wandered to the hills and coves outside, where somewhere lay a treasure chest of jewels, gleaming and glittering. Where could it be? Surely it would do no harm merely to look. She need not tell Lord Treffler if she found them. She could bring them home and report them to the authorities herself. Where would she be hiding, if she were a cache of diamonds? Perhaps in a cave in a cliff ...

Suddenly it was over, and Miss Zooth released her.

"Thank you very much," she said. "A rather vulgar transaction, I know. I am deeply grateful for your trust in me."

"Do you feel better?"

"Much." Indeed, there was new colour in her cheeks, and she was sitting straighter. "Now, we have much to discuss."

"We do?" Elinor's thoughts were still slightly vague. "Yes, how old are you? Did you say you've been sleeping for *eighty years?*"

"I was born in 1660. I am one hundred and forty-four according to your calendar. In vampiri age I am closer to twenty-nine. I am unmarried, and quite the spinster."

"A vampiri on the shelf?" Elinor squinted at her.

"I am not familiar with that idiom," said Miss Zooth, 'but if you mean I am opposed to marriage, yes." She paused. "I note that your brother is about to descend upon us. I must make myself scarce. Thank you again."

And before Elinor could blink twice, Miss Zooth turned into a bat, shrugged off the pale yellow shawl, and flew to the window. Slightly dizzy, Elinor followed and opened the latch, watching as the bat took off into the dusk. So she did have wings after all!

Elinor started, hearing not her brother's, but her mother's voice behind her.

"Are you talking to yourself now?" enquired Mrs Avely.

Elinor turned. Her mother was at the door, neatly dressed as always, her greying blonde hair pulled back tightly, and looking rather more careworn than she had a few weeks ago in London. The cat, Samuel, stalked in past her ankles, his cream-coloured fur bristling and his tail swishing as he glared around the room. Both he and her mother examined Elinor suspiciously.

"Was I talking to myself?" said Elinor. "Perhaps I was."

Mrs Avely looked at her for a long moment, her hands folded in front of her. "Not a habit to cultivate, my dear. If someone heard you muttering to yourself they might think you odd."

Samuel leapt onto the armchair, where Miss Zooth had lain, and hissed.

"Yes, Mother." Elinor glanced nervously at Samuel, hoping his behaviour would not cause any questions. Fortunately, her mother was more concerned with Elinor's own conduct.

"It is important to comport yourself beyond

reproach, so people don't watch you too closely," said her mother carefully. "They might discover your ability."

Elinor sighed. "There is no one out here to watch me."

"Which is why we have moved here." Her mother crossed the room and kissed her cheek. "Now, why don't you go to bed? It has been a wearisome few weeks."

"Yes, Mother," said Elinor. She picked up Samuel, stroking his ruffled fur, and took him upstairs with her, all the while wondering where Miss Zooth had gone.

3

IN WHICH DAYLIGHT PROVES
INSALUBRIOUS

*I*n London, before the Avelys left for Devon, they had received an unexpected and rather unwelcome visitor.

Hearing the carriage pull up, Elinor had assumed it was another acquaintance trying to gain details of the scandal of the Season. Still, she had to repress the hope that it was Beresford calling, giving her the chance to apologise. She pricked her ears, hearing a masculine voice arguing with the butler, who had been told to refuse all callers. The stupid hope caused Elinor to creep to the door of the drawing room and listen more closely.

It was not Beresford's voice.

Instead, Lord Treffler's smooth tones were disputing with the butler. "Please tell Miss Avely that I can be of assistance to her, in her present trial," said his lordship. "It is imperative that I speak with her."

Elinor frowned. What could Lord Treffler mean? She was not in the mood to accept his lordship's favours. Did he think he could somehow arrange the recovery of her reputation? As things stood, it was irrecoverable.

"And her brother, too," added Lord Treffler. "Mr Avely will also be interested in what I have to say."

It was as if he knew Elinor was listening. The reference to her brother made her pause. It was not just she who suffered in this disgrace. And her mother too, packing upstairs, was silent and grim where once she had been calm and content.

Elinor opened the door. "Admit the gentleman, Joles. And call my brother."

Alone in the drawing room with Lord Treffler, she invited him to sit. "To what do we owe the pleasure, Lord Treffler?"

His lordship looked a little uncomfortable at Elinor's direct approach, but then he shifted his narrow, handsome face into a bland expression. "I wish to express my sincere regrets as to what happened last week at the ducal garden party." He paused. "I believe you are innocent of all the claims against you."

"Thank you, my lord." Elinor was at a loss. Surely that could not be the only reason for his visit? And why did Lord Treffler, of all people, believe she wasn't guilty?

He lounged backwards, swinging his quizzing glass. "Also, I have a question for you, Miss Avely. And one for your brother."

Elinor raised a brow. "Yes?"

He examined her face closely. "How did you find that amethyst?"

Elinor noted his use of language but answered carefully. "What is it to you where I found it? I am not at liberty to disclose any details of the whole sorry affair."

"Not *where*," said Lord Treffler. "How."

There was a silence. Elinor stared at him and tried to smooth over her sudden sense of shock. "What do you mean how? I happened to look behind … something … and I found it."

"But why did you look behind … something? How did you know to look there?"

Perry spoke from behind him. "Do not say anything, Elinor."

Lord Treffler turned his head, smiling. "Ah, Mr Avely. Miss Avely has nothing to fear from me. I am merely curious as to her abilities."

"She has no abilities," said Perry sharply, but his quick denial told its own story.

"I think she does," said Lord Treffler. "I think Miss Avely is a jewel diviner."

Elinor's eyes swung to his face in shock, both simulated and real. "A jewel diviner? What, pray, is that?"

"Surely you have heard the old stories? Diviners who can sense the presence of jewels, just like some could sense water, or illness, or lies. It crossed my mind, after the ill-fated garden party, that you may have that special ability. It would explain how you found the amethyst, which one assumes was well hidden."

Perry came to stand by Elinor, watching Lord Treffler suspiciously. "So you don't believe the lies about us?"

"No. Your insults to me that day, Mr Avely, suggested otherwise. So I believe your sister found the jewel, not stole it."

Perry folded his arms and glared. "Elinor found it, but that is the end of it."

His lordship was unruffled. "Miss Avely found it using her unique gift."

Elinor interrupted, taking care to inject scorn into her voice. "Even if such a nonsensical thing were true, what has it to do with you, my lord?"

Lord Treffler leaned back, dropping his quizzing

glass and bringing the tips of his fingers together. "I have a proposition for a jewel diviner."

"We don't want to hear it," said Perry.

"It would, of course, be of great benefit to you both," said Lord Treffler. "And I speak with utmost reverence for these 'nonsensical' abilities which, in my opinion, should be harnessed, not hidden and scorned."

He spoke Elinor's own often-thought wish, but she did not allow herself to be drawn in by his attempt at charm. "You are not being clear, my lord."

"Let me be clear then. There is a cache of jewels, beyond price, that has gone missing somewhere along the coast of Devon. When I heard you are leaving for that very locality, I knew I must talk to you." He smiled lazily. "Somewhere in that county, or the neighbouring one, is a collection of jewellery. Rubies, sapphires, emeralds – but mostly diamonds. I want you to help me find them."

Brother and sister stared at him. Elinor was the first to speak, tempted despite herself, despite all that had happened. "Whose are the jewels?"

"They belong to a variety of French aristocratic families. In their haste to flee the bloodshed, they entrusted their valuables to those who were helping them cross the water to England. Whether by treachery or accident, the jewels have disappeared."

Perry was suspicious. "What do you intend to do with them?"

"Return them to the wretched families, of course." Lord Treffler widened his eyes. "Although I am sure we would be amply rewarded for our pains."

Elinor frowned. She rather suspected Lord Treffler would reward himself as he saw fit.

Perry spoke. "It sounds a noble quest, but an impossible one. The jewels must be long gone by now."

"Rumours say otherwise. Just think – if they are lost at sea, only pure luck will uncover them. But if there is indeed a power of jewel divination …" Lord Treffler turned an admiring gaze on Elinor.

Perry scoffed. "You want to ship my sister out to sea to look for sunken treasure?"

Only after he spoke did Perry realise he had tacitly admitted to Elinor's gift. There was a tense silence.

Lord Treffler smiled. "With your help too, of course, Mr Avely," he said. "I will need manpower to pull them up. Rewards equally shared. As well as the satisfaction of helping destitute families recover the only things left to their names."

Elinor could see Perry was being swayed. She stood. "I'm afraid the answer is no. You have vastly mistaken the case. I cannot help you."

Lord Treffler lowered his voice. "Ah, but you could meet my mother."

Perry let out a snort. Elinor raised her brows. "Your mother, my lord? I doubt she could do much to help us." She moved her hand to ring for the butler.

"She is a gold diviner."

Elinor's breath caught and her eyes flew to Lord Treffler's face. "Pardon me?"

"She can sense the presence of gold. Just like the old diviners of myth."

Elinor stared at him, trying to maintain her composure. Another diviner! Someone else like her, in London no less.

Elinor had never heard of there being others. She had discovered her own gift at the age of nine years old, when she found her mother's ruby earring covered in dust in a crack in the floorboards. Such abilities were thought to be the stuff of fairy tales or ancient myths, and yet here Lord Treffler was claiming his mother could divine too.

Perry objected even as Elinor stayed silent. "If your mother can indeed sense gold, why don't you use her to find this cache of jewels?"

"My mother is elderly, and she is not an adventurous type," said Lord Treffler smoothly. "She has her doubts about the whole venture, and I cannot persuade her to remove to Devon and leap into a boat."

Elinor frowned. "If your mother has doubts, I'm certain she has good reason." She turned away. "We will think about it, Lord Treffler. For now, I must bid you good day."

~

THE NIGHT after she met Miss Zooth, Elinor slept better than she had for a long time, deeply and peacefully. Yet she woke early, with the dawn light slipping through her window, to the sound of sea birds calling. She lay there a little while, listening to their melancholy shrieking, watching the play of light on the wooden floorboards. Then her mind sharpened to wakefulness. Had she really entertained – and fed – a miniature spinster vampiri in her sitting room yesterday? Or had that been a dream? She pulled her arm up and saw the two tiny pinpricks still marking her skin.

The first thing, however, was to eat some breakfast and perhaps go for a walk. Then maybe Miss Zooth would find Elinor again and they could further their acquaintance.

The rest of the house was still asleep, except for the

maid busy who was in the kitchen. After a cup of tea and some pound cake – slipping extra to Samuel, to apologise for even momentarily contemplating him as a vampiri snack – Elinor put on her cloak and left through the back door. The path there led out into the lonely fields, where no one would remark upon her talking to herself.

The day was sunny and calm after the bluster of the previous evening. The blue sky soared overhead, clear except for a few scattered clouds. Elinor relaxed into her walk, passing through the green paddocks and fields. She eyed the livestock with curiosity, wondering if any of them had supplemented Miss Zooth's meal last night. Perhaps it had been a dire mistake, to offer her own blood like that. Yet she had sensed in the vampiri a kindred spirit: an outsider, different from everyone else, yet proud.

As she walked, her thoughts turned to the last two weeks. If only she had not found that blasted jewel pendant at that blasted garden party. If only she had left it there, as Beresford had advised, instead of trying to be clever and discover whose it was. Delighted to have found something with her gift, she had wanted to locate the owner and return it, perhaps with a modest curtsy. Instead she was now a social outcast, reduced to making friends with little creatures. Still, Miss Zooth seemed a better sort than all those who had willingly slighted and believed the worst of Elinor. The last week in London had opened her eyes. It was a stark realisation to see how much social standing mattered, and how easily it was lost.

As for Beresford – well, he had not seemed to believe the worst of Elinor. He had tried to protect her, even though she had been so suspicious of him. Now, of course, he had every reason to detest her. She felt an ache as she remembered how the warm light in his eyes had gone out.

Elinor sighed. Beresford's consistent indifference to young ladies of quality provoked some to suggest the earl preferred gentlemen. Elinor knew, however, this was not true at all. He had flirted with her. Of course, he might do that anyway – gentlemen who preferred gentlemen often did – but he did so with a most disquieting gleam in his eye, and a warmth in his voice, which had made her feel quite *unsettled*. In a rather tingly, enjoyable way, she admitted, but unsettled nonetheless.

She shook her head slightly, trying to put Beresford from her mind. She would not see him for a while, and when she did, he would probably be married. The twist in her stomach at this thought was just because she was hungry.

When the trail met the larger path into the village, Elinor turned and stood a while, looking out over the solitary fields she had traversed. She could not sense any jewels nearby. She was not trying, in particular, to divine – that usually left her feeling a little out of sorts, slightly befuddled. However, if there *were* a box of jewels buried somewhere near here, perhaps within fifty yards, she would feel its presence.

Not here then. Not that she was looking.

She turned back toward home, quickening her pace. Miss Zooth was clearly not an early riser.

By the time Elinor reached the cottage again, her new acquaintance still had not materialised. Perry and her mother were at breakfast. Her mother looked up as Elinor came in.

"Restless, my dear?"

"A little."

"We will grow accustomed to country life soon." Her eyes, hazel like Elinor's, were steady in their regard. "It was kind of Lady Reeves to lend us her cottage – do you think she will visit us?"

Margaret, Lady Reeves, was one of Elinor's good friends in London, the only one who had stood by her. Margaret had offered Casserly Cottage as a retreat until the scandal died down; however, Elinor doubted Margaret would come out to Devon while the Season still ran. She shook her head. "Her father, the baron, might. I suspect we will have to make do without visitors."

"Perry tells me we received an invitation from the Countess of Beresford."

Elinor seated herself. She *was* hungry. "Yes, to morning tea at the manor. With Devonshire chudleighs no doubt, as is the custom here."

"What are chudleighs?" asked Perry.

"They are similar to the Cornish splits: yeast-leavened bread served with clotted cream and jam." Even talking about it made her mouth water. "I believe the Scots call them scones."

"Whatever they are called," said their mother, "we will not accept, of course."

"No." Paradoxically, hearing her mother refuse the possibility made Elinor want to accept. Maybe it would do no harm to visit the manor. And partake of chudleighs and cream, even if her figure was already cosy enough.

Perry spoke through his mouthful of food. "Why not? The countess might be able to sort things out for us."

"We have done enough damage to the Beresfords as it is," said Mrs Avely. "We must not impose further."

"We are here to wait the scandal out, not add to it."

Elinor helped herself to a serving of toast, giving Perry a warning glance. They had not, of course, told their own mother about the Lord Treffler's proposition in London. Elinor had learned early that Mrs Avely did not like to talk about Elinor's divining gift. She would be horrified if she knew Lord Treffler had guessed at it. Though it would give her even more justification for their flight to Devon.

The Avelys' three dark blonde heads – one with streaks of grey – bent to their breakfast without further discussion. Elinor repressed a sigh. The day stretched long before her. She told herself she was glad to have peace and quiet: time to reflect, read, walk, and sew. Yet thoughts of what she would have been doing in London intruded. Right now she would still be sleeping, after the previous night's revels. Later she would go calling on friends, and perhaps riding in the park. Here she had no friends, no revelries, and not even a chudleigh to make up for it.

Worse, she had brought it all upon herself.

MISS ZOOTH DID NOT SHOW herself all day. Remembering that she had only appeared at dusk, Elinor put on her walking boots again after dinner.

"Walking again?" asked Perry. He quirked his eyebrows. "Looking for something?"

"No!" she replied. "I am enjoying the long hours of light."

Perry looked sceptical. "Well, if you happen to find something *interesting*, be sure to let me know."

Elinor frowned at him and set off. This time she chose the path which led to the sea, winding through fields towards the dunes. The cows were huddled in groups for the evening, and a soft pink spread across the sky. Tonight there was no wind, and the evening was warmer. Elinor took deep breaths and strode quickly, trying to shake off her fidgets.

This time Miss Zooth appeared almost immediately. Elinor became aware of a small black shape swooping around her as she walked, and came to a halt. The bat hovered in front of her and dropped a small swathe of fabric on the path. Then the creature dropped to the ground, shaking herself out into the form of Miss Aldreda Zooth just before she landed.

Again, she was quite as nature made her. Quickly, Miss Zooth pulled the fabric over her head. It was a black velvet dress, at least a hundred years out of fashion, with a full skirt and low waistline. Still, Elinor was glad to see the vampiri possessed clothes.

"Good evening," said Miss Zooth formally, making a deep curtsy. Her black curls were still loose around her face and her feet were bare. Yet she managed the feat with great dignity, clasping the black velvet in delicate white fingers.

"Good evening," returned Elinor, also curtsying, though only slightly. She looked around nervously. There was no one for miles, but her mother's warning echoed in her ears. She did not want to be seen curtsying to the cows. "Do you feel better today?"

"I do indeed, thanks to you."

It was true that Miss Zooth's pale skin had lost the slightly blue-veined look of the previous evening, no doubt thanks to an amiable sheep. "Shall we continue walking?" Elinor asked, then realised this would be difficult with their varied strides. "Perhaps I could offer you a ride?"

4

IN WHICH A CONSTITUTIONAL IS EDUCATIONAL

"That would be lovely," said Miss Zooth. "If you would be so obliging as to place me on your shoulder ..."

Elinor did so and began walking again slowly, hoping her new friend would hold on tight. Miss Zooth seemed adept at this mode of transportation, and Elinor wondered how often she had partaken of it.

"Have you been sleeping again?" Elinor asked.

"Yes, I sleep during the day. I find sunlight a little taxing."

"A creature of the night?"

"That sounds melodramatic, but yes. It is why vampiri have such good complexions."

"And have you found – er – more sources of sustenance?"

"Yes, the cows are most obliging." Miss Zooth paused. "I want to thank you again – "

"No need," said Elinor hastily. "I am simply glad to know you are recovered."

"You need not worry that we are in some way bound together for life. The link will fade shortly."

Elinor sought for words. "Am I to understand it is customary to continue the exchange?"

Miss Zooth sounded embarrassed. "In some instances, yes. But I would not dream of imposing upon you." There was a silence and Miss Zooth cleared her throat. "Now, we have a great deal to talk about. If you could start by telling me what has happened in the last eighty years, I would most appreciate it."

"Goodness, I scarcely know where to start," said Elinor. She thought a while. "The revolution in France, of course." Elinor hesitated, wondering how her inter-locutor would take this news. "Twelve years ago, the French aristocracy was overturned by the common people. I am afraid there was a lot of bloodshed in the name of equality and fraternity." The losses had included Elinor's own father, who had died in the Battle of Turcoine when Elinor was only eight years old.

"Equality," murmured Miss Zooth in her ear. "There has long been talk of it, even in my time. Yet I imagine it was resisted strongly."

"Yes; in the case of France many nobles were executed. We are harbouring many French refugees here in England. The revolution hasn't left the people much happier, however. At the moment they are led by a dicta-tor, Napoleon Bonaparte. England is at war with France."

"Goodness – war?"

"Since last year. Before that we were at war with the American colonies. The Americas have departed from English rule and govern themselves now."

Miss Zooth sighed. "The world is always in tumult, it seems. I hoped to wake to a more peaceful era."

"It certainly is not that. Yet the social calendar continues in London, and everyone acts as if we are all safe here." Briefly she told Miss Zooth how King George III had succeeded his father in 1760 and had thus far ruled over agitated times. Miss Zooth asked several intelligent questions, then fell silent, digesting it all.

Eventually Miss Zooth's voice came again in Elinor's ear. "What is your gift, if I may ask?"

Elinor's step faltered. "My gift?"

"Yes. You must have one. I could sense it just before I flew into your window. Also when I – er – drank from you I could tell. Vampiri traditionally pair with Musors, and we can sense when someone is gifted. I gather you have a powerful ability."

"Musors?" repeated Elinor.

"The gifted. Those who can work magic."

Elinor felt as if she were walking in a dream. She looked at the solid cows, and the earth stretching away to the sea, trying to keep her pace steady. "Magic?"

"Do not tell me you are unaware of your power?"

It was Elinor's turn to clear her throat. "Er – no. I have the ability to divine jewels."

"Is that all?"

Elinor turned her head sharply and almost dislodged Miss Zooth. "All?"

Miss Zooth scrambled to maintain her place. "Usually the ability to divine is a broader gift. You say you can only divine jewels?"

Elinor was a little offended. "Yes. I must tell you, I have never heard of anyone else who can do so, and only one other person who can divine, and she can sense gold."

"Ah. Musors always have been secretive. And I have been asleep eighty years, remember. A lot may have changed in that time. Perhaps Musor magic is dying out, or become even more covert."

Elinor's mind reeled. Her breath quickened, though she still walked carefully. "What was it like when you were last – around?" That would have been 1724.

There was a tiny sigh in her ear. "It was a time of great change and excitement. I have spent most of my life in France, you know – it is where I was born. I became the companion of a young Musor scholar, Henri Vernet, when I was very young myself. So I grew up around culture and magic. There were secret circles of Musors, and Henri was one of the best."

"Henri was human?" Elinor asked, and Miss Zooth nodded. "What was he gifted in?"

"Memory. He could retain great masses of knowledge and charm it into objects."

This was fascinating. "And what other gifts are there? Did you know other jewel diviners? Were there many in England?"

Her traveller laughed. "Slow down. As to whether there were many in England, I do not know. I was only in Devon a few years before Henri died." Miss Zooth went suddenly silent.

"I am sorry to hear that." It explained why Miss Zooth was clad in such severe black velvet. Elinor had wondered if it was a consequence of being a 'creature of the night', but it turned out it was mourning clothes. Furthermore, if Miss Zooth had been asleep eighty years, the loss would still be fresh for her.

The little voice carried on bravely. "It is no matter, now. Henri has been dead eighty-one years. I did not imagine I would find another Musor out here in these lonely parts, and I did not feel like pairing with anyone regardless. So I went into hibernation."

"Where did you sleep?"

"In the vicarage. I have a little basket tucked away in the cellar."

Elinor laughed. "I'm sure the vicar would be horrified if he knew." She had met the vicar already. He had called on the Avelys shortly after their arrival. He was a short, stocky man with a strong grip, who seemed to take a very practical approach to his flock. The presence of a small person in his cellar would probably not be received well.

"I do not take up much space," Miss Zooth defended herself.

They reached the dunes, where the fields gave way to sand and scrub. The sea was aglow with a soft orange colour, reflecting the last of the sky's light. The path split into two – one forking down to the water, and the other along the dunes, to the cliffs. Elinor took the latter.

As she did so she saw what looked like a dark head bobbing in the waves.

"Look at that!" she pointed. "It almost looks like someone in the water."

Miss Zooth peered out. The shape showed again, black against the bright water, very much like a human head ducking in and out of the sea.

"Oh, that," she said dismissively. "That is a seal."

"Really? I didn't know there were seals along here. How lovely."

"Hm," said Miss Zooth, and Elinor could hear a frown in her voice. Perhaps vampiri had a dislike for seals, being creatures of air themselves.

Elinor changed the subject. "Please tell me more about this magic. I am dying of curiosity and I want to know *everything*."

"Goodness, I scarcely know where to start," said Miss Zooth, teasingly echoing Elinor's phrase from earlier.

"Well, there are eight different types of magic. Yours is a subset of Discernment."

"What is that?"

"The ability to Discern things usually unknown to the five senses, such as the presence of hidden jewels. It also can include Discernment of truth, or illness, or even the future, though that is a tricky art. And many other things. Whatever you turn your mind towards, really."

"Are you suggesting I may be able to further my gift to include different subjects?" It was a giddy thought.

"Yes, especially with me here." Miss Zooth coughed modestly.

"Oh?"

"Vampiris partner with Musors because we have something to offer you. You feel a little muddled after Discerning, do you not?"

Elinor's brows lifted in astonishment, though she wasn't sure why. If Miss Zooth knew all this, she surely knew the effects of divination. "Yes. My mind becomes clouded, and I feel a bit uncertain, out of kilter."

"That is called Bemusement. It happens to all Musors. But if you are with a vampiri the effect is lessened."

"Goodness."

Miss Zooth hurried on from this point. "There are seven other magics. Healing. Heightening. Illusion. Memory. Travelling. Impacting. And Diplomacy."

Elinor couldn't take it all in. She made Miss Zooth repeat them all and describe each one. But her mind turned back to Discernment. That was where her interest lay. This then, was the proper name for her gift. She felt excitement welling in her breast.

By this time they had reached the cliffs, and stopped at the large rock which acted like a lookout over the bay. It was shaped like a peak of whipped cream, coming to a point above Elinor's head. The lower, rounded part offered a place to lean against, and Elinor sat down carefully with Miss Zooth still propped upon her shoulder. The light was quite dim now, and Elinor did not trust herself to go further along the narrow path on the cliffs. Yet she did not want to turn back home just yet. She looked out over the vast gentle sea, and felt a new joy and zest rising in her. She was a Musor. There were others like her. And here was Miss Zooth to tell her all about it.

Silently, they both watched the darkening waters, moving in great slow waves to surge up against the cliffs. Elinor turned inward, testing her gift. She became aware of something, a presence, glowing nearby. With a catch of her breath, she widened and deepened her focus, and felt it humming faintly from not far off to her right. It was a jewel, or jewels: she was certain of it. Not large enough to be an entire collection, but definitely worth investigating. She might have noticed it earlier except her mind was so taken up with Miss Zooth's revelations.

"I can sense something now," said Elinor calmly.

"A jewel? Out here?"

"Yes. Odd, don't you think?" She debated whether or not to tell Miss Zooth about the smugglers' cache, and decided against it. But her curiosity was piqued by the call of the jewel. Elinor pulled herself up. This was a familiar feeling. The last time she had followed her curiosity it outcast her from London society. "Perhaps we should not try to find it. I have learned it is better to leave these things alone. Not to mention it would be tricky in the dark." Part of her, however, wanted to show Miss Zooth exactly how good she was at divining.

"How clearly can you sense it?"

"Very distinctly. It is only about forty yards away, to our right."

Miss Zooth was thoughtful. "I can see very well in the dark. Perhaps with my night vision, and your jewel vision, we shall be able to find it without too much trouble." She paused. "As for your past experiences – I don't wish to be immodest, but I am here now."

Elinor let out a huff of a laugh. "We are a pair now?"

"Indeed."

Elinor's pulse quickened. "Very well. I will walk in the direction I divine, and you warn me of any pitfalls."

Thus disposed, the two of them moved off, Elinor edging carefully and Miss Zooth leaning forwards, peering intently into the dark.

5
IN WHICH A JEWEL IS FOUND, ATTACHED

"*W*e are following a very narrow track," said Miss Zooth. "We have departed from the main path and seem to be heading away from the cliffs. Careful! Descent ahead."

Elinor could tell this much herself. Her eyes had adjusted to the dark, and she could make out a thin sliver of sand under her feet. It led them on and down. Fortunately, it was not the steep rocky descent along the front of the cliff face, but the gentler curve of the hill down the back, into a dell. Still, she went very slowly, trying to follow the faint vibration of the jewel while keeping her physical senses wide open.

She led them straight to a sheer wall of stone.

"That's strange," said Elinor, putting her hand up to the solid slab of rock. "It feels as if the jewel is another five feet in here. Do you think it is buried in the cliff?"

"Shhh," said Miss Zooth, sharply in Elinor's ear.

Elinor stilled.

"There is someone in there," said Miss Zooth quietly.

Elinor's heart sped up. They stood for a long moment

in silence, and Elinor gave the slightest tilt of her head in question.

"Two people," whispered Miss Zooth. "They are inside the cliff."

"How?" whispered Elinor.

"There must be a cave, or tunnel. I can hear them. I have ears like a bat, you know."

Elinor raised her brows. Of course. "Do you wish to turn into a bat and investigate?"

"Good idea. Only I must – er – disrobe first."

Elinor felt Miss Zooth wriggling out of her dress, and she held out her hand for the garment. The soft velvet dropped into her palm. She heard a slight whooshing sound and the sensation on her shoulder changed, then lifted.

"Be careful!" said Elinor. "They may be smugglers." Now she regretted not telling Miss Zooth the whole story.

A small shadow shot past her face and Miss Zooth disappeared into the cliff.

Elinor suddenly felt quite alone and defenceless. Which was ridiculous, really, as a miniature spinster – or a bat – would not offer much protection if there were ill-intended persons about. Well, perhaps Miss Zooth in bat form could fly into someone's face, but Elinor wasn't sure if Miss Zooth would approve of such behaviour, bat or no.

Elinor could hear the rush and roar of the sea on the other side of the hill. It seemed a long time she stood there, listening to the sea, feeling the presence of the jewel – perhaps a ruby – and wondering what Miss Zooth was doing. Images of large, violent smugglers floated across her mind, burying a prize by candlelight.

Then an unearthly shriek rent the air.

"A bat!" shrieked a female voice, in French. "A bat flew into my hair!"

Elinor bit back a slightly hysterical giggle. It sounded as if Miss Zooth was actively engaged. But what was a French woman – young by the sounds of it – doing inside the cliff? It was not Miss Zooth's voice.

Another voice came, less distinguishable, hushing the first. Then another shriek.

"I tell you, it keeps flying into me! It is attacking me!"

"Nonsense." Now Elinor could hear the other voice, also female, raised in remonstrance. "Be still and it will leave you alone."

There was a silence, then another more muffled cry. Elinor felt certain it was the second woman, now under attack.

"Let us leave this cursed cave," said the first, younger voice. "I cannot bear bats. And this one seems particularly vicious."

"We must wait here until they return for us," said the older voice.

"They did not say there were bats." She shrieked again. "Wretched creature!"

"What are bats after the revolution?" asked the older voice, aristocratic in tone, and at last Elinor put it together. These were refugees, fleeing France while Napoleon held sway. The jewel she sensed must belong to one of them.

Elinor cleared her throat. "Perhaps I can help you?" she enquired loudly in French. At the same time, she noticed she was not as muddle-headed as was usual after a divination. So Miss Zooth was right about the beneficial effects of her presence.

There was a long silence, followed by another muffled screech.

"I mean you no harm," called Elinor. "Please won't you show yourselves?" She dared not say she could call off the bat, but she hoped Miss Zooth would rein it in a bit. "My name is Miss Elinor Avely. I would like to help you." Hastily she stuffed Miss Zooth's velvet gown into the pocket of her dress, in case the newcomers emerged.

There was another shriek, then a scrabbling sound, and scraping. A few minutes later Elinor saw the weak light of a lantern bobbing some yards to her right. Shortly the lantern itself came into view, followed by two cloaked figures. They straightened as they left the entrance to the cave, and Elinor, blinking in the sudden light, saw two wary faces. One belonged to an older woman, with a patrician nose and haughty expression. The other belonged to a young and beautiful girl, with large eyes in a heart-shaped face.

The older woman took in Elinor's appearance, and seemed to find it reassuring. "Good evening," she said. "I am the Marquise de Laberche, and this is my daughter, Mademoiselle de Laberche."

"Good evening," said Elinor, dropping a small curtsy, though they were out in the dark and the wilds. "Are you in need of somewhere to stay tonight? I can offer you a bed in my mother's house, though it is very modest – a small dwelling a little way inland."

"You are too kind," said the marquise. Her accent was Parisian. Elinor could tell the jewel was hidden somewhere on her person, though she was clad head to foot in a long cloak. "We were instructed by our rescuers to stay here, but I fear we have been abandoned. We gratefully accept your offer."

Still, Elinor could feel suspicion in the glance the marquise raked over her once more. No doubt she was wondering why a girl, unattended, was walking alone after dark. She would soon find the customs out here in Devon were quite different to those in Paris.

"If you would follow me," said Elinor. "I was quite restless tonight and strayed far from home. I left before sunset, but the dark crept up on me." She found the small winding path again, easier by the light of the lantern. She could only trust Miss Zooth was keeping pace nearby.

"You speak French very well," said the young woman. "It is a relief to hear our language, I must tell you."

"I was taught from a young age," Elinor replied. "Like most women of my class. You will find we revere everything French, here in England."

"Not anymore," said Mademoiselle Laberche bitterly. "Nothing to revere about the guillotine or a common dictator."

"Your fashions, however!" said Elinor, trying to lighten the mood. With a sense of triumph, she found the main path again. "Look, here is the way along the bay. In twenty minutes we will be at my residence, where you can have a hot cup of tea."

The walk was a silent one. Elinor did not like to question the two women, and they were all occupied with keeping on the path and reaching shelter quickly. Only once did the older woman say anything, and that was to ask Elinor if she lived in a village.

"No, we – myself, my mother, and my brother – are a few miles from Deockley, the closest village. That is further up the coast, at the mouth of a river. I can take you there tomorrow, if you wish."

"Thank you," said the marquise. "But we may need to stay out of sight."

Elinor wondered at this. Why should she need to hide, now that she was safe on English shores?

By the time they reached the cottage, the moon was

high in the sky: a shining white coin, almost full. Samuel, the cat, fled across the front path and let out a suspicious yowl. So perhaps Miss Zooth was still about. Elinor called out as she pushed open the door, letting warm light flood out onto the doorstep.

"Mother? Peregrine? We have guests." She turned and smiled at the Laberches, welcoming them in. "Please enter. You must be in dire need of food and drink."

Elinor led the women into the sitting room, where she had entertained Miss Zooth the night before. It appeared that, in spite of her best intentions, life in Devon was becoming interesting.

The sitting room was small. The Marquise de Laberche took one of the hardback chairs, and her daughter sank down onto the armchair. Elinor busied herself lighting candles, examining her guests as she did so. With their cloaks removed, she could see they were dressed in expensive, well-made clothes in dark travelling colours. Both had black hair, tied back, though ringlets escaped and softened mademoiselle's face. Both looked very tired and a little sad.

There was the sound of footsteps clattering on the stairs. Perry appeared in the doorway.

"Guests? At this time of night?" He was dressed in pyjamas, with a dressing gown thrown hastily over. He took a few steps in and drew up short, the candlelight glinting on his blond hair. "Elinor, you're serious!"

"Of course I am." Elinor went and took his arm, leading him to the elder. "This is the Marquise de Laberche. I apologise for my brother, madame, he was not expecting you."

Perry sketched a bow, clutching at his dressing gown. "Madame! You have caught me unawares. I'm afraid I am not dressed for the occasion."

The marquise smiled at him, and Elinor internally raised her eyes heavenward. Perry's boyish charm always had a softening effect on matrons.

"And this is her daughter, Mademoiselle de Laberche."

"Mademoiselle." Perry turned and this time his bow was a bit more creditable. "A pleasure to meet you."

Elinor noticed again the girl was quite beautiful. Perry's type, too – he went for dark beauties. He was only just recovering from the one he had left in London.

At this point Elinor's mother arrived on the scene, and introductions were repeated once more. Mrs Avely executed a deep curtsy in honour of the marquise, incongruous in the confined space of the sitting room.

"You have fled your home country?" said Mrs Avely. "So sad. Have you only just arrived on our shores?"

"Last night," said the marquise.

"Ah! That schooner!" exclaimed Perry. "I told you, Elinor. It was smuggling these two ashore." He grinned at Mademoiselle Laberche. "Precious cargo, if I may say so."

"Last night!" said Elinor. "Have you been in that cave all day?"

"I am afraid so. We had a few dry biscuits to eat, and water, but otherwise we are quite famished."

For the second night in a row, Elinor rushed off to the kitchen to gather tea and food, though at least this time there was no request for bloodied meat. Hastily she boiled water and put together a tray, pulling out the bread and cheese again, and adding some fresh fruit. She carried it back out, hoping she had not missed too much of the Laberches' story.

Mademoiselle Laberche was describing their boat

ride. "Oh, it was awful, I was quite sick. Many times I thought the ship was going to overturn."

"Where did you land? What is this I hear about a cave?" asked Perry.

"The boat landed in a small cove – I thought we were doomed to smash on the rocks, but they managed it," she said. "Then we were led along a path to a secret cave in the cliffs."

"By George," said Perry in admiring tones. "How exciting."

Elinor set the tray down in front of her mother. "The cave is probably not secret to all the locals, but it was cleverly hid. I found them on my walk."

"How *did* you find us?" queried the marquise.

Elinor blinked. "Oh. I thought I saw a gleam of light and it made me curious. So I went off the main track, and then heard some noise – it sounded as if someone was in trouble."

"That was the bat," said Mademoiselle Laberche, shuddering. "Ghastly thing. It seemed to want to make a nest in my hair. I may have screamed a little."

"Yes, well, I heard that, and thought I had better investigate."

"You are a brave woman," said the marquise.

"In retrospect it was a bit foolish," agreed Elinor. "However, I am glad I found you."

"You are not from the locality then?" enquired the marquise. She accepted a cup of tea and a plate of food from Mrs Avely. "Thank you."

"No, we are originally from Derbyshire, and have come down from London – my health demands quiet time near the sea," said Mrs Avely. "This cottage belongs to the Baron of Reeves, a friend of ours. You are most welcome to stay with us."

Elinor spoke up. "They can stay in my room, Mother, and I can stay in the attic."

"In the attic!" said Mademoiselle Laberche. "We do not want to inconvenience you."

"We have slept in attics before this," put in the marquise, regally.

"All the more reason not to do it again," said Elinor. "It will be a novelty to me, whereas I'm sure you have both developed an ennui for attics."

Perry had not been listening. "Wait a minute – who are the fellows who dropped you off in the cave? Did they just leave you there to fend for yourselves?"

"It appears so," said the marquise. "They did say they would return for us at dawn, but we waited many hours after that."

"Did something happen to them?" wondered Perry. "Something which made it impossible for them to return?"

The marquise sniffed. "Perhaps. However, they had received payment from us already. They probably thought they had done us enough kindness. Not only that, but they also took with them our box of belongings, which contains our jewellery – chief of which is a price-less diamond necklace. They may have decided it was not worth their while to return for us, and left us there, lost in the wilds."

Mademoiselle Laberche looked sombre and gave a frightened shiver.

"The scoundrels!" Perry looked at Elinor meaning-fully. She frowned at him – it was best they did not show knowledge of such things.

"Are you saying they have robbed you?" Elinor asked. "You seem very calm about it!"

"We have suffered so much; this is just another blow,"

said the marquise. Yet Elinor could see she was, in fact, very angry and bitter. Her lips had thinned, and two spots of colour burned in her otherwise pale cheeks. "It is a shame that even in England we are not safe from those who wish to take advantage of our misfortune."

"We are truly sorry," said Elinor. "But your belongings cannot have gone far. Perhaps it is still possible to recover them."

Perry shot her another glance. "Yes, by George, we will turn the village upside down if we have to. Who are these men? Can you describe them?"

Mrs Avely interrupted. "Not now, Perry. These two ladies are both exhausted. They must eat and sleep first, and we can discuss what to do on the morrow."

Perry agreed, though a little reluctantly. The two women finished their food, while Mrs Avely made chit-chat about the weather and the village. Elinor disappeared to her room to prepare it for their guests. She gathered her few belongings and books and carried them up to the attic.

The attic was a very small room, with the roof coming in low and barely enough space to lie her bedding. Samuel followed her, strutting with his tail held high to investigate Elinor's new quarters and purring his approval. Soon after, Perry came to help too.

"I say," he said excitedly, in a low voice. "This is what Lord Treffler was talking about! Jewel thieves, stealing from the fleeing French! We must find their stash, Elinor. You can use your gift!"

"I'll think about it," said Elinor, stroking Samuel, who had made himself comfortable on her new bed. It all seemed more real, now she had met two people who had actually lost their family heirlooms. "I suppose we must help them, if we can. But I do not want to betray my ability, or lead us into danger. Whenever I sense a jewel, I seem to forget all caution. Take this evening, for example. It was only because I sensed a jewel on the marquise that I found her."

"We will be careful," said Perry. "You should take me with you on these jaunts of yours. Then if you find anything, I can help."

"Lord Treffler will be in Devon soon. He will want to help too."

"You don't trust him."

Elinor recalled Lord Treffler's narrow, handsome face. "Do you?"

Perry considered. "Not really. He strikes me as a scoundrel. I would even wager he might make off with the loot."

Elinor heard the creak of the landing and hushed him. "Bedtime now." She shooed him off and stood listening to everyone settling in for the night. Quickly she went back down to the kitchen to wash her face and hands, and waited a minute to see if Miss Zooth would come calling. Samuel followed her, rubbing against her leg and looking suggestively at the larder. She bent to stroke him and he purred loudly in appreciation. His unruffled state indicated Miss Zooth must be afar.

6

IN WHICH PRAYERS ARE RUDELY
INTERRUPTED

The following morning Elinor woke in the cramped space of the attic, feeling as if new horizons were opening around her. When would she next talk to Miss Zooth? And there was the matter of the Frenchwomen and their missing jewels. Somehow Elinor felt more justified in searching for the treasure now, if she could be of help to them. Though she hoped she would not encounter any villainous smugglers.

She came downstairs to find her mother in the dining room, preparing to host the morning meal. It was another hour before the marquise and Mademoiselle Laberche came downstairs, bleary eyed and a little subdued. Perry had bounced down earlier and had to visibly restrain himself from asking questions until the two women had made inroads into their meal.

Eventually the marquise looked up, smiling at Perry. "Is this what you call a hearty English breakfast? Eggs and meat!"

"We are accustomed to merely pastries," agreed Mademoiselle Laberche, draining the last of her tea. "But this is an admirable way to start the day."

Mrs Avely stood with the tea tray. "I shall fetch some more tea. Peregrine, do not bother these ladies until they are quite rested."

"Yes, yes," said Perry to his mother's retreating back. Then he turned to the Frenchwomen with a conspiratorial grin. "But we must hurry along, if we are to catch these thieves. Can you tell me what they looked like? I can search the village."

"They were large and ruffian-like," said the marquise ruefully. "I am afraid I cannot remember the particulars. There were two of them that brought the boat in – covered in jackets and caps. Oh, I think one had a finger missing, I remember seeing it as he rowed. Did you notice, Lucille?"

"I am afraid not, I wasn't paying much attention," said Mademoiselle Laberche. "Oh! One had red hair. I saw it glinting in the lantern light."

"Was this the same fellow as the one missing a finger?" asked Perry.

The two ladies conferred and decided it was not. Mademoiselle Laberche turned to Perry with a worried expression. "Must you really pursue them? It may be dangerous, and we would not want you hurt merely for the sake of some jewels. It is only jewellery after all."

The marquise's voice was dry. "It is all we had left."

"Surely our lives, and shelter, are enough to be content," said Mademoiselle Laberche. "I am so tired of violence and loss. I would hate for anything to happen to you, our new friends."

"A noble sentiment," said Perry, "but you must allow us to help you."

The marquise spoke. "I heard a name. I think it might be of their leader."

"Who is that?" asked Perry eagerly. "A name would be most useful."

"Beresford."

Elinor's head whipped up. "Beresford? You must be mistaken."

Perry let out a low whistle.

"Why do you say that?" The marquise raised her brows. "Who is Beresford?"

"He is the local earl," said Elinor coldly. "There is no possibility he is involved in anything so low."

There was a silence, then the marquise spoke. "Perhaps I made a mistake. Yet surely it is not unknown for your nobles to become involved in smuggling. It happens at our end of the channel also."

"Maybe for tea and brandy," said Perry. "But I must second my sister – Lord Beresford doesn't seem the type to do anything underhanded."

Mrs Avely had come back into the room, bearing a fresh tea tray. "No," she said quietly. "Quite the opposite. Lord Beresford tried to do our family a service recently."

"Tried?" asked Mademoiselle Laberche.

"The details are private," said Elinor coolly. "You may trust us when we say we can vouch for him. You are better off finding this red-haired fellow and the one with the missing finger."

Elinor did not add that she could also help, by tracking the jewels directly. Now, of course, she must do so, if Beresford was in any way accused. It was a way to return the favour he tried to do her, when she had been accused herself.

Also, Miss Zooth said Elinor would be able to divine more easily now, with a vampiri to accompany her. It was going to be a long wait until dusk. Elinor was impatient to go jewel hunting, and she would much rather Miss Zooth's company than Perry's.

Perry, however, had his own ideas. "We'll knock on every door in Deockley," he exclaimed. "Do you want to come with us, madame and mademoiselle, or would you rather rest?"

Mrs Avely gave both her children a sharp glance as she poured them more tea. "It is scarcely an undertaking for ladies. I suggest our guests rest today, after their difficult journey. Elinor, I hope you are not planning to join your brother."

"I need to go to the village anyway," invented Elinor. "To purchase some ribbons. Also, women are more likely to gossip than men – I might have more success than Perry in uncovering the whereabouts of these thieves."

Her mother knew exactly what Elinor was up to, and she was not happy. But she could scarcely challenge Elinor about her divination in front of their guests. "Very well. Just be very careful. Remember, *vincit prudentia*." She gave Elinor another sharp look, who repressed a sigh at the family motto: 'Prudence Conquers'. They both knew Elinor was prone to disregarding it.

Perry and Elinor readied themselves to go out, in spite of Mademoiselle Laberche's protests. The marquise gave them permission to mention her name, now she had some defenders. They were to tell the village the Frenchwomen had been found along the coast, destitute, homeless, and missing their baggage. "I had all our precious belongings – including the diamond necklace, and some other jewels – in a brown leather bag," said the marquise. "It is tied with a drawstring, and our crest is stamped on the outside." She received a piece of foolscap from Mrs Avely and drew it for them to see: a fleur-delis over a rearing horse.

Perry took the foolscap. "We shall find it for you, see if we don't." Rather boldly, he bent over Mademoiselle Laberche's hand and kissed it as they left. A soft pink infused her face, lending her further charm.

∿

"SHE'S A BEAUTY, ISN'T SHE?" Perry murmured to Elinor as they walked off in the direction of Deockley. It was a short walk, parallel to the coast, to where the river cut down to the village.

"Mademoiselle Laberche is very pretty," agreed Elinor.

"We must find their jewels for them. We'll be heroes!"

Elinor frowned. "I am more concerned that the marquise accused Lord Beresford."

"Ah, you want to clear his name?" Perry snorted. "The marquise didn't accuse Beresford, she merely mentioned him. They will take our word for it that he is a good fellow."

"Shh, I want to divine now." Elinor opened her senses, searching as far as she could, though it was doubtful diamonds were hidden in the fields. After walking a minute with her mind wide open, she could tell there was nothing nearby. "I will check again every hundred yards."

Perry was obligingly silent. When they reached the river Elinor shook her head, feeling muddled. Bemused, Miss Zooth called it, this unfortunate effect of divining. It was as if Elinor had partaken too freely of wine. "Nothing so far," she said, watching the quick water run, silver and green, below her feet. "Look, the river is running backwards."

Perry was used to her starts when she was divining.

"No, it's not. It's running to the sea, which is where it's meant to go."

"To the village by the sea," said Elinor dreamily. "To Deockley, where jewels await." The pebbles, covered in bright green moss, looked like emeralds.

Perry led the way on the well-worn path along the river. "I hope we'll have better luck there. It would most useful if we ran bang into a red-haired suspicious looking fellow."

"Or found a four-fingered man drinking in the pub," laughed Elinor.

They soon found themselves at the edge of the village and Elinor came to a halt. There were only two main streets, winding their way down to the harbour where the sea gleamed blue and calm. From their raised position they could see a few fishing boats, white sails furled, their brightly coloured hulls reflected in the water. Elinor watched the arcing of silver seagulls and tried to focus. She had been here before in the last week but had not previously paid much attention. The low white-washed buildings shone in the morning sun, and children and chickens were fossicking by the river where Elinor and Perry stood.

"I'll divine again," said Elinor, and she opened up her senses once more. It was perhaps unwise to try again so soon, but the matter was urgent.

Nothing but hens intruded upon her mind. She shook her head at Perry and they went forward, Elinor feeling faintly dizzy.

Perry looked a little concerned. "Why don't you start in the middle of the village, at the church? You can pretend to be praying. Give yourself more rest between attempts, Elinor. You don't want to overreach yourself."

"That's a good idea." Elinor smiled back at the chickens. "Aren't they sweet?"

"What, the children?"

"The chickens. Maybe we should acquire some chickens. I'd like to collect eggs, wouldn't you?"

"I can't say I would." Perry gripped her arm. "Let us hie to the church. Contain yourself. All this talk of chickens is unnerving me. We need to remain on point."

The church was an ancient building, made of huge stones. The vicarage alongside it, though also old, was small and squat in comparison to such grandeur.

"Do you know the vicarage is at least eighty years old?" said Elinor knowledgeably. She wondered if Miss Zooth was sleeping in the cellar as they spoke, and she sighed. It was a pity Elinor could not call upon the vampiri, or somehow catch her attention.

Perry cast her a curious look. "How do you know that?"

"Oh," said Elinor, "I can tell by looking at the stonework. Very fine stonework, that is. Very fine indeed. Good place for roosting."

"You *have* been overdoing it," said Perry reprovingly. "Next you will be telling me chickens live in there."

"Not chickens," said Elinor mysteriously.

Perry shook his head. "Now, you take a seat and rest. I'll make some enquiries."

Elinor obediently sat down in an old wooden pew at the front and struck a pose of prayer. Perry eyed her askance. "Don't move from here. I'll come back to fetch you soon."

"Yes, brother. Now leave me, I must pray." She peeked over her clasped hands and twinkled at him.

Perry shook his head again and strode from the church. Elinor took a moment to indeed pray, while she was there; she wanted to put in a good word for her careworn mother. The act of petitioning helped soothe her mind, and she drew a long, calming breath.

After a while, she looked up to contemplate the thick church walls. If Miss Zooth was next door, perhaps the bat's presence might have a counteractive effect on Elinor's Bemusement. There was one way to find out. Elinor laid her hands in her lap and opened her senses once more.

This time she could feel something. There were a couple of jewels within the village, but they were too faint for Elinor to determine much of their nature. She could not tell whether they were large or small or simply far away. She tried to follow them with her mind. After a few minutes she was certain of the direction of at least one call. Coming back to her surroundings with a lurch, she felt slightly sick and dizzy. So Miss Zooth was no help in this instance.

Elinor rested her head on her hands, appreciating the calm and peace which permeated the church. It was cool and dark, and she wondered if she could lay down on the pew and have a little nap. She shook her head slightly, trying to clear her foggy thoughts. Perry said to stay here. Did he say if she could have a nap? Or something about resting in the cellar? No, that was Miss Zooth. Miss Zooth was napping, in a basket in the cellar. All Elinor had was a cold wooden bench.

She was so lost in her muddled thoughts she did not notice when someone came into the church.

"Vicar?" A man's voice called. "Is that you?"

Elinor's head shot up. She knew that voice. Or did she?

She must be dreaming.

Her heart started pounding. Footsteps came up to her pew. Hastily, Elinor bent her head down in prayer again.

"Sorry, madam," said the voice. "Excuse me for interrupting your devotions, but I am anxious to find the vicar. Have you seen him?"

Elinor scrunched up her face, still bent away from him. What should she do? She stayed frozen in indecision, and the man's tone changed. "Miss? Are you well? Can you hear me?"

"I haven't seen the vicar," said Elinor, into her hands.

"Miss? Will you look at me? I cannot quite hear what you are saying." There was a note of suspicion in the familiar voice now.

Very reluctantly, Elinor dropped her hands and raised her face, to look into the stern grey eyes of the Earl of Beresford.

His strong jaw line and overly strong brow – too strong to be classically handsome – loomed over her, amply backed by his broad shoulders. He was dressed for riding, rather carelessly, and his dark brown hair was disordered, as if he had been hurrying somewhere. He looked, as usual, magnificent.

His eyebrows shot up. "Miss Avely!"

"My lord," said Elinor, with great dignity.

"What are you doing here?" His voice deepened, and she felt a tingle run through her. Was he still angry with her?

Elinor glanced away from those penetrating grey eyes and tried to restrain herself from adding anything else. Heaven forbid she rattle on about chickens to Beresford. "I am praying."

There was a silence.

"You know what I mean," he said stiffly. "What are you doing here, in Devon?"

Elinor thought wildly. What was she doing in Devon? "I'm staying at Lady Reeves's cottage." She tried to keep her voice composed. "To retreat from London for a while. We found it to be incommodious. London that is, not the cottage. The cottage is quite lovely."

Out of the corner of her eye, she saw him give an involuntary movement. He spoke roughly. "I left London yesterday. You should not have fled. It would have been better to brave the rumours out. Leaving the scene looks like an admission of guilt."

"I am well aware of that," said Elinor sharply, looking up at him. "My mother thought it best. I, as a dutiful daughter, followed her wishes."

Beresford gave something that sounded like a snort. "Why Devon, of all places? You must know my estate is here."

"You are not supposed to be here," she said defensively. "You're supposed to be in London. I had no intention of going near you, or your estate."

He let out a breath, frowning. Elinor put up her chin. Beresford looked around the empty church and turned back to her. "Miss Avely, this is a good opportunity, seeing as we are alone. I have something to say to you."

Something caught in Elinor's chest. He leaned forward, his broad shoulders blocking any escape, even if she had wished to flee.

"I want you to know I never intended to marry you."

Elinor's eyes widened. "Oh, really? That is very kind of you to say so, my lord."

"Well, you were so offended by my offer! It was a spur of the moment decision, made out of misplaced chivalry, which of course I had to stand by once I made it." Beresford's voice warmed to anger. "You must know I merely intended to save you embarrassment. You could have jilted me a few weeks later."

Elinor sat very straight. "I do not wish to be known as a jilt."

"Better a jilt than a thief!"

"Well, I am happy to know your intentions were purely pretence, my lord," Elinor made a show of smoothing down her skirts. "I'm sorry I didn't do you the honour of accepting a false proposal and jilting you two weeks later."

"Be sensible, Elinor! And stop calling me 'my lord.' It would have been preferable to this debacle, with you in disgrace and forced to leave London."

"I would not have found it preferable."

"Two weeks engaged to me would be so odious?" His brow became thunderous, and he drew back, his grey eyes snapping. "I deeply apologise for so insulting you."

That was not what she had meant at all. She tried to remedy her error. "You need not be offended when you have your pick of brides in London. Why don't you return there, and do as your mother wishes?"

That had not come out quite as conciliatory as she intended. Elinor shut her lips firmly together. She was Bemused by divining, she must remember, as well as confounded by his overbearing masculine presence. She should not trust herself to say much more.

Beresford took a step back and folded his arms. A glint of amusement stole into his features. "Neither one of us are very good at doing what our mothers wish."

"How can you say so?" In spite of herself, she twinkled at him. "When I am such an embodiment of daughterly virtue!"

He grinned, and she suddenly remembered that a mere ten minutes ago she had been looking for jewels in direct disobedience of her mother. Perhaps her guilt showed momentarily, for he became serious again. "You should go back to London, not I."

Elinor drew herself up. "I am in Devon now, as much as it pains you. I am making new friends."

"Is that so?" he enquired. "Anyone I know?"

"I doubt it." She thought of Miss Zooth and a small smile crossed her face. She certainly did not want to tell Beresford about the small lady who had a habit of appearing naked.

"Oh?" said Beresford, his voice haughty again.

Elinor quickly made herself expressionless. A silence stretched. Eventually she spoke, choosing her words carefully, for she needed to maintain her dignity. "I have not seen the vicar. Why are you trying to find him?"

Beresford stared at her, his face unreadable. "I have an urgent matter to discuss with him."

"Have you checked the vicarage?" Heaven forbid she mention the cellar. Elinor folded her hands in her lap.

"Yes." Beresford paused, as if he wanted to say more. Elinor looked down, and his tone hardened. "Very well, Miss Avely. I don't know why I am surprised that you scorn my advice. I wish you good day."

Elinor felt her heart drop, yet she nodded regally. "Good day, my lord."

The earl turned abruptly and left the church.

7

IN WHICH BATS AND BROTHERS
ARE PERSPICACIOUS

*E*linor laid her head on her hands again. At least she had managed to keep herself together, in the face of much provocation. He had been downright rude – as much as ordered her out of Devon! Well, she would not go. Beresford had no right to command her back to London. Why was he so angry with her? Because she hadn't accepted his illusory offer of marriage? Clearly he expected proper appreciation for his high-handed interference at the Planx's garden party.

She sighed. It befitted a lady to thank him for his efforts. In trying to stop herself from uttering some inanity, she had completely forgotten the thanks and apology she owed him. To be fair, she thought crossly, he had not made it easy to be conciliatory.

Elinor lifted her head. The countess's invitation still awaited a reply. Elinor decided she would send an acceptance. Then she could see the earl when his temper had cooled, and she was not befuddled from divining. She would make a pretty apology and thank him for his gracious efforts on her behalf. That was right, something along those lines, with a dignified inclination of her head and a charming smile. She tried it now, nodding and smiling.

A voice spoke from the roof over Elinor's head, and Elinor almost leapt out of her pew.

"Well, that was interesting," said Miss Zooth.

"You!" said Elinor, rather rudely. "Where were you when I needed you?"

"I felt your divining and came as soon as I could," said Miss Zooth. She was kneeling on a high stone ledge, her pale white flesh apparent in the shadows of the ceiling. "Even though it is inconvenient for me to be abroad in daylight. Fortunately, this church is fairly dark, and there is a passage from the vicarage cellar."

"Well, you are too late," said Elinor. "I've been divining, and became completely Bemused – is that what you call it? I just made a mess of things."

"Who was that tall, brash fellow?" asked Miss Zooth. "And what is all this about guilt and leaving London?"

"*That* was the Earl of Beresford," said Elinor bitterly. "He tried to clear my name when I was accused of stealing a priceless pendant. But I wouldn't let him do it."

"*Did* you steal a jewel?"

"Of course not!"

"I am afraid I don't quite understand."

"I found the jewel at the Duchess of Planx's garden party," said Elinor. "Using my cursed ability. Then the jewel was found upon me. I did proclaim my innocence, but no one believed me."

"Except for the Earl of Beresford?"

"Yes, and now he thinks I'm an ungrateful wretch."

"Hm."

"Well, he shouldn't have tried to betroth us publicly when there was no such agreement between us!"

"Oh," said Miss Zooth. "Did he ask for your hand in marriage?"

"No! Yes!" Elinor put her head on the wooden backing. "He *stated* it, publicly, but he did not mean it, though of course he felt he had to stand by it afterwards."

"Hm," said Miss Zooth again. "And you publicly rejected him?"

"Yes," muttered Elinor. "It was for his own good. He was offering under duress, not because he really meant it."

"Are you certain of that?"

"Yes!" Elinor did not want to elucidate further. There was good reason to believe Beresford had not meant his offer, including his own words a few minutes ago. "However, I never thanked him properly for trying, in his backward way, to rescue me."

"I see," said Miss Zooth.

"Do you?" Elinor looked up at the ceiling, where Miss Zooth sat. "I'd like to know what you see!"

The vampiri merely contemplated her.

Elinor grimaced. "And here I am talking to a miniature spinster who can turn into a bat. Unclothed too! I hope you are certain Beresford is not going to come back and see me talking to the roof."

"No, he has gone," said Miss Zooth. Elinor felt a pang. "But your brother is coming back."

"You had better make yourself scarce," said Elinor.

"Oh, he won't look up. I am safe here."

Elinor raised her brows. That seemed a rather foolhardy assumption. But she clasped her hands again and bent her head. Sure enough, she soon heard the hasty footsteps of Perry coming back into the church.

"Elinor! Lord Beresford is here!"

Elinor heaved a sigh. "I know. I just met him."

"Good Gad, what did you say to him? He looked like thunder when I saw him marching down the street just now."

Elinor sniffed. "You should rather ask what he said to me! I was quite restrained in response."

Perry came to a halt and gave her a measuring look. "Ah, I see."

"What! What do you see?"

"Composed, were you? All dignified and proper? Hah – cold as ice and about as comfortable. Poor fellow."

"I was Bemused! I still am!"

"Bemused? What do you mean? From divining?"

"Yes." Elinor was glad her useless brother at least retained some measure of acumen. "I was trying not to mortify myself."

"And managed to put him off entirely," said Perry.

On second thoughts, her brother was completely lacking in any intelligence whatsoever. "Lord Beresford doesn't need to be put off!" Elinor bit her lip. Perhaps she had been a little too repressive. Beresford had tried to help her, after all, in his misguided way.

Perry rolled his eyes, and then jumped, staring upwards. "Egad, what is that in the roof?" He rubbed his eyes. "I swear it ... oh, it's a bat. Shouldn't be in here though."

A black shape fluttered crossly to the darker reaches.

Elinor stood hastily. "Goodness, I hope not. You must be mistaken." She grabbed his arm. "Let us leave. Did you have any luck at the inn or the baker's?"

"Yes," said Perry, permitting her to usher him up the aisle. "I've discovered the names of three red-haired fellows – Harris, Rusty, and Clodder. Harris is the vicar's man, so out of the question as a jewel smuggler. However, Rusty is a smith's apprentice, so bound to be large and ruffian-like as the marquise described. And Clodder is a fisherman. Highly suspicious."

"You indict a whole profession?"

"Yes: fishermen have boats, and an excuse to be out on the ocean. Easy for Clodder to smuggle French ladies on the side."

Elinor pursed her lips and acknowledged this perhaps had some truth. "What of the four-fingered man?"

"Ah, that's Floy, another fisherman. My bet is on him and Clodder, his red-headed fellow in trade. I'm going down to the docks to see if I can find them."

Elinor squinted as they came out into the sun. "How will you approach them? I hope you are not considering violence."

"No, no, merely a combination of blackmail and bribery," said Perry, with insouciance. "I will tell them they are in danger of arrest, but they can make a recovery if they lead me to the loot."

"It sounds fraught with risk," objected Elinor. "What if they lead you somewhere deserted and turn on you?"

"Lord Treffler will assist me. Besides, what is a little danger in the name of a lady's honour?"

Elinor tutted.

Perry grinned. "What of you, sister? Did you divine any jewels?"

With a sense of surprise, Elinor remembered she had. She had been so taken aback by Beresford she had clean forgotten it. "Yes, there are a few jewels at the other end of the village. Not many, however, and I don't think it is the cache of missing jewels."

Perry shot her a look. He seemed to decide she had suffered enough for one day, and agreed. "Back home then," he said. "I will drop you off, then wander down to the docks."

"You must wait for Lord Treffler! You can't go down there alone."

"I won't confront anyone yet," said Perry. "Just have a look around, see if I can find Clodder the red-head and Floy of the four fingers. See the cut of their jibs."

Elinor reluctantly accepted this, but she was anxious. Goodness knew what trouble Perry would waltz into if he was given half the chance. It was far better to find the jewels without relying on ruffians to lead the way. However, she was already overtaxed from the morning's exertions. She needed Miss Zooth present with her, so she could divine more easily. That meant waiting until dusk.

It was a long time until then. What could she do meanwhile? There was one thing she intended to do straight away: write to the countess to accept her invitation to tea. Elinor did not care if her mother thought it unwise. There were many reasons to accept, and the first was that she needed to unbend a little with Beresford. She was beginning to think Perry was right – she was too proud and held herself too aloof. The very least she could do was apologise to Beresford with real warmth, not a chilly nod. Which meant she had to brave tea with the countess, as there was a good chance the earl would be at his ancestral home at the time.

Besides, there was cream tea to be had.

When they arrived home, she and Perry went straight to the sitting room. Mademoiselle Laberche and the marquise were reading, but they looked up eagerly to hear the news. Perry boastfully told them of the names he had discovered and was rewarded with Mademoiselle Laberche looking quite pale.

"They sound ghastly!" she exclaimed, shuddering. "Even the name – Floy – it casts a shadow into my heart. I beg of you to leave them alone."

"Clodder is scarcely a name to strike one with fear," said Elinor. "Though I must agree with you that Perry should proceed with caution."

"Perhaps Lucille is right," said the marquise, unexpectedly. "Two burly fishermen will not be easy for you to overcome."

Whatever the marquise's intention, the comment stirred up Perry's pride.

"I am trained in boxing, and I will have my gun," he said stiffly. Mademoiselle Laberche gasped in horror. "Besides, I'm not going to confront them straight away," he added. "I'm merely going to look around, see the lay of the land. Identify the men, and observe if they behave suspiciously."

Mrs Avely was quietly sewing in the corner. "You must take the parish constable when you do confront them, Perry. It is madness to do it by yourself."

"Yes, yes," said Perry, but it was apparent to Elinor he was placating them. He wanted to take all the glory himself, and he might not even wait for Lord Treffler. Elinor frowned. It was imperative she find the missing jewels as soon as possible.

Before Perry left, Elinor went over to the dresser and quickly penned an acceptance to Lady Beresford. After some hesitation, she showed it to her mother in silence.

Mrs Avely put down her sewing. "I thought we decided it was not a good idea," she said, frowning up at Elinor.

"Matters have changed somewhat. I met the son in the village today."

Her mother raised her brows, but aware of the

Laberches in the room, did not press for an explanation. "You must take Perry with you," she said. "The invitation is to all of us."

"If I must," said Elinor. "Do you want to come too?"

"No," said her mother, after a pause. "I will stay here to look after our guests. Tell Perry to hire a carriage for tomorrow. I do not want you walking."

8

IN WHICH AN ALLIANCE IS
PROPERLY FORMED

*T*hat afternoon, Elinor rested, trying to conserve her energy for the evening. Her plan depended on Miss Zooth visiting, but Elinor was confident curiosity would bring the vampiri. After dinner, Elinor claimed to have a headache and retreated to her attic. There she opened up the small, square window and hung a red ribbon from it. She sighed, looking out to sea, where the water glimmered golden with the last of the sunset. She would much prefer to invite Miss Zooth in for a civilised cup of tea, and a chat about magic. Instead, they would have to venture out into the dark.

Elinor turned back to her sewing basket. Samuel was asleep on her makeshift bed, and she wondered what he would do when Miss Zooth arrived.

She soon found out: twenty minutes after sundown Miss Zooth fluttered to the window and landed upside down, swinging from the curtain rail. Samuel opened one eye, then leapt two feet in the air, snarling. To Elinor's horror, he made a lunge at the window.

Elinor leapt after him, feeling his soft tail slip through her fingers. Luckily, Miss Zooth seemed unfazed, perhaps aware she was out of reach. Elinor saw there was a roll of fabric hanging from the bat's jaws, which now dropped onto the sill. Samuel swiped at it, hissing.

"I do apologise!" said Elinor, bundling Samuel up her arms. He was a spitting, heaving ball of fur, and showed no compunction in baring his teeth at Miss Zooth. Elinor opened the attic door and thrust him down the steps. "Samuel dear, I'm sorry but you must learn some manners! I do believe that was Miss Zooth's dress you were trying to shred!"

She shut the door firmly. Miss Zooth was now on the window sill, in her human form, looking rather embarrassed. Elinor politely averted her eyes while Miss Zooth clothed herself. This time she was wearing a black bombazine mourning gown. Again, it was a century out of date.

They exchanged greetings, and Elinor put something on the sill before the vampiri. It was a dress Elinor had been working on that afternoon, made of black silk, in the modern high-waisted style. An offering, as it were. She had a proposition to make.

"What is this?" asked Miss Zooth.

"A gown I am making for you. It is cut in the current style, which does without corsets. You might find it easier to wear, and – er – disrobe. May I take your exact measurements?"

Miss Zooth looked pleased and allowed herself to be measured. "I must say, it does look comfortable," she said, fingering the soft fabric. "I wonder if my old dressmaker is still in France. She would keep up with the fashions."

When Elinor finished with her tape measure, Miss Zooth sat on the bed, folding her hands in front of her.

"Yet these are trivial matters. I gather from your red ribbon that you are in need of assistance."

"Yes." Elinor paused, feeling a little awkward. "Actually, I was going to propose that we – er – form an alliance."

Miss Zooth raised her brows. "Oh?"

Elinor hurried on. "You are in need of proper sustenance. I imagine cows are less than satisfactory. And I am in need of help with divining – or Discerning, if you will. Today demonstrated what a fool I become when I try to divine too much. Yet it is imperative I find this smuggled treasure, before my brother does something stupid." She smiled. "Therefore, I propose we help each other."

"What *is* all this about smuggled treasure?" asked Miss Zooth. "I gather it is not only the jewels missing from the Laberches?"

Elinor eyed her. "No – remember, Perry mentioned it on that first evening, when you were under my shawl? Several French aristocrats have lost their jewels on their way over to England. There is speculation they are hidden somewhere along the coast. A certain Lord Treffler has approached me, guessing my gift, and asked me to help him find it all. Initially, I refused."

"Why?"

"I had just sunk myself into strife at the Duchess of Planx's garden party," explained Elinor, "using my gift. I didn't want to chase more trouble. Besides," she added, "I don't trust Lord Treffler. He is a charming rogue, and I am not sure of his morals."

"Why do you want to pursue the matter now?"

Elinor gazed out the window. "In some measure, it is because I have met the Laberches – people who have suffered from the thieves. And partially it is because the marquise said Lord Beresford's name was mentioned as the leader of the gang." She gave Miss Zooth a glare. "There is no way that is possible."

Miss Zooth held up her hands. "I have not accused your Lord Beresford! He seemed a gentleman to me, though a little stern. Not one likely to steal from refugees."

Elinor dropped her eyes. "He is not my Lord Beresford. Yet I can assure you he would not steal from the helpless. There is also the matter of my brother, who is set on chasing down some large fishermen and forcing them to lead him to the diamonds."

"Oh dear." Miss Zooth was silent a few moments. "Very well. I understand more what is afoot. Let me explain to you how an alliance between us would work, before you commit yourself."

"Go on," said Elinor, though she was impatient to begin.

"Firstly, it is not just sustenance you provide. Traditionally, in a Musor–vampiri alliance, the Musor provides shelter and food. That would mean I move into your residence." Miss Zooth looked around. "I could set up a basket somewhere in this attic, if you do not object to such an intimate arrangement. Or I could find a corner in another part of the house. Attics or cellars are my usual domains."

"Certainly, that would be fine." However, Elinor felt a little unsettled. It would be a radical change, then, not just a distant partnership.

Miss Zooth continued. "You would undertake to protect my sleeping hours during the day: to provide a safe place for when I am most vulnerable. In return I would protect you at your most vulnerable – when you are Discerning."

"How does that work?" asked Elinor. "Must you be present?"

"For the best effect, yes, but the very fact of our linked blood – from your feeding me – will provide some lessening of your Bemusement."

"So, for best effect I must divine in the night hours?"

Miss Zooth nodded. "With me somewhere in a radius of twelve yards. However, for urgent matters I can be active during daylight, as long as I am in deep shadow, like I was in the church. It weakens me, but I can still be present and aid you. Also," she added, "my assistance is not limited to assisting your divinations. I am little, agile, and sharp of hearing. I can be your eyes and ears when needed."

Elinor smiled. "That sounds very helpful indeed. I may as well add I am desperate to quiz you more about Musors and magic, and all the rest of it. Do you think you can teach me more about it, as part of our arrangement?"

"I am not a Musor," cautioned the vampiri. "I don't understand the arts very well. Traditionally you would receive training and guidance from another Discernor. But of course I would be happy to tell you all I have gleaned."

"Very well," said Elinor. "It sounds like we have come to an agreement." She began rolling up her sleeve. "Shall we begin? We don't have much time. I was hoping to go divining with you tonight."

"Certainly," said Miss Zooth, and Elinor sat down beside her.

Again, came the odd sensation. Elinor felt a momentary panic at the pricks in her skin, but soon she was dreamy and placid like before. This time it was much quicker, perhaps because Miss Zooth had already dined on sheep that evening. Whatever the reason, soon the vampiri sat back, with a certain brightness to her eye.

"Well, then!" said Miss Zooth. "Off on an adventure, are we? How exciting. Shall we creep downstairs, with me on your shoulder? I would rather stay in human form, so we can talk."

"Certainly," said Elinor. She pulled on some gloves, a cloak, and shawl, and tucked Miss Zooth onto her shoulder. They sneaked out of the house, relying on Miss Zooth's superior hearing to assure them the rest of the household was abed. The only person to disturb their passage was Samuel, who leapt out of the shadows to utter a parting hiss, then slunk off in the opposite direction.

THE MOON WAS ALREADY UP, now full and round. Elinor carefully lifted the lantern from the front door just in case, though the sky still had a faint tinge of gloomy light, the not-quite-darkness of a Devon summer night.

Where should they look? The treasure could be hidden anywhere in the wild reaches of Devon. It was a daunting prospect to search the whole county by night: cliffs, moors, and coves. After some thought, Elinor decided it was best to start where they had found the marquise and her daughter – out by the cliffs. If there was one hidden cave there could be others. Also, the smugglers were last seen on that side of the bay. Perhaps they did not go far to drop off their stolen goods.

Elinor explained this in a whisper to Miss Zooth, and they set off on the path towards the sea, Miss Zooth perched in the folds of Elinor's scarf. They walked in silence at first, both preoccupied with their own thoughts. Then Elinor asked Miss Zooth how many people were able to do magic back in France, in her time.

"In 1724?" said Miss Zooth. "It is hard for me to say. I only knew Henri's circle."

"How many Discernors did you know?" Elinor asked eagerly.

"Hm, perhaps four personally," said Miss Zooth. "I heard of others, but did not meet them."

Four seemed very many to Elinor, who up until recently thought she was alone in the world, apart from Lord Treffler's mother.

"Could any of them divine jewels?"

"I imagine so. As I told you, Discernment usually has a wide application. However, jewel divination may be different in some way."

Elinor wanted to ask more, but she fell silent as they approached the cliffs, in case the smugglers had returned. They were drawing close to the sea and could hear the hush and crash of the waves. Elinor slowed her steps, tentatively opening her other senses. So focused on her search for jewels, she was taken by surprise when they came up to the large whipped-cream rock and found a man sitting with his shoulders leaning against it.

The moon had just come out from behind a cloud. Elinor's eyes had adjusted well enough to see he was a singularly beautiful young man. He had long black hair, tied back with a ribbon in the old-fashioned style. His profile was aquiline, with a strong jaw and high cutting cheekbones. His lips were full, and his eyes, when he turned to face Elinor, were liquid pools of black.

Elinor pulled up short, and Miss Zooth muttered something in her ear. It sounded like a curse. For a long minute Elinor simply stared at the man. He stared back, with a dark brooding gaze that suddenly, surprisingly, broke into a mischievous smile. This was, if possible, even more attractive.

"Ah! Two mysterious ladies." The man rose to his feet in one graceful movement and bowed deeply.

Miss Zooth hissed in Elinor's ear. Elinor understood her distress. The stranger had spotted Elinor's companion, yet strangely he did not seem discomposed. Miss Zooth must have been caught by surprise as well, which was strange considering her bat-like senses.

"A mysterious gentleman," Elinor returned, attempting to keep the civilities afoot. She dropped a curtsy. "I must confess, the wilds of Devon are turning out to be far more populated than I was led to believe."

"Likewise, I find my solitude interrupted," said the young man, smiling with devastating beauty. "Delightfully surprised, in my case. It is not often I meet ladies by the light of the moon."

Miss Zooth hissed again.

"May I enquire as to your name?" asked Elinor carefully, putting her hood up over her head to provide more shelter for Miss Zooth.

"Jaq Delquon, at your service." He bowed. It was a deep and flourishing bow, as if he took great pleasure in it.

Miss Zooth muttered in her ear. "He is a selkie."

"Spoilsport," said Jaq, rising out of his bow with grace. "To give away my secrets so soon!"

"A selkie?" asked Elinor.

"A seal shapeshifter," said Miss Zooth. "He is only part human, which is why I did not sense him. A demon of the oceans."

"One could call you a demon of the night," pointed out Jaq, with considerable aplomb. "No part of *you* is human. I, at least, do not suck the blood of innocents."

"I am honourable in all my dealings! That is more than can be said of your kind," said Miss Zooth, a tense bundle of hostility on Elinor's shoulder. Elinor wondered why; Jaq Delquon seemed quite charming to her.

The moonlight made the man's skin gleam like dusky pearls. "An unjust accusation," he said, "but far be it for me to contradict a lady."

"You are a seal?" asked Elinor.

"Sometimes."

"Was it you I saw swimming last night?" She remembered the human head diving in and out of the waves.

"It may have been." Jaq gave her a smug smile. "Was it you I saw wandering around alone at twilight?"

"Yes," said Elinor. She almost asked him about the Laberches, but bit back her words.

Miss Zooth sniffed. "What business do you have here? Where is your pod?"

Jaq waved a languid hand out towards the ocean. "Somewhere out there."

"Don't you have to stay near them?" asked Miss Zooth accusingly.

"I am not a child," said the man, though in fact Elinor thought he seemed quite young. "I can venture ashore to see the moonlight shimmering on the water if I wish."

"The moonlight shimmering, my foot," said Miss Zooth.

Jaq gave them a limpid gaze. "The moonlight is beautiful tonight."

Elinor glanced over the water. Indeed, it rippled and glittered with silvery light, giving some credence to his story.

"Not as beautiful as the ladies," added Jaq. Elinor gave him a sharp glance. She rather thought he was mocking them. Aldreda tutting in her ear supported this impression.

Then, just when Elinor thought the night could not become more confusing, she heard another voice ten feet behind her.

"Jaq," said Beresford brusquely. "Who are you talking to?"

9

IN WHICH GRATITUDE IS REFUSED

*E*linor stiffened. She brought her hand up to pat her shawl, tucking it closer around her neck, hoping Miss Zooth took the opportunity to hide herself. She swung around. "My lord!"

Beresford stared grimly. "Miss Avely." He gave a short bow, which made a mockery of Jaq's earlier extravagances. "What, may I ask, are you doing out here in the dark?"

Elinor took offense at his censorious tone. "If it comes to that, what are *you* doing out here in the dark?" she asked coldly.

"You know each other?" asked Jaq, with interest. "Two such attractive humans are already acquainted?"

"Indeed we are." Beresford gave Jaq a quelling look. "I take it you have just met Miss Avely?"

"Yes," said Jaq. "Charming. I did not expect to meet a lady by my rock tonight." He put a slight emphasis on the singular *lady* and winked at Elinor. Obviously he did not intend to expose Miss Zooth just yet.

"Don't be impertinent," said Beresford. He looked at

Elinor. "Jaq here is a young friend of mine. He is prone to wandering off to explore the coves and tends to lose track of time."

So Beresford either did not know Jaq was a selkie, or he was trying to hide it from her. Elinor was prepared to go along with either possibility. "He has my sympathy. I do the very same thing. So lovely to walk along these paths."

His lordship regarded her narrowly. "You, however, are a lady, and should be indoors at this time of night. I cannot imagine what your real reason is for being out here, but whatever it is, I advise you to abandon it, Miss Avely."

"You are fond of giving me advice." Elinor matched him stare for stare. She vaguely remembered her intention to humble herself before him, but she couldn't bring herself to do it when he was being so abominably ... abominable.

"It is a pity you are not fond of following it," he returned. He jerked his head at Jaq. "Come along. Let's find you dinner."

Elinor wondered what selkies ate – fish? – and cast a speculative glance at Jaq. He bowed once more, another deep and graceful flourish. "A pleasure to meet you, Miss Avely."

Beresford turned. "She is coming with us."

"Oh, am I?" Elinor was incensed.

"I cannot leave a lady unattended out here, alone on the cliffs. It is not safe."

"I am perfectly capable of looking after myself!"

"Really?" His sardonic expression called to mind the circumstances which had delivered her to Devon in the first place. "Nonetheless, it is my duty as a gentleman to escort you back home."

"We are hardly on the streets of London, my lord."

"Yet you are chatting with two men all the same, unchaperoned." A gleam of humour lit his expression. It was a familiar look, and she felt something soften within her.

She smiled back at him. "You are both perfect gentlemen, so I have nothing to fear."

"There may be others out in the night," Beresford said. "Others who are not so gentlemanly."

"That reminds me, my lord," Elinor said, gathering her courage. Here was her chance. "I don't believe I have properly thanked you for your attempts to protect me in London. I am deeply grateful for your very flattering offer –"

"No need, Miss Avely." He cut her off. "As the offer was unwanted, thanks are not appropriate."

His voice was caustic. Elinor felt a stab somewhere in the region of her heart. "Nonetheless, I appreciate you were trying to save me from embarrassment," she said awkwardly, inclining her head and lowering her eyes. She only hoped she looked the picture of humility, not aloofness.

Jaq's voice was curious. "Great sea gods, what did you do in London?"

Elinor looked up crossly. "Nothing terrible. It was a monstrous fuss about nothing."

Beresford's arms were folded, his broad shoulders implacable. How like him to refuse her thanks. He was not even looking at her! Rather than showing a proper appreciation for her efforts, he was scowling out at the ocean.

"Indeed, a fuss about nothing," said Beresford. He turned away. "Now, let us go."

Elinor seethed. Then she heard Miss Zooth whisper in her ear. "Follow them. They might know something."

Elinor fought with herself, then let out a sigh. Ostensibly it was a reluctant concession, though perhaps it sounded more like a huff. "Very well. I will come with you."

As Beresford turned, Elinor noted Jaq's eyes sweeping admiringly over Beresford's – admittedly attractive – masculine figure. Then Jaq turned the same appreciative gaze on Elinor. Elinor huffed again and hurried to follow Beresford. What a brazen young man. At least with Elinor walking behind the earl, Miss Zooth was more likely to remain hidden, even if Jaq had a good view of them all.

Beresford made an effort at polite conversation as they walked, to give the whole late-night expedition a veneer of decorum. He asked after her mother and brother, and how long they intended to stay in Devon. As to that, Elinor could not say. Part of her wished to tell him they would leave immediately, but she feared their stay was indefinite.

Beresford scowled back at her, and Elinor sighed. She was so clearly *de trop* in Devon. Now, of course, she was more determined to stay. And not simply because a beautiful selkie was lurking around.

Miss Zooth prodded her neck. "Ask them about smuggling," she whispered.

Elinor cleared her throat. "I have heard rumours of smuggling in these parts. Is that true? Is that what you meant by ungentlemanly types about?"

"Unfortunately, yes," said Beresford curtly. "We are close to the French coast here, and with taxes so high with the war, there is a roaring black-market trade in tea and gin."

"As well as laces and silks," put in Jaq.

Beresford spoke shortly. "It is only a matter of time before the Crown comes down on it."

It did not sound from his commentary as if Beresford condoned the free trade. "Not only tea and gin," said Elinor. "People as well."

There was a silence from Beresford as he strode ahead of her. "Yes," he said at last. "People as well. How do you know of that?"

"We met two of them last night."

Beresford stopped and swung around. "Pardon me?"

Elinor pulled up short, and Jaq nearly crashed into her.

"The Marquise of Laberche and her daughter," she said. "They are staying in our house at the moment. They are refugees from France."

Jaq nodded. "Ah, the black-haired ladies lurking around the cliffs. I heard them last night."

Elinor turned on him. "Why didn't you help them?"

"You were there first," said Jaq, holding up his hands.

"Staying in your house?" Beresford repeated.

Elinor explained. "Their rescuers abandoned them, so I offered them our hospitality."

Beresford turned and started walking again. "The Baron of Reeves cottage must be rather full."

"They are charming guests," said Elinor.

"Are they?" asked Jaq. "The young one is pretty, I must say."

"Mm, is she?" said Beresford. "How did they find the trip over?"

Elinor wondered if he was trying to determine how much the Laberches had said about their 'rescuers'. Could Beresford possibly be involved, after all? He was out here tonight, lurking around the cliffs in the dark.

81

Elinor was willing to wager his meeting with Jaq was pre-arranged, not a result of him chasing down Jaq as he claimed. She wondered what business they had together.

She decided to be bold. "Did you help them across to England?"

Beresford laughed. "Me? No."

"Nor I," said Jaq helpfully from behind her, though she had not thought to direct her question at him.

"Do you know who did?"

There was a silence, broken only by the sound of their footsteps on the sandy path. "I have a few ideas," said Beresford at last. "Smuggling is rife in this community. In fact, it could be almost anyone from Deockley, bringing a few extra passengers over with the brandy." He cast a quizzical look back at her.

Well, that narrowed it down, thought Elinor.

"What about you, Mr Delquon?" she asked. "Did you see anything, in your amblings among the rocks?" She did not mention Jaq might have seen more from the waves themselves.

"I am afraid not," said Jaq. "I came out to these cliffs only late last night, by which time I believe the ladies were already in residence."

"The Laberches lost their jewels," said Elinor. "The people who helped them apparently decided they needed an extravagant payment for their services. There is a diamond necklace and other jewels missing."

"Ah," said Beresford. "It all becomes clear. You are determined to throw yourself into a jewel mystery again, after the last one went so well. You are foolish beyond permission, Miss Avely. I recommend you stay out of it, rather than allow your curiosity to run rampant again."

By this time they had reached the last field before

Elinor's house. She could feel a hot flush of anger in her cheeks, and was glad the darkness hid her complexion.

"I thank you for your advice, once more, my lord," she said. "Now I must bid you adieu. We do not want to wake the household by talking too close to its doors."

Beresford must have seen a flash in her eye, because he let out a low laugh. "I have offended. I apologise. But truly, Miss Avely, please don't seek to solve this mystery. I will look into it. You can leave it to me. It is not a matter for ladies."

"I have already been looking into it," she informed him coldly. "With my brother. Furthermore, we have discovered the names of the men possibly involved."

"Oh?" said Beresford sceptically.

She cast her mind back to what Perry had told her. "Clodder and Floy. And Rusty. They are all fishermen, red-haired or four-fingered, which is how the Laberches described the men who took them across. One – or all – may be the jewel thieves."

Beresford frowned. "Yes, I know those men, and they are most likely smugglers, though not necessarily jewel smugglers. And if they are, they will be answering to someone higher up. It is a risky venture, with higher penalties. They need someone to identify the targets, and fence the jewels in London." He pinned his gaze on Elinor. "Chasing fishermen will not lead you very far."

Elinor bristled. "I am not chasing fishermen, my lord." She was chasing the jewels directly, but he was not to know that.

"Good." Beresford smiled and made his tone placatory. "Please keep out of it, Miss Avely. I only wish to keep you safe from harm."

"Thank you, my lord, for your chivalry, once more," she said evenly. "Good night. Mr Delquon, good night."

Both gentlemen bowed: one a curt nod, the other an elegant dip.

Elinor curtsied regally and left.

BACK IN HER ATTIC, Elinor was given plenty of opportunity to seethe alone. Miss Zooth disappeared, following Beresford and Jaq to see what they might say when they were by themselves. The momentary pang Elinor felt at this underhanded dealing was soon burned away by the recollection of Beresford's arrogance. To think she had once held him in esteem! He was odious, utterly odious. To flat out accuse her of *rampant curiosity* and being *foolish beyond permission!* To be fair, he did not know of her divining gift, which was the reason she had embroiled herself in these matters – she could help where others could not. But Beresford thought she was only a hindrance: inquisitive and misguided.

Well, she would show him otherwise.

When Miss Zooth returned, she reported the two men had not discussed the missing jewels – at least not explicitly. Beresford had been eager to question Jaq as to the whereabouts of a man named Harris. Apparently Harris, from the village, had gone missing a few nights ago, and Beresford thought Jaq might possess information.

"Oh goodness – Harris! That was the fourth name!" Elinor sat down abruptly on her bed. "The one name I did not mention to Beresford. Perry said Harris was the vicar's man, and dismissed him as a possible smuggler." Too late, she remembered Beresford had been making urgent enquiries at the vicarage that morning. He must have been asking after Harris. "Harris appears to be an interesting fellow. He is missing, you say? Maybe he has gone off with the jewels."

Miss Zooth, once dressed, sat primly on a stack of books in the corner. "Perhaps. Jaq denied all knowledge, but said he would look for Harris."

"Do you think he meant – look in the ocean?" asked Elinor. "Does Beresford know Jaq is a selkie?"

"I am not sure. Maybe not. Selkies are good at fooling humans. If I was not there, you would have assumed him to be merely a young man."

"Not merely," said Elinor. "He is quite astoundingly beautiful."

"Yes, selkies are," said Miss Zooth grumpily.

"Are vampiri also?"

"Hmph. Flatterer," said Miss Zooth. She paused and spoke delicately. "Do you think Jaq and Beresford are having *une affaire?*"

Elinor shook her head, though the thought had crossed her mind. "No, Beresford treats him more like a pesky young man than a lover. Though I must say Jaq appreciated Beresford's – er – physical attributes."

"Selkies' romantic entanglements are a bit more – variable – than humans'."

"Oh really? Such relations are not unknown in London, and I suppose romances are – variable – everywhere. Yet I don't think Beresford is that way inclined." Elinor sighed. He did not seem to be inclined towards her either. "Never mind that – the question is why *did* they meet at night?"

"If it were merely to recite poetry to each other, I would be glad," Miss Zooth sniffed, and Elinor giggled. "However, I suspect something more nefarious is afoot if the selkies are involved."

"Why are you so taken against selkies? Jaq seems harmless enough to me."

"He might be," acknowledged Miss Zooth. "However, I have found selkies to be untrustworthy and selfish." She paused, and Elinor waited. "They treated my Henri badly. I would even say they drove him to his death."

Elinor was silent in sympathy. She wondered what story lay behind that claim, and whether Miss Zooth's tragic history had unfairly prejudiced her. However, Miss Zooth gave no more details.

"I am sorry," Elinor said at last. She stood and went to the window, peering out at the distant, dark coastline. "Either way, I think we should regard everyone with suspicion. Jaq has the run of the seas, I imagine. Might he be able to slip a hand above decks and snatch a leather bag away from unsuspecting sailors?"

"I do not doubt it."

"That doesn't help us find the blasted things," Elinor sighed. "If Jaq took them, they could be at the bottom of the ocean. That would make it difficult."

"Indeed," said Miss Zooth darkly. "Selkies always make things difficult."

"Well, if worse comes to worst we can take a boat out," said Elinor. She turned back to face Miss Zooth. "A gentleman by the name of Lord Treffler is coming to Devon, and he mentioned something of that nature when he visited me in London. Let us hope the jewels are somewhere on shore." She rubbed her eyes. "I should rest. I am visiting the Countess of Beresford tomorrow."

"Oh, are you?" said Miss Zooth with interest. "You decided to accept after all?"

Now she had said her piece to Beresford, Elinor realised she no longer had a reason to accept – except for the cream tea, of course. That was a very good reason. The thought of seeing Beresford's scowling face again had nothing to do with it.

"The jewels may be hidden somewhere in that part of the county," Elinor said coolly, walking back to the bed. "I don't suppose you can join me tomorrow to help me search?"

Miss Zooth hesitated, shifting on her stack of books. "In point of fact, there is something I have not told you."

10

IN WHICH PERRY IS AFFRONTED

*T*he vampiri looked embarrassed, fidgeting her delicate hands in her lap.

"Oh?" asked Elinor.

"It is a confession of sorts."

"Do tell." All sorts of things flashed through Elinor's mind, like a secret vampiri romance, or a penchant for cream tea.

"I have another motivation for forming an alliance with you."

Elinor took a moment to digest this and began to feel uneasy. "Oh?"

"I am hoping you will help me find a lost pearl necklace."

Elinor sat back and regarded Miss Zooth. Suspicion kindled in her breast. "Is this why you flew into my window?"

"No! At least −" the vampiri coughed. "I did sense you were a Musor, but I had no idea you were a Discernor. I could not believe my luck, for I am desperate to find a priceless necklace. It belonged to my Henri − a string of large pink and purple pearls, set in silver. He hid it somewhere here in Devon before he died. It is of great sentimental value to me and I would be grateful if you could help me find it."

"But I cannot divine pearls," said Elinor. "Only precious stones, like rubies or sapphires. Pearls are made of a different substance."

"I believe you can," said Miss Zooth, standing on the books now in her eagerness. "You are a Discernor. You can learn to extend your gift. Obviously you have a natural affinity for precious stones; it is amazing you are so adept at finding them, without any training. With practice you may very well be able to find other things such as my pearls."

Elinor had been wondering – secretly, hopefully – the same thing. "But I have no idea how to begin. You will have to teach me what you know." A new thought occurred to her. "What has this to do with tomorrow?"

Miss Zooth coughed. "I believe the Moria Pearls may be hidden at the Beresford Manor."

THE NEXT MORNING Elinor awoke feeling unsettled. It took her a moment to remember why – Beresford had been dreadfully rude to her last night, and yet here she was about to set off for tea at his house. She had not even told him of the invitation from his mother. Please, Elinor prayed, let Beresford be out looking for Harris. She did not want to run into his lordship again, especially as she had other business to conduct.

Miss Zooth – Aldreda, she had begged Elinor to call her, seeing as their friendship was growing so intimate – had returned to the vicarage cellar for one last night before she was to take up residence in the attic. Nonetheless, she had arranged to be a stowaway in Elinor's carriage the next day. Elinor had promised to call on the vicar and allow her small passenger to board with minimum exposure to sunlight. She would wait in the church while Perry spoke to the vicar, and conduct Aldreda to the carriage in her reticule. Elinor had chosen her largest, heaviest one, hoping it would provide enough protection from the sun. Perry would be there too, so the whole thing had to be managed carefully.

Even so, Aldreda was eager to come to the manor and help Elinor divine in the area. She would find a place to hide until nightfall, and then Aldreda too would search the house, she said, going where only a bat could go. Henri used to be a tutor for the Beresford's young children eighty years ago, and had lived in the manor. There was a good chance he had hidden the pearls somewhere there.

"Why are you only looking now?" asked Elinor. "Did you look before you went into hibernation?"

"I was too distraught," said Aldreda. "I was so miserable when Henri died, I could not face it. Also, he had commissioned a protective spell on them, to last seventy years. That seemed forever back then. I thought I had time, but now the spell has worn away. Anyone could find them now."

"Is anyone likely to be looking, other than us?"

Aldreda pursed her lips. "Yes," she said. "The selkies. Thankfully, they are mostly bound to the sea. I would keep a sharp eye on Jaq, however."

Elinor thought she'd rather enjoy keeping a sharp eye on Jaq.

So after breakfast, Elinor set off with Perry in the hired carriage from the village. Perry was a little impatient; his trip to the docks on the previous day had given him no luck. Very inconsiderately, all the fishermen had been out fishing. Perry wanted to try again today, but Elinor persuaded him the trip to Beresford Manor would allow them to widen their search for the jewels. She even convinced him to call in at the vicarage, by the simple expedient of telling Perry the vicar's man, Harris, had gone missing.

"Where did you hear that?" Perry asked.

"The maid," Elinor replied, crossing her fingers and hoping Harris's disappearance was common knowledge. "It sounds suspicious to me. Don't you think we should ask the vicar about it?"

So they stopped at the vicarage, and Perry went to offer his help. Elinor went into the church, ostensibly to pray. Sure enough, Aldreda appeared on the stone ledge and dropped her gown onto the floor. Then she changed into a bat and flew rather haphazardly to Elinor's lap. Elinor stuffed both the dress and the bat into her bag, and hoped God did not disapprove of such things. God made all creatures, and made them naked, so surely a naked vampiri was no exception.

Quickly, Elinor made her way outside to the carriage. Once inside, Aldreda unexpectedly popped her human head out of the reticule. "Oooh, dreadful sun," she said weakly. "I may need a drink."

"Quick, onto my lap." Elinor stripped off one of her gloves.

She lifted Aldreda onto her lap, ignoring the vampiri's state of undress, and felt the pricks in her wrist. Miss Zooth was slower to drink this time, perhaps needing more or affected by the sun. She had only just finished when Perry came back down the path. Hastily, Elinor held open the reticule. However, Aldreda, clumsy and drowsy, stumbled as she tried to climb in, falling down into Elinor's skirts.

Thankfully, the soft fabric cushioned the vampiri's fall. As Elinor watched, Aldreda became a bat and clung to the skirts upside-down. Afraid Perry would see, Elinor quickly threw her green shawl over the vampiri and stared brightly out the window.

Perry clambered aboard. "The vicar says Harris went missing the night you found the Laberches. Apparently he went out that afternoon and did not even come back for dinner. Highly suspicious." Perry almost rubbed his hands together.

"You think Harris grabbed the jewels and made himself scarce?" Elinor watched her shawl and her skirts out of the corner of her eye, thankful to see that Aldreda had the sense to keep still.

"Or he stumbled on the plot and was forcibly made scarce," said Perry ominously.

Elinor bit her lip, taken aback. "You mean ... ?

Perry suddenly stiffened. "Aaaahk!" he shrieked.

Elinor jumped. "What?" she demanded. "Don't squawk like that when you have just mentioned the possibility of foul play!"

"Something moved under your shawl! In your skirts, down there!"

"Nonsense." She stared down at the soft swathes of fabric: her lilac skirts and forest green shawl. They remained obediently still.

"It did, I swear it," said Perry. "Should you not look? There might be a rat clambering into your petticoats."

Elinor shuddered and thought she heard a sniff. "Don't be absurd, Perry. Now quieten yourself. I wish to divine now."

Perry glared at Elinor's skirts for a long, suspicious

moment, then relaxed back against the upholstery. He shrugged. "If you don't mind the possibility of rats, why should I?"

Elinor drew a sigh of relief, and was careful not to move her limbs.

The journey passed in companionable silence. Every now and then, Elinor would do a spot of divination, in the off chance the jewels were hidden somewhere near the main road. She was pleased to note she was able to do so without much ill-effect. She could still feel traces of Bemusement, but it was much fainter, a vague softening of her usual acute mind. As if she only had half a glass of wine, not two glasses.

But perhaps it was this softening that made her completely forget to be on her guard against Perry. When the carriage went over a bump, he let out a sudden yell. Elinor jumped.

"Good Gad!" shouted Perry. "What is that!?"

Elinor looked down. The rock of the carriage had dislodged her shawl. Aldreda lay exposed – thankfully, still in bat form – clinging upside-down to Elinor's dress and fast asleep. The little ears twitched, but she did not wake.

"Oh, goodness me," said Elinor. "It appears to be a bat."

Perry glared at her. "On your skirts! You are taking it very calmly."

Elinor folded her hands together. "What is there to fear in a bat?"

"What is it doing there?"

"Perhaps the carriage was a refuge for little creatures. This is Devon, after all."

"Well, I don't like it being so friendly with you," stated Perry. "Shall I rescue you?" He grabbed the shawl and made as if to pick Aldreda up to throw her out the window.

"No, wait!" It was Elinor's turn to shout.

"What?" Perry stared suspiciously.

"Poor little thing. Maybe we should let it sleep."

"You're mad!" Perry paused. "Did you put it there? There's something you're not telling me."

Elinor widened her eyes innocently. "Why would I keep a bat in my skirts? It is certainly not fashionable in London, whatever the custom may be in Devon."

This attempt at levity may have succeeded in distracting Perry. However, Aldreda chose this moment to wake up. She lifted her little bat head and shimmered into human form, blinking her deep blue eyes sleepily. As usual the transformation was conducted without the benefit of clothing, and she slid naked down Elinor's skirts to the floor of the carriage.

Perry shrieked for the third time. "Aaaaahk!"

"Oh dear," said Elinor.

"Oh dear," echoed Aldreda, blushing a deep pink, in a tangle of limbs on the floor. Elinor hastily passed the reticule to assist her modesty, and Aldreda clutched it up to her shoulders. "I do apologise, Mr Avely. I am a little addled from the sun. Please may I have the shawl back?"

"How does she know my name?" shouted Perry, fixing on a rather irrelevant detail, Elinor thought. He had turned a bright pink.

"This is Miss Aldreda Zooth," said Elinor, pulling the shawl back from Perry's limp hands. She wrapped Aldreda up, and placed her back on the seat. "She is a friend of mine."

"What?!" Perry spluttered. "Elinor! You have naked faery friends now?"

Aldreda tutted and frowned at Perry. "I am not a

faery."

"You are naked," pointed out Perry.

"She is a vampiri," said Elinor. "Quite different to faeries, I believe. Clothing hampers Miss Zooth's ability to transform into a bat."

Perry did not look reassured. He demanded further explanation. Carefully Elinor told him she had met Miss Zooth two nights ago, and that Miss Zooth was able to help her with divination.

"Good Gad," said Perry. "Does she have to be naked to do that too?"

Aldreda had been attending to this matter. She had fished the black bombazine out of the reticule, and after some shuffling around under the shawl, emerged triumphant. "Here are my clothes. A momentary lapse only, Mr Avely, I do assure you."

Perry did not look assured. "Are you turning into a witch now, Elinor? Is this your familiar?"

"Don't be rude, Perry," chastised Elinor. "You can speak to Miss Zooth directly."

Perry cleared his throat. He turned his eyes reluctantly to Aldreda. "Are you Elinor's familiar?"

Aldreda sniffed. "No. I am merely offering my help. I am able to lessen the confusing effects that Elinor's divination may have on her." Elinor was glad Aldreda did not go into the full details of their arrangement. Perry did not seem to be taking the news of a vampiri alliance very well.

"How?" demanded Perry.

Aldreda lifted her chin. "By the gift of my very presence."

Perry did not appreciate this with due reverence. "Does this mean you are going to attach yourself to Elinor like that all the time?"

"No," explained Elinor. "She merely has to be in the same vicinity."

"Twelve yards," put in Aldreda.

"Well, the countess better not see you clutching Elinor's skirts," said Perry.

"She will scarcely scream louder than you," said Elinor, somewhat waspishly.

"I will hide in Elinor's reticule, never fear," said Aldreda.

Perry did not approve of this notion. "You're both touched in the upperworks! If people see Elinor carrying a bat in her bag, they will think she is a witch!"

Aldreda put her hands on her hips. "She is not a witch. She is a Musor."

Elinor grinned. "There, see, I am a Musor."

"What the hell is that?" spluttered Perry, careless of language.

"A person who has a gift," stated Aldreda.

"That's all very well, but everyone else will simply think Elinor is a witch."

"That is possibly true," allowed Aldreda.

"Miss Zooth will stay out of sight," said Elinor. "No one is going to look in my reticule. I will put it down behind me, and when the coast is clear she can sneak out."

Perry shook his head with gloomy foreboding.

Aldreda ignored him. "Now, perhaps if I may take up residence of the said reticule?"

Elinor helped her into her bag and drew the drawstring lightly. Perry watched the proceedings with a frown, but there was nothing he could do. He was too much a gentleman to throw a small lady out of the carriage.

11

IN WHICH CREAM TEA IS HAD

*B*efore they knew it, they were breasting the long driveway of Beresford Manor. Broad green lawns swept down with oak trees on the edges. To the left of the driveway a lake glimmered, with a quaint boathouse perched on its shore, painted in blue and white. A river ran along the edge of the property towards the sea, and the gardens closer to the house were crowded with roses, low hedges marking out elegant beds. The house itself was a sprawling, white, Restoration structure, and behind it lay orchards.

Elinor felt her nerves increasing as the carriage pulled up. She picked up the reticule carefully, under Perry's censorious gaze, and allowed herself to be handed down by one of the footmen who came out to greet them. Perry leapt down behind her and they were led indoors. Elinor dared not try a divination just yet – she wanted all her wits about her for meeting the countess.

The butler, a tall, thin, white-haired man, greeted them and took Perry's card before leading them to the drawing room.

"Mr Peregrine Avely and Miss Elinor Avely," announced the butler, and ushered them inside.

Elinor held her head high and walked forwards, aware of an airy room in light colours of yellow and pink. Then she noticed something she should have thought about earlier – the estate's dogs. Two gold and white spaniels ran up to her and started barking. One even tried to jump up and nip her reticule.

Elinor swung it up, her heart beating rapidly. Clearly they could smell Aldreda. Elinor looked across at the other occupants of the room, hoping they would not suspect anything amiss.

"Down, Hamilton! Down Harper! Dear me, I am sorry, Miss Avely. Such unusual behaviour!" This was from an older lady who could only be the countess. She was seated by a window, dressed in an elegant grey silk gown edged in lace, and wearing a diamond necklace which thrummed quietly at Elinor. The glittering stones and the white of the lace accented the countess's pure silver hair. "Do you have some food in your reticule?" she asked curiously. "They are not normally so bad mannered."

"Er, yes, I believe I might have put biscuits in there yesterday. I'm afraid I don't have them anymore. Sweet little things," Elinor added, eyeing the canines with disapprobation.

Lady Beresford laughed and clicked her fingers again. The dogs reluctantly left Elinor's ankles and trotted back to their mistress, their gold and white pelts gleaming and tails wagging.

No longer surrounded by dogs, Elinor could better take in her surroundings. Lady Beresford's drawing room was large and elegant, though its furnishings were old-fashioned. The countess had her son's intelligent eyes and thick hair, though it had completely gone to silver. Her skin was very clear and hardly lined, and she was smiling, though also examining Elinor closely.

Belatedly, Elinor dropped a deep curtsy. Next to her, Perry bowed. Elinor hoped they made a creditable picture, dressed in their best: she in her favourite lilac-coloured gown with forest green ribbons, and Perry smartly attired in buckskin breeches and a morning jacket. Elinor was relieved – wasn't she? – that Beresford was not in the room.

"Good morning Mr Avely, Miss Avely," said Lady Beresford. "May I introduce you to my companion, Miss Tabitha Trent. She helps me while away my days in this lonely corner of the county."

Miss Trent was a round, cheerful-looking sort of person. A poor relation, thought Elinor, unable to be married and in need of shelter. Miss Trent smiled at her. "Good morning." Her voice had a low timbre, warm and comfortable. "So lovely to have fresh faces."

"We find Devon most refreshing also," said Elinor. The countess gestured for her to sit, and Elinor did so, careful to hold the reticule on her lap. This was going to be tricky. She had counted on being able to slip it under her chair and allow Aldreda to depart unseen. She hadn't thought of the dogs, who sat at Lady Beresford's feet, still staring with interest at Elinor's bag. Also, the drawing room was rather full of light, which Aldreda would find difficult to manage. Heaven forbid Aldreda, weak and dazzled by the sun, should stumble towards the dogs. They might suspect she was someone who occasionally snacked on canines.

"It is an odd time for you to be visiting Devon," said Lady Beresford. "Were the festivities not in full swing in the metropolis when you left?"

Elinor was still uncertain whether or not the countess knew what happened in London, though by the shrewd look in her eye, Elinor suspected she did. She decided to follow her hostess's lead.

"Yes, London is rollicking," said Elinor. "I am afraid we found it necessary to depart. Partially for my mother's health," she said, stating the official reason they had given out.

"And partially because London thinks you are a thief," said Lady Beresford.

Miss Trent laughed awkwardly. "Oh dear, Anne – always so blunt!"

Elinor let out a sigh of relief. "I am glad of plain speaking." She smiled. "Yes, we were accused as thieves. Very unfortunate. Untrue, of course."

"I am glad to hear it," said Lady Beresford.

"Of course it is untrue!" said Perry. "We were falsely implicated, and vicious rumours were spread about."

Lady Beresford smiled. "I did wonder, though my son declared you to be innocent."

"That is very kind of him," said Elinor. She hesitated nervously, and concluded she might as well address the matter. "Lord Beresford spoke out on my behalf when it all happened. I am deeply grateful for his intervention."

"That is not exactly how James described it," said his mother. "He said you snubbed him."

Elinor flushed, at a loss for words.

"Elinor is a little proud," said Perry anxiously. "Sometimes she does not accept help easily."

"I may have been ungracious," said Elinor, stumbling through her words. "In my defence, I was rather put on the spot, and feeling under strain at the time."

"What you mean is my son put you on the spot," said Lady Beresford judiciously. "I am not surprised. He tends to be high-handed sometimes. Believes he knows best, and does not think to ask anyone else's opinion."

"Exactly!" said Elinor, with a bit too much fervour. She dropped her eyes, embarrassed. "Lord Beresford's motives were noble, and I am very grateful."

"Hm," said the countess. "Now, let us have some tea." She rang a small bell, and when the thin butler came in, she asked that the spaniels – who still showed too much interest in Elinor – be removed. Elinor was relieved, and finally put her reticule down, tucking it behind her skirts. Aldreda might now sneak out, except … Elinor glanced around at the bright light slanting in from the windows, and chewed her lip. What excuse could she give for leaving the drawing room?

"Tea will be lovely," said Elinor, turning her mind to the civilities. "Dare we hope for cream tea the traditional way?"

"Oh yes," said Miss Trent. "There will be chudleighs with cream. Can you not tell by my figure that we partake freely of both here?"

"And plum jam?" asked Elinor. "I believe the Beresford estate itself makes the jam?"

"Of course," said Lady Beresford. "You must try the Beresford jam. We are famous for it."

"So I have heard," said Elinor wryly. Beresford himself had told her about the charms of his estate's jam, back when they were friends. He had claimed it was the only reason he was a sought-after bachelor. Nonsense, of course. Jam, while a necessary and delightful aspect of life, did not really compete with his deep, grey eyes and rare smile; his fine figure and intelligent, wry humour; his brown tousled hair or … Elinor frowned and brought her attention back to the gathering.

The conversation had turned to gossip from London.

The countess kept to the country as she was still mourning her husband, who had passed away three years ago. But she showed an avid interest in all the goings-on, and knew even more than Elinor did of the latest *on dits*.

Elinor's eyes wandered to a painting on the wall. It was of the late earl.

"He doesn't look much like his son," observed the countess, seeing the direction of Elinor's gaze. "The dear man was more handsome than my rough-and-ready boy."

Miss Trent demurred. "Oh, but Lord Beresford is so striking, in a different way. He has your lovely thick hair and sea-grey eyes, Anne."

Elinor said nothing. By this time the tea and chudleighs had arrived, and regardless of how striking Beresford was, there were more important matters to consider. Such as whether to place the cream or the jam on first.

"Most definitely the cream," said Lady Beresford. "Though in fact it is a highly contested point, and for Cornish cream tea I believe it is jam first. Barbarians," she added.

"When in Devon," said Perry bravely, and smeared on the thick clotted cream. Elinor followed suit, and Lady Beresford placed a large dollop of the acclaimed jam on top. It was heaven: the soft, slightly salty chudleighs sweetened by jam, all melting in the mouth with the luxurious cream.

"The jam has a lovely hint of tartness to it," remarked Elinor.

"Yes, not too sweet, which is why it is so good," said the countess complacently.

Everyone nodded fervently, their mouths full of the yeast-leavened treat.

The tea was also divine – though milk was not permitted in the event of the cream on comestibles. Elinor took a sip and let out a sigh of content, the fragrant brew restoring some of her equanimity. Perhaps she should try a divination now, when everyone was taken up with their devotions.

"Free trader tea," said Lady Beresford. "Only the best at our house."

Elinor raised her brows in surprise, forgetting her divination. "You mean smuggled?"

Lady Beresford smiled. "Oh, we openly confess it. Everyone smuggles in Devon, so of course we benefit from it. The price of tea is just too high otherwise, with all these ridiculous taxes for the war."

"Well, it is delightful tea." Elinor wondered if the lace on the countess's dress was also free trade.

At that moment, the butler came back into the room and announced a new visitor: Lord Reeves.

A large man bounded into the room, and Elinor turned to examine him curiously. This was the Baron of Reeves, to which the Avelys owed their hospitality at Casserly Cottage: father to Elinor's friend Margaret, and kind enough to allow Margaret's scandalous friends a refuge.

Lord Reeves was tall like Margaret, who was built on fine proportions for a woman, and he had Margaret's rich auburn colouring, though the father's cheeks took on a more rosy hue. He was holding a newspaper in his hand, and seemed surprised to see Lady Beresford had guests.

"Oh, pardon me," he said. "Frobisher did not warn me you were receiving."

"Frobisher is growing old," said Lady Beresford. "These are the Avely siblings. Mr Peregrine Avely and Miss Elinor Avely. They are staying in Devon – in one of your houses, I believe."

"Yes, of course," said the baron. "You must be Margaret's friends." He gave a bow. "I hope Casserly Cottage is proving suitable?"

"Indeed, yes, we are most grateful," said Elinor, going to curtsy in front of him. "We do not know where we would be if it were not for your generosity."

Perry added his thanks also, remarking on the lovely views and walks.

"Pooh, least we could do," said the baron, waving them away. "Never use the place anymore, good for it to be aired out."

"Is that the London paper?" enquired Lady Beresford.

"Yes, brought it straight over," said Lord Reeves. "Napoleon has been announced Emperor of France. Bad news."

"Such arrogance."

"Yes, and he is becoming more aggressive in our waters. Needs to be sorted out."

Perry looked eager. "Oh, would that I could be in the navy and help!"

"You are a sea-faring man?" asked Lord Reeves.

"I would like to be," said Perry. "Can't quite afford my colours just yet."

"Dangerous thing, the sea," said the baron. "Just this morning they found a body by the cliffs, drowned. I think it was the vicar's man too. He probably couldn't swim and found himself in trouble."

Elinor's eyes widened in shock. "The vicar's man is dead?"

"Harris?" exclaimed Perry. "Harris is drowned?"

12

IN WHICH THE EARL IS
TYPICALLY HIGH-HANDED

*T*he baron looked surprised. "Yes, Harris is his name. How do you know that?"

Perry cleared his throat. "Er, we were at the vicarage this morning. We heard Harris was missing. He must have only just been found, as the vicar didn't know where he was when we called earlier today."

Elinor's mind was working quickly, and she could see Perry's was too. Why had Harris been by the cliffs? Was it merely an accident, as the baron said?

"Yes, only just happened. I heard it when I stopped at the tollgate," said Lord Reeves.

"This is terrible," said Lady Beresford. "Poor vicar. He will be dreadfully upset. Did this Harris have a family?"

"He was unmarried," said Lord Reeves. "His parents must be told, of course – think they are in another county altogether."

"Oh, how awful," said Miss Trent. She put her teacup down, and Elinor saw her hand was shaking slightly. "Poor Harris. I knew him a little. He was kind to me."

"You must be careful by those cliffs," said the baron.

"Best to keep away from them altogether, Miss Avely, Mr Avely – even though there are walking paths there."

"Are the paths not safe?" asked Elinor.

"Not particularly," said the baron. "The waves weaken the rocks sometimes. Or a freakishly large wave might take you by surprise. That is probably what happened to Harris."

"Surely he would have known to be careful," said Miss Trent. "Even though he was from inland."

Lady Beresford shook her head. "Ah, but the inlanders don't have proper respect for the ocean. If you grow up next to the sea, you know you have to be on the lookout."

"On the lookout for what?" asked a voice from the door. It was Beresford, dressed for riding, his muscular legs admirably set off by his buckskin breeches. His shoulders were barely contained by his grey woollen coat, Elinor observed.

"Good morning, Mother." Beresford strode into the room and pulled up short. "Miss Avely!" He raised his brows. "You are always turning up in unexpected places."

The countess tilted her head curiously. "What sort of unexpected places, James?"

"Oh, like the church," said Beresford, smoothing over his accidental reference to certain night-time strolls. "I met Miss Avely there yesterday morning, praying." He quirked an amused eyebrow at her, and Elinor found she was blushing.

"Nothing unusual about that, surely?" asked the baron.

"It is when the church is in Devon," said Beresford smoothly. "The last time I saw Miss Avely was in London. I was not expecting her out here."

Elinor stiffened. Was that a rebuke again? "Your

mother invited me," she said. "I do apologise for not warning you of my presence."

"Hello, Lord Beresford," said Perry hastily.

"How do you do, Mr Avely," said Beresford. "What were you saying about being on the lookout for something?"

"We were warning the Avelys about the sea," said the countess. "Apparently the vicar's man was drowned last night."

Beresford stilled. "The vicar's man? Harris?"

"Found this morning," put in the baron.

"Where?"

"By Sea-Catcher Cove," said the baron. "Must have fallen in. Terrible accident."

Beresford's face was unreadable. "Where is he now?"

"I imagine he has been taken to the vicarage."

Beresford turned. "I must go. See if the vicar needs my help."

"Why would he need your help?" asked Lady Beresford. "He will have the doctor if he needs anyone."

"Still, at such a time," said Beresford cursorily. Elinor knew, suddenly, that Beresford wanted to look at Harris's body, to see if he could learn the manner of his death. She shivered. Suddenly this jewel hunt had taken on more sinister overtones.

"By the way," added Beresford, pausing at the door. "Miss Avely found some French aristocrats wandering around those cliffs. She has them staying with her. Mother, don't you think we should offer our hospitality instead?"

"Goodness me," exclaimed Lady Beresford. "French aristocrats? Refugees, I suppose, smuggled over? How many?"

"Two, ma'am," said Elinor. "The Marquise of Laberche and her daughter, Mademoiselle Laberche."

"Oh, the Laberches. Very good family," said Lady Beresford. "I have never met them but of course we must have them here. They must be living quite below their usual standards – no offence meant, Lord Reeves, but your coastal residence is not very large."

"None taken," said the baron cheerfully.

"That will be delightful," said Miss Trent. "Guests! Noble guests too! Shall I tell Mrs Paige to prepare the Green Suite, Anne?"

"Yes, lovely," said Lady Beresford. "Will you please extend our invitation to the Laberches, Miss Avely?"

Perry looked reluctant – no doubt he wanted to keep Mademoiselle Laberche where he could flirt with her – but Elinor graciously accepted on behalf of the Frenchwomen. "I will tell them today, and send them over tomorrow," she said. Privately she wondered whether the marquise would want to accept the hospitality of the Beresfords, a name the marquise associated with the smuggling gang who had stolen her jewels.

"Good," said Beresford. Before Elinor could say anything else to this high-handed ordering of her affairs, he turned and strode from the room.

"Dear boy," said the countess fondly. "Always thinking of others."

Elinor tried not to huff.

LADY BERESFORD HAD many questions about the Laberches, and it was only when conversation turned back to the war with France that Elinor felt she could safely make an excuse to stroll around the room and look at the paintings. With Perry, the countess, and the baron arguing about Napoleon's sea prowess, Elinor pretended to be admiring the picture of the late earl. She opened her senses, wondering whether Aldreda was still safe inside the reticule.

Immediately, Elinor felt the presence of the countess's diamonds more loudly, as well as the sapphire ring that adorned her hand. There was also a jewel, Elinor realised, nestled in the large bosom of Miss Trent – perhaps a generous gift from the countess. Elinor widened her focus. The first floor of the house, in the immediate vicinity, was empty of riches. This made sense, as it was the kitchens, dining room, and perhaps a library. Lady Beresford's private rooms and jewellery collection would be on the upper levels.

Cautiously, Elinor checked her own mind. She was not too befuddled. Glancing around the room to confirm the others were still debating, she reached her senses carefully to the second floor.

Ah, there it was: a mixed humming, Lady Beresford's private collection. Many fine pieces, if Elinor was any judge, with perhaps a few diamonds among them. It seemed there were two piles – one, perhaps, in her dressing table, and another secretly glowing in what might be a safe.

Now Elinor had located the house jewels, she began to look for anything else that seemed suspicious. Of course, she didn't believe there would be anything hidden at the manor. She could prove it to herself, even if she could not prove it to the Marquise of Laberche.

Tentatively Elinor extended her senses to the gardens outside. She felt nothing. It was just as she supposed: the Beresfords were innocent.

She felt something move against her side, and almost

jumped out of her skin before realising it was Aldreda, still bound in the reticule. The light, airy drawing room must be too well lit for the vampiri. Elinor looked around, and saw Miss Trent watching her. Elinor smiled, and quietly slipped out of the room, trusting it appeared she was going to use a chamber pot. No one would dare bring attention to that.

Outside the drawing room the hall was darker, but Elinor did not want to take any chances. She hurried down the hall and peered into the next room. The masculine tones of a study met her eyes: leather couches, and a large oak desk sat there, with books scattered around. Beresford's domain. Elinor repressed her desire to investigate further. The room was fairly dim – that was the important thing – and she could find a dark hiding place for Aldreda.

She dared not risk the drawers of the desk. Beresford might be out all day on the matter of Harris, but he might also come home, open his study drawer, and find a sleeping vampiri there. Elinor looked around, feeling anxious to go back before her presence was missed. There – near the fireplace, a box of wood. The fire would not be used in this weather, and the box was in a dark corner. Elinor hurried over to it and opened the reticule.

"Quick," she whispered.

Aldreda stuck her head out, black locks in disarray. "Where are we?"

"Beresford's study. There is a wood box here for you. I'm sorry I couldn't find anything more comfortable."

"Never mind." Aldreda clambered out of the reticule and slipped into the box. "I will be a bat. Bats don't need much comfort."

"Very good," said Elinor. "I had best be going. I will

see you tomorrow." They had agreed Aldreda would fly home in the night, though it was a long flight for a little bat.

Aldreda nodded and disappeared under the logs. A minute later a small white hand held out the black bombazine dress for Elinor to take. Best not to leave *that* lying around, even though not having it increased the risk of scandal should Aldreda be discovered. A tiny naked lady was more disconcerting than one wearing bombazine, or so Elinor thought.

She made haste back to the drawing room and took her seat by Lady Beresford again. Elinor was drawn into the conversation, which was now upon the subject of French fashions. Miss Trent was enthusiastic, and wanted to know if the Laberches were fashionably clad.

"They do not have much," said Elinor. "Though their travelling clothes certainly are very elegant."

Lady Beresford nodded regally. "I will loan them some good English dresses." However, Miss Trent looked apprehensive, perhaps fearing the countess's taste was not French enough.

Elinor sighed, feeling rather bored. She wondered if she should try extending her gift, just as Aldreda had told her was possible. How would she do that? Perhaps she could just raise a question in her mind and see if her divination sense gave her any answers. Elinor tapped her fingers on her lap, wondering what she could divine. There were Aldreda's pearls, but that felt too close to jewels. She needed a different kind of subject altogether, something new to try out 'Discernment'.

She remembered Aldreda said it was possible for some Discernors to identify lies. Perhaps Elinor could simply look for something that was hidden.

A secret.

Elinor felt her pulse quicken with the idea. She might find something interesting that way. A secret, she thought to herself, opening her mind again. Something hidden. *Is there anything hidden here?*

To her sixth sense, the house felt empty, and she was a little disappointed, or afraid that it simply wasn't working. Then she felt something beckoning to her from afar, the faintest whisper on the edge of her mind. Tentatively, Elinor stretched her senses to the gardens again. That was when it became clear: something niggling at her from outside. A secret.

A thrill of excitement shot through her. Not only for the fact that she had found a secret, but the fact that she had managed to turn her gift to something else. It had not occurred to her before to even try, but now, on her first attempt, she was successful.

Elinor reined her senses back in and looked up from her cup of tea. The discussion had narrowed down to the correct height of a waistline, though Lady Beresford was looking at her.

"More tea, Miss Avely?" she asked.

"No, I thank you," Elinor replied. She cast about for an excuse to go outside. "We should leave soon. Do you think I could take a walk in your rose garden before we return to our carriage?"

"Of course," said Lady Beresford, inclining her silver head. "Our roses are greatly admired. Miss Trent can show you around if you like."

"Thank you," said Elinor, though she would rather do without company when she was ferreting out secrets.

13

IN WHICH A SECRET IS FOUND, PERHAPS

*M*iss Trent led Elinor outside, chatting about how the war had brought even more French fashions to English shores. "Such lovely styles," said Miss Trent, with a hint of wistfulness in her voice. "Not for my figure, of course. I wish Lady Beresford would wear more modern dresses, but she is so old-fashioned."

Elinor made vague replies and focused on her divining sense. It called her straight and true to a large oak tree on the far side of the rose garden. It was huge, and majestic with the greenery of spring. Elinor eyed it eagerly. What could it hide in its leafy branches? With impatience she allowed herself to meander through the roses with Miss Trent, bending to smell the fragrant blooms and remark upon the colours and arrangements.

At last they reached the farthest bed. Looking up, Elinor exclaimed admiringly that the oak tree was a magnificent specimen and strode purposefully towards it.

There *was* something hidden behind the tree, or in it. For a brief moment she almost faltered in her stride, wondering if there was a person hidden behind the tree – it was large enough to hide three people – but she dismissed the thought. When she reached her goal, she placed her hands on the huge, smooth trunk.

The secret glowed from within the tree. Elinor felt a surge of triumph.

Belatedly, she realised Miss Trent had hurried up behind her. How was Elinor to investigate with Miss Trent hovering about? Cursed companions, always in the way.

Miss Trent puffed a little. "Oh yes, a splendid tree. Lord Beresford used to climb it when he was a boy, I believe. A real scamp he was, by all accounts."

At any other time, Elinor would have been interested to listen to accounts of Beresford as a boy, but at the moment her first thought was whether he had hidden anything in the tree. If that was the case, she was even more determined to investigate.

"It is a pity us ladies cannot climb it," she said to Miss Trent, and stepped back to examine the huge trunk. There – a hole, in the middle of the spreading branches. It was just out of Elinor's reach. She looked around for something to stand on, careless of how that would appear, eager with the thrill of the chase. A large stone lay nearby, and she briefly considered rolling it to the tree, or even asking Miss Trent to give her a leg up. She felt as if she were a child again, on a treasure hunt, and eagerly spotted the small foothold cut into the wood. Of course – whoever used the secret hole would also need help to reach it. Elinor was a tall woman herself, as tall as many men.

She glanced back at the house. The drawing room windows faced the opposite direction, so no one would see her scandalous behaviour. Quickly she placed her foot on the ledge and pulled herself upward.

"Miss Avely!" exclaimed Miss Trent. "What in heaven's name are you doing?"

"Er, a spot of climbing," murmured Elinor, reaching her arm into the hole, praying there were no spiders. "I used to climb trees as a girl. This one is irresistible."

"I must protest!" said Miss Trent. "If you should fall! Please come down at once!" She sounded very worried, and even tugged at Elinor's skirts.

"In a minute." Elinor's probing fingers had found something. Some kind of rough material. Her pulse quickened.

"I really must protest," repeated Miss Trent. Suddenly Elinor found herself being wrenched away from the tree. Miss Trent was pulling her down. The force of her yanking was enough to tumble them both to the ground.

Elinor hit the dirt rather hard, as even the presence of Miss Trent's ample figure was not enough to cushion the fall.

"Excuse me!" said Elinor. "What did you do that for?" She stood up, dusting her skirts down, glaring at Miss Trent.

"Oh dear, I'm so sorry." Miss Trent stood also, looking rather flushed. "I was trying to stop you climbing the tree. Most unseemly. Lady Beresford would not want you to climb her oak tree. Very irregular. Besides, you might hurt yourself."

"It is most unseemly to pull me to the ground," said Elinor. She stared at Miss Trent. "There is something in that tree. I'm going to see what it is."

"I wouldn't!" said Miss Trent, and with great agitation she tried again to prevent Elinor from breasting the tree.

Elinor shook her off. "You know something about it! What is it?" With difficulty she retained her foothold in the tree and reached in again. Her fingers grasped the heavy cloth. She pulled, but it was too weighted. "Oh, what is it?"

"Leave it, leave it," said Miss Trent. "It is only the tea and laces the gentlemen have left us."

Elinor stopped clawing at the fabric and turned to frown at Miss Trent. "The gentlemen? Are you saying Beresford's friends left smuggled tea in here?"

"Oh no," said Miss Trent hastily. "The smugglers call themselves gentlemen, éven though they are from the village. It is a polite way of referring to the free traders. They drop off goods for the house in that tree."

"Funny way of referring to smugglers," said Elinor. Reluctantly she stepped down from her foothold. "You're telling me it is tea and laces in there?"

"Brandy as well," said Miss Trent apologetically.

"Probably gin too," said a voice from the other side of the tree. Jaq strolled out, immaculately dressed in morning clothes, with a fine waistcoat of striped purple. He bowed low in his extravagant fashion. "Miss Avely, how charming to see you again. Miss Trent, good morning."

"Mr Delquon!" said Elinor. He was obviously at his ease, and familiar with Miss Trent. "Are you looking for Lord Beresford? He has gone into the village."

"Oh no," said Miss Trent. "Mr Delquon is staying with us."

"Yes," said Jaq, winking at Elinor. She saw that his pupils were oddly dilated. "I sometimes stay with the Beresfords. Old friends and all." He grinned at her. "The countess is very fond of me."

"You scamp," said Miss Trent indulgently. "What are you doing out here?"

Elinor narrowed her eyes. "Do you know anything about the free trade laces in the tree?" she demanded.

"Laces?" Jaq put on an air of innocence. "I thought it was all gin. Of course, all the big houses receive special deliveries from the *gentlemen*."

"Hmph," said Elinor. "They are not gentlemen in my estimation."

"Let us leave it," said Miss Trent anxiously. "Your brother will be wondering where you are, Miss Avely."

"Does Lady Beresford know about this?" asked Elinor.

"Oh no, don't mention it to her," said Miss Trent. "The countess knows the house buys smuggled goods, but she is not cognisant of the details. Best not to worry her about it. I believe she thinks the cook buys the goods in the village, but in fact they are delivered to the tree."

Reluctantly, Elinor allowed Miss Trent to take her arm and start walking back to the roses. There was something else going on here, she felt it. "So how do you know about it, Miss Trent?"

"I hear the servants talking," said Miss Trent. "I hear more than the countess, as you can imagine."

Elinor thought this was probably true – Miss Trent would hear gossip from both sides of the house. She wondered what else Miss Trent knew.

"What of you, Mr Delquon?" asked Elinor. She was willing to bet Jaq himself had made the delivery. She remembered how he had been waiting out by the rocks – probably with free trader stash tucked away somewhere. What's more, he had probably helped himself to some, which would account for the slight flush to his cheeks and the glint in his dilated eyes.

"I don't do deliveries," said Jaq, and there was such a note of scorn in his voice that Elinor almost believed him. He waved a hand languidly, and a sapphire ring glinted on one of his fingers, catching in the sun. Then he leaned forward and whispered in her ear. "I don't like gin myself; disgusting stuff. I much prefer coral cutthroat, it's a stronger brew."

~

ON THE TRIP home Perry was eager to discuss the news about Harris.

"You know what this means," he said. "Harris was murdered, just like I suspected. He stumbled upon the plot, and being a God-fearing man, threatened to turn them all in. The fishermen then lured him out to the cliffs and knocked him into the sea, leaving the treacherous waves to do the rest." He looked all too pleased about this theory.

"That may be so," said Elinor. She recalled what Beresford had said the evening before. "Have you thought maybe the fishermen are under the direction of someone higher up?"

"You mean someone from the gentry or nobility?" Perry nodded thoughtfully. "That would make sense – it is an ambitious scheme for a poorly fisherman. I imagine most of them wouldn't think much beyond the whisky smuggling. Jewel thieves hang."

"Who could be directing them?" Elinor paused. "Miss Trent was behaving very suspiciously today."

"Miss Trent!"

Elinor explained how Miss Trent had violently accosted her rather than allow her to gain a foothold in the oak tree. "It was very strange behaviour. Quite inappropriate."

"Hm," said Perry. "Miss Trent pulling you down, or you trying to climb it in the first place?"

"Oh that," said Elinor. "I could sense something in there. Not jewels necessarily." She told him about her attempt to divine a secret.

Perry was duly impressed. "And Miss Trent tried to stop you?"

"She claimed it was the usual delivery of tea and laces." Elinor raised her eyebrows expressively.

But Perry frowned. "Miss Trent scarcely seems villainous material."

"Poor relations are often treated as little more than servants," argued Elinor. "She might resent being at the beck and call of Lady Beresford. Jewel smuggling would allow her to set up her own wardrobe, in the French fashions she admires so much – not to mention give her independence and wealth."

"You think she was hiding the jewels in the oak tree?"

Elinor considered. "No. I was so focused on a finding a secret I was not listening for jewels. But I would have noticed the presence of a large stash." She paused. "It might have been something else."

"A murder weapon!" said Perry.

"Goodness Perry, you don't seriously believe Miss Trent was marching around the cliffs brandishing a poker?" Elinor shook her head. "I imagined it was a note, perhaps from her man in the village. From the fisherman who *did* kill Harris."

"Rusty or Clodder, the red-heads. Or Floy, the four-fingered one."

"Indeed."

"I'm determined to question them," said Perry. An apprehensive look crossed his face. "Does this new ability of yours mean I won't be able to keep any secrets from you? That's no way for a brother to live."

Elinor squinted at him. "Thus far, I have only been able to uncover physical objects. I think the secrets of your mind are safe. For the moment, at least." Perry looked relieved. "Why, are you keeping something from me?"

"Oh no," Perry hastened to reassure her. "It is the principle of the matter." He gave her a stern look. "You are the one who has been hiding things from me. Bats and whatnot."

Elinor waved a hand. "Pooh, just a very little bat."

"A little person, in fact!"

"I only met her three nights ago," Elinor defended herself.

"Still, Elinor, do you think it wise to become friends with her? How do you know she is trustworthy?"

"I don't know, but I feel she is." Elinor leaned back against the upholstery, trying to become more comfortable in spite of the brotherly interrogation.

Perry shook his head. "We know nothing of these ... vampiri. Yet you have left her in Beresford Manor. Goodness knows what mischief she might make."

Elinor yawned. "Maybe she will make friends with the bats on Beresford's property. I must ask her if she can speak bat language. Or indeed if bats have a language."

"Stop rambling on," said Perry. "Listen to me for once. Take care with this vampiri. Don't trust her completely until you know more about her."

"Yes, brother dear," said Elinor.

"And be more friendly to the earl, for goodness' sake."

14

IN WHICH THE EARL CHARMS
THE WRONG GIRL

*W*hen they arrived home, Elinor informed the marquise of Lady Beresford's invitation. As expected, the marquise was reluctant to accept.

"The Countess of Beresford?" she asked. "The wife of the earl you spoke of?"

"The mother," corrected Elinor. "The earl is unmarried."

The marquise considered this. "Why does Lady Beresford extend her hospitality?"

"It is customary in England to be hospitable," said Elinor, smiling. "She thought, rightly, that you would be cramped in our small abode."

"I don't want you to leave," put in Perry. "I will only allow it if you promise I can call upon you at the manor." He smiled at Mademoiselle Laberche.

The marquise shot him a quelling look. It appeared she did not approve of his flirtatious attitude towards her daughter – understandable, as Perry was untitled and far from wealthy. Elinor knew Perry was well aware of his ineligibility, but the marquise clearly felt it had to be established.

Mademoiselle Laberche appeared torn. "It sounds quite grand," she said. "Perhaps we are better here, Mother, away from such society. We are still recovering from our recent trials, after all."

The Avelys had discovered the Laberches had lost their patriarch in the troubles. The details were still obscure, but Elinor feared it had been in the worst possible way – at the guillotine.

However, the look Mademoiselle Laberche cast Perry was far from mournful. The marquise, seeing it, decided.

"We shall accept," she said regally. "I should like to meet this Lord Beresford."

Elinor stiffened. "The earl? Why?"

The marquise turned a calm gaze upon her. "To meet someone who has done your family a service, of course."

Several thoughts jostled in Elinor's mind. First, that the marquise still suspected Beresford's involvement in the jewel smuggling. Or worse, that the marquise planned to matchmake her pretty daughter with the unmarried earl.

ELINOR WENT TO BED EARLY, for she wanted to be ready when Aldreda came back. Unfortunately, she found Samuel had taken up residence on her bed again. He was curled up in creamy splendour, fast asleep. Elinor pursed her lips. She had installed a basket for Aldreda, but Samuel would probably make objections when the vampiri returned. However, he usually departed into the night to go adventuring, so he might be gone before Aldreda arrived at their arranged time of four in the morning. Elinor sighed and left him sleeping, feeling too guilty to oust him once more.

It was difficult to fall asleep. Her mind was busy with all the implications of the day. Harris dead – in suspicious circumstances. Whoever had the jewels was prepared to kill for them, which was an unsettling thought. Though, of course, it may have simply been a tragic accident.

She mulled over the smuggler's loot in the oak tree. With the benefit of distance, she began to doubt herself. Jaq had come out from behind the tree. Why had he been hiding there? Was it merely his presence she had sensed, as something hidden from common sight? Worse, was it Jaq's sapphire ring that had called Elinor out there? Perhaps it was simply coincidence that there were laces in the oak tree. Perhaps she had just followed her sixth sense to a jewel, as usual.

The thought made her despondent. She had allowed herself to be misled, filled with misguided pride. No hidden secrets for her, then. Unless they were jewels, of course.

She shook herself. That was all that was needed in this case. Luckily, the secret here *was* the jewels. She would find them, given time. Furthermore, she would delight in seeing the surprise and respect on Beresford's face when she did.

With this beatific vision Elinor drifted off to sleep.

Sometime in the early hours she awoke to the sound of a soft creak and tap at the window. She sat up in bed and saw Aldreda collapsing on the sill in human form. Elinor hurried to throw a small blanket over her, and saw thankfully that Samuel had gone off on his nightly jaunt.

"Aldreda?"

"I am exhausted," said the vampiri. "I searched thirty-two rooms tonight."

"Did you find anything?"

"Only Henri's old room. It still has a trunk of his clothes in there, can you believe?" Her face wrinkled for a moment, in grief. "As if he still lived there, but covered in dust. Unfortunately, I was not strong enough to open the chest."

"You think the pearls might be inside?" Elinor carried the bundle that was Aldreda across to the bed, and passed across the black silk gown, which was now finished. Aldreda gratefully slipped it on.

"Unlikely, but it is better to check. We will have to go back together so you can lift the lid for me."

Elinor considered her. "That might be tricky. If you think it is an unlikely hiding place ... ?"

"If not the pearls, there may be some clue. I would not want that Jaq Delquon to get there before me." Aldreda smoothed down the silk and folded her hands together in her lap, sitting on the end of the bed.

"I saw Jaq on the grounds today," remarked Elinor.

"Yes." Aldreda tutted. "Lurking. He is up to no good, I am sure of it."

"Apparently Jaq is a guest of the Beresfords."

"Hmph," said Aldreda.

Elinor smiled. "I asked him if he was a smuggler, but he was scornfully dismissive."

"It is true selkies rarely involve themselves in human affairs." Aldreda furrowed her brow. "Odd for him to be staying at the manor."

"Hm," said Elinor. "You think he is there to look for the Moria Pearls, like you?"

"Maybe." Aldreda sighed. "I feel there is more going on than I understand."

Elinor hastened to tell her the news of Harris's death on the cliffs.

Aldreda was intrigued. "You think it wasn't an accident?"

"I think we should find these jewels quickly. When can you next accompany me on a hunt? We did not make it very far last night with the advent of Mr Delquon."

"I wonder if he is a mister," mused Aldreda. "He could be from selkie nobility. He has the arrogance for it."

"Do selkies have rank?" enquired Elinor.

"Of course. Right up to their monarch, Queen Glowdon. Followed by Ducs, Erls, Barones, and Llords. 'Mister Delquon' could be any of those."

"He does strike me as a spoiled aristocrat," said Elinor. "Why do you think he is ashore? The adventures of a bored young lord?"

"It is possible." A thoughtful look crossed Aldreda's face. "Unless Jaq is ... " Her voice trailed off.

"Unless Jaq is what?"

"Never mind," said Aldreda firmly. "What about you? Did you find anything?"

Elinor recounted her divining adventures, including the 'secret' stash in the oak tree, and her subsequent doubts. Aldreda was unwilling to give her opinion. "We shall have to investigate ourselves," she said. "Then we will know for certain what is in the tree."

"Yes, but how?" asked Elinor. "Shall we creep back in the dead of night to open dusty chests and climb oak trees?"

"I don't see why not," said Aldreda bracingly. "If needs must, ladylike conduct can be sacrificed."

"Certainly. I will show Miss Trent I am above such concerns."

"I would not assume she is the jewel thief mastermind."

Elinor sighed. "When you put it like that, it sounds

unlikely. Apart from when Miss Trent was violently attacking me, she seemed a comfortable sort of person. Yet who else would steal heirloom jewels?"

"The countess," said Aldreda. "Or the baron. They are both well connected and locally situated."

"But what reason could possibly motivate them?" asked Elinor. "Regardless, our first priority is to go back along the coast and look there for the jewels. Can you come with me this evening?"

"Indeed," said Aldreda. "This time I think we should walk parallel to the cliffs but further inland. In case any selkies are lurking along the coast."

Elinor agreed. Without further discussion, she tucked Aldreda into her newly appointed basket, and threw a dark cloth over the top of it. Both of them needed to sleep.

THAT MORNING ELINOR'S slumber was rudely disturbed by the sound of Samuel yowling. Elinor's eyes shot open, and she rolled out of bed hastily. Samuel was hissing and batting at Aldreda's basket, his fur standing on end. He crouched low and wriggled his rear slightly. Elinor leapt forward before he could.

"Samuel, stop!" She grabbed him. "That is Miss Zooth's bed. You cannot disturb her!"

Hoping they had not woken Aldreda, Elinor bore Samuel downstairs and received a scratch on the arm for her pains. She placated him with some kippers, and she slipped back upstairs to dress. She had a task before her – to persuade Perry to stay away from the docks and villainous fishermen.

This was no mean feat and was only accomplished by

pointing out it was the last day the Laberches were staying with them, and the ladies required the escort of a gentleman into Deockley to purchase a few necessities. Perry accepted this burdensome duty with some hesitation, only finally convinced by Elinor's observation that Mademoiselle Laberche would be terribly bored without him.

"Can't have that," he acknowledged, grinning.

The marquise was quite determined to accompany them, perhaps thinking Elinor would not be sufficient chaperone for her daughter. Accordingly, they all set off on foot together, even Mrs Avely.

Deockley was becoming familiar to Elinor. The wooden framed houses gleamed in the sun, and the church tower struck ten as they approached. Mademoiselle Laberche exclaimed at the prettiness of the harbour, even though the tide was out and it looked much like a mud flat.

The first order of business was to visit the leather-maker, to purchase new bags and shoes. These were, of course, far from the fashionable accoutrements to which the Laberches were accustomed, but beggars could not be choosers, as Mademoiselle Laberche said rather proudly. Elinor was pleased to see Perry dancing attendance on the Frenchwoman; he appeared to have forgotten all the fishermen.

Next on the agenda was the haberdashery, where, true to the village's reputation, an astonishing array of laces and silks were laid out for such a provincial port. Mademoiselle Laberche chose a few of the more serviceable fabrics, determined to make a few practical dresses, but was prevailed upon by Perry to buy some exquisite French lace to adorn them.

Elinor admired the purchases. "I believe Miss Trent,

the companion to the countess, is handy with her needle," she remarked. "Miss Trent avidly follows French fashions. Perhaps she can be prevailed upon to help you make some new dresses."

"We do not want to impose," said the marquise stiffly. Elinor wondered if this was humility or snobbery.

The marquise insisted on buying a small pistol as well, from the armoury, to offer them some protection in uncivilised England. "We have learned our lesson," she said. "I will not be so ill-used again." Elinor felt quite sorry for any smuggler who tried to steal the marquise's jewels in the future.

Then it was the inn, as by this time the party was quite famished. They ordered a vast amount of pies and pastries and a hot pot of tea. Just as they were finishing, Beresford came through the door.

Beresford was in his riding gear again and looked very masculine and stern. Seeing their party, however, his expression changed to polite urbanity. He walked over to bow to Elinor's mother.

"Good morning, Mrs Avely. Are these your new guests?"

"Let me introduce you, my lord," said Mrs Avely, looking rather flustered. She hastily introduced the Laberches.

Beresford bowed – much more deeply and creditably than he had for Elinor, she noted crossly. He was scrutinised carefully by both the marquise and her daughter.

He raised an eyebrow. "Am I the first English earl you have been privy to meet?" he enquired. "I feel I am rather being examined."

"Indeed," said Mademoiselle Laberche, blushing. "I did not expect English earls to be quite so ... tall."

This comment – and the flirtatious intonation in

which it was uttered – caused quite a stir. Perry stiffened up, Elinor felt a stab of irritation, and the marquise frowned at her daughter.

Beresford laughed. "Are all Frenchmen short?" he asked. "I suppose your lovely *petitesse* would not look quite so well on your countrymen, mademoiselle."

Elinor tried not to glare, and Mademoiselle Laberche blushed even more at this charming return. "I do not mean to impugn my countrymen," she said. "Merely to compliment the Englishmen." She widened her gaze to include Perry, but he looked a little put out. "You all seem so ... noble."

Beresford laughed. "The crossing must have addled your perceptions if you think all Englishmen are noble. I hear you had a rough journey?"

Elinor didn't know how he had heard that, as she certainly hadn't given him any details. Mademoiselle Laberche gave a delicate shiver and nodded. "Oh, it was terrible, the waves were like mountains."

Beresford looked at her sympathetically, and Elinor was irked to find herself experiencing a spasm of jealousy.

He spoke soothingly. "Yet now you are safe on these noble English shores, mademoiselle."

"I do not know about safe," said the marquise coldly. "Our jewels were taken by your compatriots." She gave her daughter a black look.

Elinor could only be glad the marquise had not said the jewels were taken by Beresford, although *compatriots* could be interpreted widely or narrowly. "The smugglers have failed to return the Laberche's diamonds," Elinor hastened to explain. "Do you know the identity of any smugglers in Deockley, my lord? Could you have a word in their ears? Perhaps an edict from the lord on high might persuade them to return the jewels."

Beresford quirked his brows. "It is more a question of who *doesn't* smuggle." Amusement glimmered in his eye but then he turned a sombre face to the marquise. "I am sorry to hear your jewels have gone missing, madame. I shall endeavour to put the word around. I shall recover them, do not fear. We cannot have our national image tarnished by such a crime."

The marquise narrowed her eyes at him. "Or the earldom tarnished."

Mademoiselle Laberche coughed. "Thank you, my lord." She was apparently trying to make up for the rudeness of her mother, but Elinor did not think it required the fluttering of eyelashes. "We greatly appreciate your efforts on our behalf."

Beresford gave her one of his rare smiles, which lit his face into attractiveness. Elinor grit her teeth. His lordship would not find the jewels, because Elinor was going to find them first.

The earl cast Elinor a glance, and then turned back to the marquise. "I believe we can expect your company at the Beresford Manor tomorrow?" he asked. "I hope you will be comfortable there, though it will not compare with the home you left behind."

"Yes," said the marquise, unbending a little. "I thank you for your hospitality. I look forward to meeting the countess."

"As she does you," said Beresford, and conversation turned to less threatening channels, such as the weather and English food. Beresford mentioned the estate's jam, promising the ladies would find it most delicious. Elinor felt a pang. Once she had been the lady to whom Beresford bragged about plum jam, even if he was only funning.

With the others debating the merits of Devon's cream tea over Paris's croissants, she took the opportunity to quietly ask Beresford about Harris. "Have you visited the vicar again?" she asked. "When is Harris's funeral to be?"

"Tomorrow. In his home town in the next county, so do not plan on attending, Miss Avely."

"I had no such intention," she replied. "Has anyone discovered what happened to him?"

"No." Beresford gave her a grim look. "However, the huge lump on the back of his head indicated a violent blow. It could have been from either a fall on the rocks, or from a more human agency. The latter possibility is what worries me."

"Surely it was just the fall," protested Elinor. "Harris was a religious man – he would not have been involved in anything dangerous."

Beresford raised an eyebrow, the amused glint back. "I am afraid to inform you that the vicarage is a well-known smuggling house."

Elinor's mouth fell open in astonishment. Beresford continued, taking some pleasure in her surprise. "Much of the loot is hoarded there, as an independent third party. The vicar and Harris were up to their necks in it. There is every possibility Harris was involved with something even more nefarious, such as this jewel caper." He grinned at her, then caught himself. His expression settled back into sternness. "Not that any of this is your concern, Miss Avely."

"Of course not," she said gently. Her mind seethed with the new information. The vicarage a hotbed of smuggling! Perhaps Aldreda should move back into the cellar. Indeed, the passageway between the cellar and the church was probably a route for illicit activity.

She ignored Beresford's frown, and looked around to see if Perry had heard this latest information. Then she realised Perry wasn't there.

"Excuse me." Elinor stood abruptly. "I think Perry has wandered off. I am going to join him."

15

IN WHICH FISH AND FISHERMEN
ARE UNSAVOURY

She was right: Perry was striding down the cobbled avenue, heading towards the sea. Elinor hurried after.

"You can't go down there by yourself!" she huffed at him.

Perry shot her an irate look. "Plum jam! As if that would attract a lady!"

Elinor blinked. "No, indeed. Beresford is quite ridiculous."

"Mademoiselle Laberche thinks he is ... tall."

"More likely she thinks he is droll."

"A real gentleman wouldn't brag about jam."

"No," agreed Elinor.

"What are us mere mortals supposed to do, who don't have plum orchards?"

"I really do not know."

Perry practically stomped. "I'm going to interrogate these fishermen now. You go back to the inn and hang on Beresford's every word."

Elinor ignored that insult. "I can divine. Please let me

come with you. Remember, *vincit prudentia!* Prudence is certainly wise in this case."

Perry looked annoyed. "You pull out the family motto when it suits *you*," he snapped. "And your divinations don't seem to be working. Besides, why can't I resolve this in a normal fashion? Why do you have to always lurk around divining things?"

Elinor raised her brows. It sounded as if Perry was nursing some resentment toward her.

"You have never complained before," she remarked.

"You've never had a small bat assisting you before."

"Miss Zooth is asleep now."

"Good," said Perry and mumbled on about how he was perfectly capable of finding the jewels without the help of women and bats, and that they should all go and fill their faces with plum jam instead of bothering him.

Elinor let him ramble on, but she took his arm and slowed their pace as they approached the jetties.

"So, red hair and missing fingers?" she murmured.

The boats lay on the mud flats, looking somewhat forlorn. Their colours still showed bright under the sun – reds, blues and yellows – but now Elinor could see the peeling undersides. Without water lapping at their planks, they lost some of their glow and polish, looking more disreputable, like drunks recovering from revels. A strong smell of rotting fish assailed Elinor. She could see carcasses lying on the mud.

A few men were sitting around in the sun, while a couple more worked on one of the boats.

"Hallo there," said Perry. "Tide's out, I see?"

One of the fishermen, a tall skinny fellow slouched against a post, grunted. It was difficult to tell the colour of his hair, as it was hidden by a voluminous cap which also cast a shadow over his face. Furthermore, his hands were thrust in his pockets, so Elinor could not even count his fingers.

"Does that mean no fishing at all today?" Elinor tried to peer under the cap. "Or will you go out later?"

Another grunt seemed to indicate an affirmative. Elinor wondered if grunting was the skinny fisherman's only mode of communication, and whether Mademoiselle Laberche would recognise a dastardly grunt if she heard it.

"Would you like to buy some fish?" asked another fisherman (brown-haired), waving a sun-spotted hand (fully-fingered) towards a crate of cod in the shadow of a boat. Flies buzzed around the crate.

"No, I thank you," said Elinor politely. "We are simply admiring the view from the pier."

"Sorry to hear about Harris," said Perry, going out on a limb.

One of the men looked up at that, and gave Perry a long, slow look. "Harris weren't one of us."

Perry did not quite know what to say to that.

"He shouldna been by the cliffs," put in another. This one *did* have red hair, as exhibited by the facial hair covering his large jowls. Elinor and Perry examined him closely. Before they could make wild accusations that he went by the name of Clodder or Rusty, another fisherman spoke.

"Stupid," he said, busy knotting a net with fingers that seemed all present and correct. "I wouldn't fall off no cliffs."

The tall, skinny fisherman grunted again, this time in apparent agreement. But he still didn't pull his hands out of his pockets.

"Indeed not," said Elinor, attempting flattery. "You are

all men of the seas and know exactly how to handle the cliffs."

This comment seemed to meet with some approval, in that two fishermen expectorated firmly.

"Did Harris ever go out in the boats?" asked Perry.

All heads raised and looked at him as one. Then all bent back down. No answer was given.

Perry continued boldly. "I heard Harris went out with a fellow called Floy. Do any of you gentlemen go by the name of Floy?"

The gentlemen in question merely stared at him. The tall, skinny one did not even vouchsafe a grunt, but his eyes narrowed under his cap.

"Well," said Perry. "I am eager to talk to Floy. Or a fellow by name of Clodder." He waited, but no response was forthcoming. "If you could let them know, I would appreciate it. I will make it worth their while to meet with me."

Silence again. This line of questioning had fastened the fishermen's mouths.

Elinor changed the subject, asking what kind of fish they caught. But from then on, any comments were met with grunts – not only from the skinny man this time – and they all avoided meeting her eyes.

Reluctantly, Perry and Elinor moved on, making a show of walking along the pier and back again. Elinor could feel they were being watched. She chatted glibly about the village and the shops, hoping that they had not raised too much suspicion.

Once out of hearing, she pinched Perry. "You were a little obvious, brother!"

"How else was I supposed to broach the subject?" said Perry sulkily. "I wasn't to know they would all clam up like that."

"Now they will never tell us anything. Better to have started them chatting about other things."

"They weren't chatty types," said Perry, and Elinor had to admit he had a point.

She took a deep breath to calm herself, and became aware someone was following them. Elinor turned her head slightly. It was the red-haired large-jowled fellow from the docks, fifteen paces behind. Elinor tightened her grip on Perry's arm. Somehow she didn't think this was Clodder or Floy coming to volunteer information.

"Keep walking, Perry," she muttered. "I think someone is following us." Perry turned his head. "Don't look!" Elinor hissed.

They strolled along through the village, following the winding cobbled path. The fisherman stayed fifteen paces behind. Elinor felt distinctly uneasy. What if he were to follow them home? Or murder them in their beds? Or sell them some of that dreadful fish?

She expressed these concerns to Perry. He shook his head. "It might be Clodder or Floy. Or Rusty, with a beard like that. Maybe we should see what he wants. Maybe we *should* buy some fish, to put him in a forthcoming mood."

Elinor did not feel so sanguine about it, but she allowed Perry to stop at a corner. They turned to face their shadower.

The man kept walking: slow, steady steps. He was solid, with pale arms reddened by the sun and wind. He drew abreast of them and stopped.

"What do you want?" asked Perry sharply. "Are you Rusty?"

"Who I be is not for you to worry on." The fisherman spoke in a rounded Devonshire accent that still managed to sound menacing. His gaze travelled from

Perry to Elinor. "Nawt of this is your affair. Ye keep out of it."

Elinor straightened. "I don't know what you are talking about, my good sir."

"Oooh yes, ye do," said the man, sharpening his pale blue eyes on her. "Ye've been poking around in the Beresford oak."

Elinor felt a frisson of alarm. How did this man know about that?

"I fancied some laces," she replied. "That is where the laces are delivered, no?"

The man squinted. "How should ye know? A lady like ye, new to our little corner of the world?"

"Your practices are common knowledge," said Elinor, repressing her first inclination, which was to name Miss Trent as her informant. Elinor did not want to put anyone else in trouble just to save her own skin. Besides, it could be Miss Trent who had told this man about Elinor's oak tree investigations. "You did not expect the oak tree to be such a secret, did you?"

"Ye strike me as a curious young lady," said the man. "Too curious, like your brother here. I'm merely telling ye not to be too inquisitive. Ye may end up over those cliffs like Harris."

Elinor's eyes widened.

Perry stepped forward. "Is that a threat? Are you threatening my sister?"

"Just a warning," said the man, and he smiled. One of his teeth was missing, making a dark hole in his red bearded face. "A friendly warning, that's all. Your sister is too pretty to end up over the cliffs."

Elinor swallowed. Perry took another step forward and raised his fist menacingly. The red-haired man stepped backwards and shook his head. "I aren't looking for trouble. Just letting ye know, that's all."

Perry took another step, and the man turned and walked off, his pace offensively slow. Then he turned back. "Did ye want to buy some fish, perhaps? I have some fresh mackerel ye might enjoy."

"No, I thank you," said Elinor. She grasped Perry's arm, as her brother was about object strongly to the various affronts. "We are about to return to our friends. Let's go, Perry."

ELINOR CONVINCED PERRY not to inform the rest of the company what had occurred. They did not want to make Mademoiselle Laberche feel nervous, Elinor argued, and it was best if Mother did not become worried. Elinor had no doubt that half of Deockley had seen the confrontation, so perhaps news of it would carry back anyway, through the servants. Or perhaps the red-haired fisherman was feared by the rest of the village, and everyone would keep silent.

Elinor was relieved to go home and divest herself of her companions. She needed an afternoon nap to prepare for the night's activities. She left Perry playing piquet with Mademoiselle Laberche, making the most of their last afternoon together, and snuggled into her attic bed, comforted by the knowledge that Aldreda was also sleeping the afternoon away, in her basket a few feet away.

The evening came, blustery and cold with sea winds. After a family dinner, Elinor joined her brother and their guests for a game of whist, watched by Mrs Avely, after which she made her excuses and slipped off to bed.

Opening the attic door, Elinor saw Aldreda sitting on her bed, reading one of her books.

Elinor smiled. "I hope Samuel did not disturb you? He seems to regard this attic as his domain."

"He did come hissing at the door," admitted Aldreda, "but he could not push in."

"It is a problem; he might alert someone to your presence," said Elinor. "Will he grow accustomed to you, do you think?"

"Unlikely," said Aldreda. "Cats generally perceive me as an evil sort of rat."

Elinor declaimed such a rude interpretation, but she felt rather worried. Such an animosity between two of her friends was upsetting.

Aldreda pursed her lips. "There is one thing I could do to change Samuel's mind."

"Oh?"

"I could drink from him." Aldreda hesitated uncomfortably. "When I have some of his own blood within me it will change how he responds to me. It is a protective effect that vampiri have on cats particularly, because they are our predators." She paused. "However, I do not like to do it. It doesn't seem like fair play."

Elinor raised her brows. "Do you have that effect on all those you drink from?"

"No, only cats," Aldreda hastened to reassure her. "I believe you are immune from it."

Elinor cast her mind back – she had been pleasantly disposed towards Aldreda before she offered her own blood. "Speaking of which, is it not time for your evening drink?"

Aldreda nodded, looking somewhat discomposed. Elinor tried to put the vampiri at ease, cheerfully rolling up her sleeve and joking she was happy to be of some use in the world, even if it was only to be dinner for a small lady.

Soon after, they sneaked out of the house, but just as they slipped out the front door Samuel leapt out of the shadows and let out a yowl loud enough to wake the dead. Fortunately, Perry did not stir, and the rest of the household must have dismissed it as feline adventures, for no one came to the door.

Samuel looked as if he wanted to stalk them, but Elinor shooed him away and quickly set off along the track through the fields. The moon showed its uneven face intermittently through the scudding clouds. It was a bit too bright, in these moments, for Elinor's liking. She no longer assumed that no one else would be out and about of an evening, and she did not want to be seen. She was careful to tuck Aldreda into her shawl, on the off chance they might run into Beresford again. Not that Elinor wanted to run into him again.

The two ladies talked as Elinor strode along the narrow path. Elinor told Aldreda what had happened that day with the fisherman.

"He was threatening me, or warning me," she said. "Telling me to stop looking around. Of course, that makes me more determined to look."

"Hm, yes," agreed Aldreda. "Did he actually threaten to throw you over the cliffs? You think he is the brawn of the enterprise?"

"Yes, someone told him about my oak tree investigations. My first thought, of course, is Miss Trent. She was right there."

"Someone else might have seen you poking around," said Aldreda. "Jaq Delquon, for example. Or the countess herself could have been informed. It strikes me that Miss

Trent and the countess enjoy an intimate relationship. Miss Trent is likely to tell her everything."

"Oh?" Elinor lifted her brows. "You mean ... ?"

Miss Zooth nodded. "When I was exploring the house at night I saw Miss Trent – er – slip into Lady Beresford's room."

"Goodness." Elinor considered this new information. "Yet Miss Trent claimed Lady Beresford doesn't know about the oak tree."

"Perhaps Miss Trent did not want you discussing the matter with her mistress. Perhaps, in fact, she is keeping something from Lady Beresford."

"I wonder what. It appears suspicious, but it could be as innocuous as some new silks."

"And it could be a servant or gardener who saw you at the oak tree, who might be connected with the smuggling."

"I suppose so." Elinor sighed. "We don't even know if this threatening fisherman was Rusty or Clodder. All the men at the docks clammed up when Perry questioned them."

"Nonetheless, I am glad we are taking the farmland paths tonight."

16

IN WHICH COMPANY IS MOST
INOPPORTUNE

*E*linor agreed with Aldreda's assessment. The path through the paddocks was narrower and less frequented, but as far as Elinor was concerned, that was a good thing. The expanse of fields meant they could see if anyone approached. A copse of birch trees huddled on a nearby hill, shaking their branches in the strong sea wind, but that was all that disturbed the emptiness of the landscape.

Elinor turned the conversation to the Moria Pearls.

"These pearls of yours – are they of sentimental value only?"

"They are enchanted," admitted Aldreda. "With Memory. Memoria is Latin for Memory. Henri placed much of his knowledge into that necklace. It is the equivalent of a rare library."

"What kind of knowledge?"

"I suspect it is the teachings of the eight arts."

"Goodness." The necklace was suddenly much more intriguing to Elinor – something Aldreda probably intended. "Could we access the knowledge inside, if we found it?"

"Yes, especially as you are a Discernor. A Memor would be best at it, however."

"How exciting," said Elinor eagerly. "You will have to come to London with me, so we can find any other Musors together." With a pang she remembered she was no longer welcome in London. Yet Elinor would skulk around if she had to, if only she could find some other Musors in the metropolis. She knew of at least one: Lord Treffler's mother.

Elinor suddenly halted. Something was pricking at her mind.

"I sense something," she breathed. "A jewel."

"Out here?" asked Aldreda.

"Close by."

"Well, let us be careful it is not attached to somebody again," cautioned Aldreda.

Elinor knew it wasn't so this time. The jewel was close, and she could not see anybody for miles.

She took slow steps in the direction that called her, and with a thrill saw there was a small cairn by the path: a pile of rocks stacked on top of each other as a marker. The whispering hum of the jewel took her directly to it.

"In there." Elinor pointed.

"Left there as a signal?" wondered Aldreda. "Or for pickup? Should we leave it there?"

"What if it belongs to the Laberches? We must look." Elinor could not restrain herself. She knelt in front of the cairn and started unstacking the rocks. They were rough but light, and she worked quickly, sensing her way to the jewel hidden inside.

"Elinor," whispered Aldreda suddenly. "Someone approaches! Thirty paces to the east!"

Elinor looked around. Moving quickly across the moors, from the direction of the copse of trees, was a masculine figure. At first Elinor's heart leapt with the thought it might be Beresford, but she soon saw the figure was not as broad-shouldered or as tall as he.

Yet he was familiar. Jaq, or Perry? Elinor stood, brushing down her skirts, hoping he could not see what she had been doing. She squinted in the moonlight, trying to make out his features. A black hat shadowed the man's face.

Aldreda became a bat and took off into the air before he was close enough to see. Elinor hastily reached for the silk gown and shoved it into her reticule. Looking up, she finally realised who approached.

Lord Treffler, in Devon at last. What was he doing lurking about in the dark on the fields? Elinor realised, wryly, that he could ask the very same thing of her.

The answer, of course, would be similar. Elinor faced him, chin at a defiant angle.

Lord Treffler came up to her, but did not bow. Perhaps he thought the circumstances excused him from civilities. Elinor soon put him straight on the matter. She curtsied. "Lord Treffler. A surprise to see you here."

"Ha," said his lordship, his narrow features breaking into a smile. It was a charming smile, one that had won him the rights to any drawing room in London. "Miss Avely. I cannot say the same. I quite expected you to be here, sooner or later. Were you looking for my ruby?"

"What do you mean?" Even as she spoke, Elinor realised, and inwardly cursed herself.

Lord Treffler pulled out his quizzing glass and examined her through it, the silver circle catching in the moonlight. "The ruby I hid in those rocks. The one you were scrabbling about for. Proving you are indeed a jewel diviner, despite your protestations."

Elinor stiffened her spine infinitesimally. "A lowly trick to play on a lady, my lord."

"If the lady would be open with me, I would not have to resort to such unchivalrous behaviour." Lord Treffler let the eyeglass drop and swung it idly, though still watching her closely.

Elinor resisted the urge to fold her arms in front of her. "Very well, I confess. I am a jewel diviner."

"A jewel diviner wandering around at night, unattended. I am most pleased," said his lordship. He bent to shift a few rocks, retrieving a gem that glinted momentarily in his hand. "You were looking for this? I am glad to see you are pursuing our quest."

"Yes," said Elinor, as she could not deny it. "At least, I was looking for some jewels that were stolen from a friend. I have good reason to believe they are being kept with the other missing jewels."

"A friend?" enquired Lord Treffler, tucking the ruby away. Elinor told him about the Laberches and their missing diamonds, thinking he would discover it soon enough – it was common knowledge now in the village.

Lord Treffler raised his brows. "The Laberches, you say? Their jewels have also been stolen?"

"You know them?" asked Elinor in surprise.

"I made their acquaintance when I was in France." Lord Treffler did not seem pleased to hear they were now in England. "Is Mademoiselle Laberche well?"

"She appears none the worse for her trials. If you know her personally, you will find it a pleasure to return her diamonds to her."

"Hm, yes," said Lord Treffler, though Elinor rather thought he was irked by the fact of this personal connection, as it impinged upon his plans to claim the treasure for himself.

"You arrived in Devon today?" she asked, trying to move the subject away from jewel hunts, and wondering if Aldreda was hovering far above their heads.

"Indeed. Sorry I am late to join you. London's delights tempted me too long." He smirked. Elinor knew he was probably referring to his affair with a particular lady of the nobility. "Have you found anything in my absence?"

"No."

"Are you certain, Miss Avely?"

"Would I be out here digging around for rubies if I had found anything?" she replied tartly.

"I suspect you would scrabble after any jewel you divined," said Lord Treffler. "We are partners now, Miss Avely. I would not want you recovering any treasures without me."

"We are recovering treasures only to return them to the rightful owners," stated Elinor. "I can do that by myself."

"Of course," agreed Lord Treffler. "Yet, you are a lady. You should not be alone, unattended, undefended. Harm may come to you. You must allow me to accompany you."

Elinor examined his face. She suspected there was a threat hidden beneath the gentlemanly expostulations.

"I am not undefended," she said slowly. "My brother, Peregrine ..."

"Ah, yes, Peregrine, where is he at this moment?" Lord Treffler took a step closer to her, closer than she liked. "I must call on you tomorrow and chastise him for leaving you so ... vulnerable."

Elinor swallowed. Then she waved a casual hand, trying to keep the tone light. "Oh, you must not mention this in front of my mother. She would highly disapprove."

"Mothers are so conservative," agreed his lordship. "My mother is also against the whole notion. Yet I am sure she would be delighted to meet you."

Threats *and* bribes, thought Elinor. Lord Treffler was indeed eager to obtain her cooperation.

"Certainly, I would greatly enjoy meeting your mother," she said calmly. It was better to pretend he had it.

"Where were you going now?" he asked, stepping back again. "May I accompany you on your search?"

"I hardly see how I can stop you," she said mildly, and began walking along the path again.

Elinor was determined Lord Treffler would not halt her quest for the night. She would still divine near the cliffs; she need not tell him if she sensed anything. In fact, his presence might be quite useful, if any villainous fishermen appeared on the scene.

Elinor kept up a brisk pace, with Lord Treffler trailing close behind her. He quizzed her on the village and any gossip about smuggling and the Laberches, but she kept her answers short and uninformative. She claimed she had to keep a quiet mind for divining, which did succeed in closing his mouth. Elinor hoped a small bat was flying above them, out of sight. It was comforting to think if anything happened – if Lord Treffler turned nasty – Aldreda could fly for help. Only it might be a while before the vampiri would be able to rouse Perry from his customarily deep slumbers.

They reached the whipped-cream rock. Elinor was relieved to find there was no devastatingly handsome selkie brooding on the ocean view. She stopped where Jaq had sat the evening before, on the aft of the stone. A strong wind blew in her face, blasting in from the sea. The water was choppy this evening: white caps showing on the grey. Elinor scanned the waves, looking for a head, seal or otherwise, but could not see any.

She turned inward, doing her first real divination for the night. This time there was nothing hidden in the cave nearby where the Laberches had sheltered – or at least nothing resembling a precious stone. Elinor widened her reach to a radius of about fifty yards. Nothing.

"Well?" asked Lord Treffler, to her left. "Can you sense anything?"

"No," she said shortly.

"Where to now?"

"I suppose we walk along the cliffs. I should warn you that someone died a few days ago, on these rocks."

Elinor turned to examine his face as she said this. Lord Trefller seemed surprised, and wary. "Really? Falling off?"

"How else?"

Lord Treffler shrugged. "Maybe they were swimming, and were thrown against the rocks."

Elinor had not considered this. She made a note to ask Beresford if Harris's clothes were wet when he was found, though that fact would not be decisive. He may have become wet once he fell.

"Near here?" asked Lord Treffler.

"I am not sure. Sea-Catcher Cove, wherever that is. I am not yet familiar with the exact contours of the shoreline. However, it behoves us to be careful. Please may you lead the way, my lord?"

She smiled at him, a beguiling young lady. Lord Treffler was not fooled. "Ah, you would much rather I slip on the rocks than you. Very well, Miss Avely." Squaring his narrow shoulders, he set off down the path winding along the cliff tops. "Let me know if you sense anything."

Elinor followed him, giving a quick glance around to see if she could spot any bats. She knew Aldreda was close by, as the divination had not addled her mind very much.

Every five minutes Elinor called Lord Treffler to halt, and did another search for the jewels. Each time she shook her head in a negative.

On the fourth stop, she found them.

It was utterly clear. The voices sang together, a rich mixture of tones, like a clarion call to her senses. Excitement thrilled through Elinor. Carefully, she tried to keep her face blank and passive, so Lord Treffler would not realise. Then she listened, following the call with her mind to pinpoint its exact location.

It came from the sea, forty yards out in the water.

Elinor narrowed her eyes, peering out at the grey waves. There were white buoys floating atop the surging currents, now that she looked. Markers for crab pots perhaps, or kegs of gin. One of them would mark the pot of jewels. She could even hazard a guess as to which one – the small one, third in from the right. It bobbed erratically in the waves, a small beacon in the sporadic moonlight.

"Anything?" asked Lord Treffler.

Elinor shook her head, hoping she had not paused longer here than elsewhere. "Nothing." She almost asked to turn back, but she thought it wiser to end the night's search in another place. So they kept walking along the narrow track.

Lord Treffler was disposed to make conversation. "You know, it is a pity I could not prevail upon my mother to join us. A gold diviner would be useful out here."

"Yes," agreed Elinor. Jewels were often set in gold. "No doubt gold necklaces are part of the treasure."

"Not only that," said Lord Treffler. "There are French spies about. Apparently they smuggle English gold back to France, to pay Napoleon's soldiers. It is called the Guinea Run – a boat load of guineas across the seas. Imagine if we could find that before it left our shores."

"An honourable venture," agreed Elinor.

"Ah yes," said Lord Treffler. "It would be bounty we could rightfully keep."

"Would we not return it to the king?"

"I would insist on our own reward," said Lord Treffler firmly. "I don't suppose you can stretch your talents to gold?"

"No," said Elinor. She was not going to tell him Aldreda's belief that it was possible to learn to divine other things. "Let us stop here. I will try one more time."

She did so, and duly reported a negative.

"Are you absolutely certain?" A harsh note suddenly entered Lord Treffler's voice. The sudden change in his manner was so marked that Elinor almost jumped.

"I am certain," she said, turning to stare at him. She was determined to show no fear. "I am weary now. Let us return."

Lord Treffler took a step closer. "I hope you would not keep anything from me, Miss Avely."

"Of course not. Why should I do that?" she asked, not dropping her eyes.

The charming smile came back into place. "Exactly. I am glad we understand one another."

"Yes, and I rely upon your escort back home." Elinor

smiled, trying for a modicum of charm as well. She stood aside, allowing him to lead the way back along the path.

She felt the jewels again as they passed them, and an urgent thought occurred to her. What if the smugglers came back this very night, before she could bring Perry on the morrow? She needed to signal to Aldreda that this was the spot. Perhaps the vampiri could keep watch. Elinor eyed Lord Treffler's back ahead of her. Suddenly she waved her hands around wildly and jabbed her finger, pointing out to sea.

Then Elinor kept walking, the picture of feminine decorum. Lord Treffler might prove to be a problem, if he were to attempt to keep her company all the time. She spent the remainder of the walk considering ways and means to occupy his lordship elsewhere the following day.

WHEN ELINOR HAD SAFELY LOCKED the door in Lord Treffler's face, she hurried up to the attic. Aldreda was waiting on the bed, a shawl wrapped around her tiny form.

Aldreda raised her brows. "What was that strange dance you did out there? Dare I hope you have found the treasure?"

"I have! Clear as day. It is sunk in that cove, under one of those buoys."

"How exciting!" Aldreda smiled up at her.

Elinor sat next to her on the bed. "Could I ask you to keep watch over it tonight? I have a fear that the smugglers will whisk it out from under our noses."

"Of course. I have the whole night ahead of me, after all."

"Not the whole night. It must be after two in the morning already."

"You had better sleep. But first tell me about this new gentleman."

Elinor sighed. "I don't think he is much of a gentleman. He is Lord Treffler, the one who approached me in London after the garden party debacle, guessing I could divine jewels. He wants to find these ones, but I don't think his motives are noble."

"It sounded as if he was threatening you," observed Aldreda. "No way to talk to a lady."

"I agree. Terrible manners."

"You bore it well."

"I thought so." Elinor smiled. "Yet I am exhausted now. In a few hours Perry and I will pick up the jewels." She carried Aldreda over to the window and placed her on the sill. "Thank you for guarding them. I am hopeful that by the time I see you next, it will all be resolved."

17

IN WHICH A CAT COMES UNDER SUSPICION

*E*linor woke late that morning, with the sun slanting in through her attic window. She felt bleary and in need of more rest, but the day's quest awaited. Sitting up, she rubbed her face, and glanced over at Aldreda's basket.

The cloth lay gaping, exposing the bed to light.

Elinor leapt to her feet, hoping to save Aldreda from ill-effects. But Aldreda was not in the basket.

Elinor stared at the small, untouched blankets, and felt a wave of foreboding. Quickly she searched the room, in the vain hope that Aldreda had decided to sleep somewhere else.

The room was empty.

Had Samuel chased the vampiri out? Or had she not returned from her watch overnight?

Hurriedly Elinor dressed and rushed down to search the house. She found Samuel sunning himself in the back garden, his fur golden in the morning light. The cat raised his head sleepily, and batted his tail slightly. Elinor stared at him, praying desperately he had not eaten Aldreda. Surely that was impossible:

the vampiri would have defended herself. Samuel looked unharmed, and no more smug than usual, as one might expect if he had eaten a vampiri for breakfast.

Elinor shuddered, and went inside for her own breakfast. She was late; the others were already finishing, the four of them sipping their tea or chocolate.

"Slug-a-bed," said Perry.

"Are you well, Elinor?" asked her mother. "You look a little pale."

"Merely hungry," said Elinor. As she sat down she widened her eyes at Perry in a meaningful fashion.

"What?" said Perry.

"Pass me the chocolate, brother." Elinor frowned at him darkly.

"No need to be so grim about it." Perry passed the jug, then seemed to realise that something else might be afoot beyond a pressing need for chocolate. "What are your plans for the day, sister dear?"

"I'm going for a walk along the cliffs," she replied. "It would be nice if you would join me, Perry."

"Oh, I am escorting the marquise and mademoiselle to the manor," said Perry, but a look of doubt came into his face.

Curse it. She needed Perry. "That is a pity," Elinor said with emphasis. "Such a lovely day today."

Mademoiselle Laberche pouted at Perry. "So sad this is our last breakfast in your house!"

"We have much appreciated your hospitality," put in the marquise. "However, we do not wish to overstay our welcome."

"Impossible," said Perry, looking in some indecision from Elinor to Mademoiselle Laberche. "Why don't you stay another day? Leave tomorrow?"

Mademoiselle Laberche giggled. "Lady Beresford is expecting us today. We cannot be rude."

Elinor was eating with unseemly haste, though the food stuck in her throat. A vision of Aldreda, injured and stranded on the cliffs in the sun, was cutting at her insides.

Perry observed her behaviour and turned to his own food with renewed vigour.

Mrs Avely was watching the whole. "I can accompany madame and mademoiselle," she offered. "It is more seemly if I go, to pay my respects. I have not called upon the countess yet. Elinor, you should have a companion when you walk. It is not appropriate to charge around the countryside by yourself."

Perry agreed through a mouthful of food, much to Mademoiselle Laberche's barely hidden surprise.

"Very well, Mother," said Elinor meekly.

In short order, she and Perry finished. Elinor stood to leave, only to hear a knock on the front door. Soon after, a flustered maid came up to Mrs Avely and announced the Earl of Beresford was in the sitting room.

Elinor wrinkled her face impatiently. For once she did not feel like seeing Beresford. Yet what if he knew something of Aldreda? Though Beresford did not even know the vampiri existed, unless Jaq had told him. Biting her lip, Elinor followed her mother into the sitting room. She would quickly see if Beresford knew anything, then depart for the cliffs.

"My lord." The Avely ladies curtsied. Elinor examined him closely. He did not seem overly distressed or afoot with news. He was clad in morning clothes, his thick brown hair neatly arranged, his cravat beautifully tied.

"How do you do, Mrs Avely, Miss Avely?" Beresford too examined Elinor, but did not seem to like what he saw. "Miss Avely, did you sleep well? You look a little peaked."

"Not so well, thank you, my lord," she replied. "I am about to go walking, for some fresh air."

Beresford narrowed his gaze. "I would love to accompany you. However, I have come to escort the Laberches to my home."

"Of course," said Mrs Avely. "That is very kind."

"Very," said Elinor. Even in her worry about Aldreda the thought crossed her mind that Beresford had come especially to accompany Mademoiselle Laberche on the journey. He had not seemed immune to French feminine wiles yesterday.

"A simple duty," replied his lordship. "Where are you walking, Miss Avely?"

"Along the cliffs." Already her mind was there, wondering where Aldreda could have taken any shelter. There were precious few trees on those windswept rocks. Caves – maybe she was in a cave. Elinor's eyes turned towards the windows, staring out at the cursedly sunny blue skies.

"In which direction?"

She barely heard him, and turned back. "Sorry?"

"In which direction will you walk?"

"Away from the village." It occurred to her that she should tell him the whereabouts of the jewels. Elinor blinked at him, considering. She did not really care anymore who found them. Perry, however, might object strongly to being deprived his chance to play the hero. "I must go now. Good day, my lord."

"Good day, Miss Avely," said Beresford to her departing back, and she was vaguely aware his tone was slightly cool.

PERRY WAS WAITING by the front door. Outside, he put out his arm, and Elinor took it gladly, dragging him down the path.

"So?" Perry asked impatiently. "Have you found the jewels?"

"Yes," said Elinor. "Never mind that. Miss Zooth is missing."

"Who, the bat?"

"The lady vampiri, yes."

"Oh," said Perry. "Where is the treasure? When did you find it? Are we going there now?"

"Perry, listen to me. Either Samuel ate Miss Zooth, or she didn't come home last night."

"What? She lives here?" exclaimed Perry, showing a callous disregard for the notion Miss Zooth had been consumed by Samuel.

Elinor kept marching along the path. "Yes. In my room. She wasn't there this morning."

"That's no great problem," said Perry. "It is an excellent thing if a bat is not in your room. But I doubt Samuel ate her. She wouldn't go down easily; she'd cause Samuel no end of indigestion. She must be out and about still."

"She can't bear sunlight!"

"As in she doesn't like the stuff, or she crumples up and dies in it?"

"Perry! It may very well be the latter." Elinor thought grimly that she had never enquired as to the particulars.

The sun was well into the sky by now. The winds of the previous evening had dropped away, and it was a beautiful, calm, light-filled day. Elinor muttered to herself. Some large grey clouds would have been most opportune.

Perry, taking in the general radiance, finally seemed to grasp the situation. "But where is she?"

"I don't know! I left her guarding the treasure last night, in a cove along the cliffs. We are going there now."

This, at least, met with Perry's approval. "Oh good."

Elinor let go of his arm, to surge on ahead. "Don't be too excited. The jewels are sunk in the sea, about forty yards out in the water. It won't be easy to recover them."

"Pooh, what is a little bit of water? Well done, Elinor! You've done it!"

"I have put Aldreda in danger, that's what I've done."

The rest of the walk was in silence, as Elinor set a cracking pace. When she reached the cove with the white buoys, she felt a sinking sensation.

No jewels pricked at her senses.

She pulled to a halt on the cliff top. The wide blue seas stretched out before her, meeting the lighter blue of the sky. A faint breeze caressed her face. Elinor closed her eyes, opening her inward sense.

Nothing. She extended the search further out, but still nothing met her mind.

"The jewels are gone," she said bleakly.

"What!"

Elinor turned, her face grim. "Whoever took the jewels must have taken Miss Zooth. She was probably trying to stop them."

"I can't believe it!" Perry was aghast. "How could you let them slip out of our hands like this!"

"Never mind the cursed jewels," shouted Elinor. "What about Aldreda?"

"She's probably fine. Hiding in a cave somewhere," said Perry. "I'm more concerned about the loot. It could be halfway to London by now – with Miss Zooth, I might add. Have you considered she might have arranged this disappearance?"

"Don't be ridiculous," said Elinor crossly make a good point about a cave. We mus' where I found the Laberches."

However, it was not so easy to find the (did not contain a jewel-wearing marquise less hour of combing the cliffs and scrabt rocks, Elinor felt quite desperate.

"I can't find it," she wailed. "What if ι yards from us, injured, and I can't even reac

"She is probably sleeping," said Perry reasc

"She is not, I can tell," said Elinor.

"What, you have developed other power: asked Perry.

"Maybe I have." Elinor suddenly lifted her head. "I have a distinct feeling she is far from us."

"Maybe you should try divining Miss Zooth," said Perry. "Even though I would much rather you divine the jewels. Besides, they may be in the same place."

Elinor sat down, careless of her gown. She needed to rest, and to listen. Putting her head in her hands, she closed her eyes, and turned inward once more.

All she felt was lonely. No whisper of Aldreda came, only a sense of the vast expanse of ocean before her. No, there was something on the ocean, a faint presence. She opened her eyes and saw a small boat on the horizon, its white sails unfurled in the sun. As she watched it grew bigger, heading to shore. Not Aldreda then.

Elinor closed her eyes. Behind her was the more solid feeling of cliffs and hills. But no human presence, or vampiri, filled it.

Wait. Something moved nearby. Elinor's eyes shot open.

It was not the message of her sixth sense, but the sound of footsteps. They approached, attached to an elegant figure with long black hair.

"Well met, Miss Avely," said Jaq Delquon.

Elinor stood wearily. "Mr Delquon. This is my brother, Mr Peregrine Avely."

Jaq executed one of his flawless bows. "A pleasure." He gave Perry a charming smile, and then turned his head to Elinor and gave her a broad wink. When she stared at him blankly, Jaq waggled his head and wiggled his eyebrows.

Elinor raised her own brows. "Yes, Mr Delquon?"

Jaq lowered his voice. "Your little friend is safe, Miss Avely."

Elinor almost allowed her posture to droop with relief. But not quite. "Miss Zooth?"

Jaq shot a look at Perry. "Yes, the same."

"Oh, don't worry about Perry, he is acquainted with Miss Zooth. Where is she? What happened?"

"Well," said Jaq. "I went for a – walk – early this morning. In fact, it was just before daybreak."

Elinor thought this sounded highly suspicious, but she was too eager to hear the rest. "Yes?"

"I saw a little ruckus occurring in a cove further up. A couple of men were rowing a small boat to the buoys, but they were behaving in a most peculiar fashion. Flapping their arms around, rocking the boat, generally carrying on as if they were under attack by an invisible force."

"The smugglers!" said Perry.

"Dear Aldreda," said Elinor. "She was trying to stop them."

"That may be apparent to you but it was far from apparent to me," said Jaq. "I moved closer, utilising some stealth." Elinor wondered if that was a euphemism for being a seal. "I saw them grab a small black creature out of the sky and shove it into a sack."

Elinor gasped.

"Indeed," said Jaq. "Couldn't have that. Gruesome treatment of a lady, even if she was a bat at the time. So I intervened. Took the sack."

"Hold on," said Perry. "Did you swim out to the boat?"

Jaq looked shifty. "I did. Hauled myself aboard, snatched the sack and swam off." He grinned at Perry. "An early morning swim."

Perry was impressed. "A bold move. I don't know that I would brave the cold ocean for Miss Zooth. Did the smugglers fight back?"

Jaq smiled at Perry approvingly, and raked his eyes over him a second time. He seemed to like what he saw. "A little, but I easily bested them."

"Never mind that. What did you do with the sack?" cried Elinor.

Jaq cleared his throat. "I am aware that the small lady is somewhat averse to sun. That in fact a vampiri will burst into flame if exposed to light for too long." Elinor caught her breath, horrified. Jaq continued with aplomb. "The glorious globe was just breaking over the horizon as the contretemps took place. Therefore, I dared not remove her from the unfortunate receptacle."

"Where is she?" demanded Elinor, her voice shaking slightly.

"Well, I could not walk up to your residence and knock on the door in the early hours," explained Jaq. "Such an irregular time for a morning call. Your family might look askance."

Perry did look askance at him. "Reach the point, good sir."

"I took the lady to the only place I could think of that would be safe and dark," said Jaq. "Beresford's boathouse."

IN WHICH A SELKIE PROVES
USEFUL

*E*linor let out a breath of relief. "Really? Where is that?"

"On the lake at the manor."

Now she thought of it, Elinor remembered seeing the quaint boathouse when they drove up to the manor. "I assume you allowed Miss Zooth out of the sack?"

"I did, though I regretted it," said Jaq. "She was vitriolic and virulent in her criticisms of me. However, she dared not leave the boat house. So post haste I came, to inform you of her whereabouts." A brilliant smile lit up his handsome countenance. He was obviously quite pleased with himself, and Elinor wondered if had been imbibing coral cutthroat again. It seemed odd behaviour for the selkie to rescue Aldreda, when the vampiri was so hostile towards him.

"Thank you," said Elinor reluctantly. "You probably saved her life. I am deeply grateful for your chivalrous action."

Jaq winked and smiled charmingly.

"Did you see where the men went?" asked Perry. "And their loot?"

"I am afraid not," said Jaq. "I had my hands rather full."

Elinor highly doubted he had not seen anything of note. Jaq might have his own reasons for rescuing Aldreda, but he may very well have known the smugglers personally.

"They were picking up the stolen jewels," she told him. "Did the thought not cross your mind?"

"No!" he said. "I thought they were just after the usual serving of gin. Besides, wouldn't you rather I value a small lady's life over a bag of jewels?"

Elinor had to concede the point. "Still, it is most irksome you cannot tell us where the jewels went."

"Can't, or won't?" said Perry, menacingly.

Jaq threw up his long white hands, his finely tended nails shimmering in the sunlight. "Can't, I promise! Stop bristling at me, young man. Of course I would like to know where those jewels are. Beresford is going to have my hide when he hears I let them slip away."

"Does Beresford know Aldreda is hiding in his boathouse?" Elinor asked suddenly.

"Oh no. I thought the lady has not made his acquaintance?"

"Has she not?" said Perry. "Thank God for that."

"Take me to her straight away," demanded Elinor.

ALDREDA, when they found her, was extremely grumpy. If she had been sleeping, she was woken by the two humans and selkie intruding upon her refuge. She was not pleased.

"Close that door!" The small, irascible voice carried surprisingly well in the dark space of the boathouse.

Bright sunlight poured through the door, so Elinor hastily shut it behind her. Before she did so, she saw a glimpse of four boats tethered to a small jetty. Two were rowboats, and the others larger.

Elinor adjusted her eyes to the gloom of the windowless wooden structure.

"Aldreda! How are you?" she asked anxiously.

"I have been worse," replied the vampiri, though her tone implied it was only slightly. "I am – or I was – sleeping, and now I am in a boat. It is damp and keeps moving."

The three newcomers became aware of the soft lapping upon wood. Occasionally a boat creaked.

"Were you harmed by those men? Or by the sunlight?"

"If I were not a vampiri I would have bruises and broken bones from those thugs," said Aldreda. "Fortunately, I have superior healing powers. They would not have caught me if I had not been discommoded by the advent of the sun." She sniffed. "As for the sunlight, a few minutes more and my complexion would have been ... irreparably damaged." She paused and added reluctantly, "I owe a debt to Mr Delquon."

She did not sound grateful.

"He is here," warned Elinor.

"I know," Aldreda's voice was cold. "Good afternoon, Mr Delquon. Good afternoon, Mr Avely."

"She sees like a bat," explained Elinor.

"I can't see a blasted thing," grumbled Perry. "Good afternoon, Miss Zooth. I am glad you are safe. Did you happen to see where the smugglers went, by any chance? And did any of them have red hair or four fingers?"

Aldreda ignored him. "Are you here to take me home, Elinor? I wish you would not." Her words became pointed. "I do not want to travel during the day, especially in a sack. I would rather stay here until nightfall and make my own way back."

"Oh," said Elinor, taken aback. "If you wish. I just wanted to see you were unharmed. I brought your dress as well." She laid it down on a post of the jetty.

"Good Gad," said Perry. "You mean to say Miss Zooth is unclothed again?"

Aldreda's voice sounded caustic in the dark. "Where was I to obtain a gown in that sack? Thank you, Elinor. Now, if you don't mind, I need to sleep. I cannot think clearly during the day."

The three trespassers sheepishly retreated. Just as they were about to close the door to the boathouse behind them, Aldreda's voice came sharp once more. "Elinor? May I have a word?"

"Certainly." Elinor hurried back in, closing the door on Jaq and Perry. Perry averted his gaze, in fear of sighting a bare Miss Zooth again, but Jaq showed no such compunction, looking curious at the last-minute summons.

"Second boat on the right," directed Aldreda's voice.

That was one of the larger boats. Elinor edged forward cautiously. "I can't see. I don't want to end up in the water." She stopped. Sure enough, a bat soon swooped in to hang from her skirts. "You are lucky I am not squeamish," she said reprovingly. "Bats in the dark would make another girl shriek. Not to mention one crawling into my pocket and turning into a naked lady. Thankfully I have an iron constitution."

Aldreda paid Elinor's banter little heed, and stuck her head out. "Listen carefully. I overheard the smugglers say something about the jewels."

"Oh?" Elinor stilled.

"I distinctly heard one say that the 'stash' would be off their hands, once it was delivered to the manor tonight."

"The manor tonight?" repeated Elinor stupidly. "They are delivering the jewels to the Beresford Manor?"

"Perhaps to the oak tree," suggested Aldreda. "You will have to sort it out with Perry."

"What are you going to do?"

"I am staying here. There is gold in one of these boats."

"Pardon me?"

"A whole boat-full of guineas. Sacks and sacks of them."

Elinor did a quick divination. "There are no jewels. Are you sure there is gold? Which boat?"

Aldreda directed her towards the largest, a dim shape of a jolly boat, commonly used to ferry goods out to a ship. It was tethered at the end of the jetty. Elinor's eyes were adjusting to the dark. Determined to see for herself, she clambered aboard, the boat rocking under her weight.

"Where?"

"Under the seats."

Elinor heaved the wooden cover up and felt within. Rough material met her fingers. She made out the shape of sacks and tried to haul one out. It was heavy.

"Open it," said Aldreda.

Elinor did so. Even in the dark she could see the truth of what Aldreda said. Piles of round fat coins glimmered softly in the sack.

With a sinking feeling, Elinor remembered what Lord Treffler had told her.

She repeated it to Aldreda. "This must be a shipment, ready to run across to France. Lord Treffler told me

French spies take guineas across to pay Napoleon's soldiers."

"In Beresford's boat?"

Elinor spoke quickly. "I don't for a moment believe Beresford knows anything about this. Someone must be using his boat without his knowledge."

"Ah," said Aldreda. "Yet Beresford came to the boathouse this morning."

"To check the boats?"

"Apparently."

"Did you see him look at the gold?"

"No," admitted Aldreda. "Yet don't you think it odd for Beresford to be 'checking his boats' when one of them contains sacks of guineas?"

"It could be coincidence," argued Elinor, drawing the sack tight and folding it back. She replaced the seat with a snap. "Or maybe he saw Jaq leaving here and came to investigate. That must be what happened."

"Perhaps. However, you must entertain the possibility he is responsible, Elinor."

There was a long silence. It was broken by Perry's voice from outside. "Elinor?"

"I am coming," Elinor called back, climbing out of the boat. "I don't believe it," she said in a harsh undertone to Aldreda. "Beresford would never do such a thing."

"There is one way to find out," said Aldreda. "I will stay here tonight. If he is planning on taking the gold across to France, I will soon see."

"Miss Avely." This time it was Jaq's voice calling. "You may wish to know that Lord Reeves is riding up the driveway. Perhaps we should not be lurking out here."

"You cannot put yourself in danger again," said Elinor to Aldreda. "Who knows who will come along tonight? It won't be Beresford, I can tell you that much. It could be one of the men from the boat this morning, who will recognise a pesky bat when he sees one. He could make short work of you this time."

"I am not going to sleep in the boat like a fruit-bat," said Aldreda. "I will watch from afar, and I won't try to stop whoever it is. I will inform you immediately."

Elinor considered this. "I don't like it. However, we must do something. I think we should tell Beresford. He has a right to know someone is using his boat for nefarious purposes."

"*He* might be using his boat for nefarious purposes."

"Elinor!" Perry's voice was an urgent mutter through the door. Then she heard another voice outside.

"Gentlemen," called Lord Reeves. "Going for a swim?"

Elinor froze in the dark. "Do you think it could be the baron's gold?" she whispered.

"Perhaps," whispered Aldreda. "You had better go out there."

"Very well. If you insist on staying the night here, so be it. But please don't do anything foolish."

"Nor you," said Aldreda. "Good luck retrieving the jewels." Elinor felt Aldreda shift and then a brush of bat wings against her arm.

Elinor walked back towards the crack of light at the door and stopped to listen.

Perry was babbling to the baron. "Just admiring the view, Lord Reeves. Such a fine prospect, the lake, with this picturesque little boathouse. It quite makes me wish I had a knack for painting. To capture that lovely shade of blue–green. Wouldn't you agree, Mr Delquon?"

"Teal, you mean?" said Jaq. "I prefer cobalt. Maybe we should go for a swim, Mr Avely. Good idea, I think."

Elinor thought it best to make her presence known,

before the boys leapt into the lake. She opened the door and blinked in the sunlight.

"Miss Avely!" said Lord Reeves in surprise. "What are you doing in there?"

"I was looking for bats," said Elinor. An approximation of the truth would serve. Too late, she remembered her mother would not approve.

"Bats? My word! What can you mean?"

"I have a fondness for bats," Elinor explained. "I thought this boathouse might be a haven for them. I have not yet had an opportunity to examine the bats of Devon."

"Goodness me," said the baron. "What an unusual pursuit for a young lady."

"Is it not?" said Perry, frowning at Elinor. "My sister has a few odd quirks, which she usually doesn't announce so boldly."

"I am sure bats are harmless enough," said Lord Reeves uneasily. "Did you find any, Miss Avely?"

"No," said Elinor. "Lord Beresford's boathouse is all too clean and tidy."

She watched the baron closely as she spoke, wondering if he was afraid she had found his gold. His expression remained a little confused.

There was an awkward silence. "Well," said Lord Reeves. "I was about to call on Lady Beresford. Are you walking to the house, or are you indeed going for a swim?"

Perry declaimed the swim, though Jaq looked reluctant to abandon the idea. The baron led his horse, with Perry and Elinor walking alongside him. Jaq declined to accompany them and strolled off downriver. Elinor wondered if he was going to change into a seal and dine on some fish in the lake. He must be starving after his morning's exertions.

Come to think of it, Elinor was very hungry herself. She hoped they were in time for morning tea.

The Beresford carriage was in the driveway and must have disposed the Laberches at the manor already. The countess's carriage was old-fashioned and ornate. It made the hired job that Jaq had acquired to drive them from Deockley look very shabby.

When the butler showed them in, the countess and Miss Trent were having cream tea with the Laberches. The delicious smell of fresh-baked morsels met Elinor's nostrils and she suddenly felt weak at the knees. Not to mention Beresford was standing in the corner by the window, the light illuminating a brooding frown as he turned to greet her.

The spaniels were there again. They acknowledged Elinor with a more decorous display of enthusiasm this time. She herself was able to greet the dogs with more equanimity now they were not potential spinster devourers. Really, they were beautiful creatures, with big brown eyes and soft coats. Elinor cooed at them, ignoring Beresford's examining look. Had he seen her come out of the boathouse?

"Miss Avely!" said Lady Beresford. "Please join us for cream tea. You see your friends are quite settled in already. We are so glad to have them."

"As we are so glad to be here," said the marquise, sipping from her cup.

Elinor was relieved to see the marquise was willing to be gracious. Perhaps the size and grandeur of the manor had convinced her that the Beresfords' acquaintance was to be cultivated. Taking a chair next to Mademoiselle Laberche, Elinor gratefully accepted a cup of tea.

As the countess passed the cup, she spoke to her son. "James, please sit down. You are making me nervous, brooding over there."

"I am not brooding."

"Sit then. You must be tired, coming in so late last night. I cannot think what you have to do on the estate that requires you to be out after dark."

Elinor glanced at Beresford to see him give his mother an admonitory look.

The tea in her mouth suddenly tasted bitter. What *was* Beresford doing in the dark? Why was he trying to keep his mother from mentioning it?

Mademoiselle Laberche let out a giddy sigh. "Lord Beresford, allow me to tell you how much I admire your jam."

Beresford looked slightly cheered. "Ah yes. The Beresford jam is always popular with the ladies." He cut a sideways glance at Elinor, who pointedly ignored him. "Do you like our jam, Miss Avely?"

She responded with only a hint of sarcasm. "Of course, what lady would decry such a divine compote?" Unfortunately, the jam *was* divine – rich, slightly tart, and sweet all at once.

"Perhaps a lady who likes bats," put in the baron.

"What can you mean?" asked Mademoiselle Laberche. "No lady likes bats."

"Miss Avely does," said the baron. "She was bat hunting a moment ago, in your boathouse, Beresford."

Beresford turned a hawk-like gaze on Elinor, so she felt rather like a bat herself. "Is this true?"

"Indeed," she said bravely. "Much like others watch for owls, I watch for bats. Fascinating creatures."

Mademoiselle Laberche gave a shiver. "Oh, you should look in the cave where you found us. There was a bat there, though I do not recommend seeking it out. It was rather vicious."

Elinor glanced at Perry and saw from his expression he had only just put two and two together to realise this vicious bat was none other than Miss Zooth. He glared at Elinor.

"Bats are not usually aggressive," Elinor hastened to say.

Surprisingly, she had an ally in Lady Beresford. "Bats are normally harmless; I give you that. But when I was a child there were tales of bats that could turn into tiny women." A faraway look appeared in Lady Beresford's eye. "Apparently one lived in this very manor. She could transform into a comely maiden, although of a miniature variety."

Goodness, an old story about Aldreda! Everyone stared at Lady Beresford. She continued in sepulchral tones. "The pretty little bat–woman would then seduce men to be her dinner."

There was a gasp of fascinated horror.

"Oooh, how ghastly." Mademoiselle Laberche widened her eyes. "You mean like the stories of blood-sucking vampires in Europe?"

Elinor pointed out acerbically that it was unlikely a miniature lady would feed on a whole gentleman.

"What nonsense," said Beresford. "I confess, Miss Avely, I find it hard to believe you have a partiality for bats, whether or not they consume gentlemen for dinner."

"Oh, merely the normal variety," said Elinor. "I think they are the sweetest creatures. You probably have not examined a bat closely. They are just like kittens."

"I cannot say I have," said Beresford. "However, I refuse to believe they are like kittens."

Elinor amended her statement. "Perhaps more a cross between a kitten and a butterfly. The soft furry body, with the sweet little eyes and ears, and the large delicate wings." She sipped her tea. "A most charming combination."

Miss Trent looked impressed. "Do you think one would make a good pet?"

"There are still the sharp teeth to think of," put in Beresford. "And apparently the blood-sucking partiality. Miss Avely is overly poetical." He looked at her suspiciously, as if he still had strong doubts about her purpose in his boathouse. Elinor wondered, with a sinking feeling, why he cared.

"Not poetical, my lord. Merely descriptive of the facts."

"Well," said the baron. "If I find any bats on my property, I will be sure to inform you, Miss Avely."

"Be careful it does not dine on you first," said Beresford sardonically.

The marquise had been following this conversation with some difficulty; perhaps her English did not extend so far. However, when her daughter rapidly explained in French, she nodded sagely. "Ah yes, we have heard of such things in France. The vampiri."

Elinor thought it best to change the subject. "How is the war progressing?" she asked brightly.

19

IN WHICH A LADY'S SLUMBERS
ARE DISTURBED

*B*eresford excused himself from the gathering. Elinor nervously watched him leave, and soon afterward she made an excuse to walk over to the window where he had stood. It was just as she feared. She had a clear view down to the boathouse. Striding towards it was Beresford, walking with a dire and purposeful air.

"Oh dear," murmured Elinor.

Suddenly she became aware of the countess at her shoulder.

"What was that, Miss Avely?" enquired Lady Beresford. "Ah yes, my son." She looked down fondly on his long-legged stride. "I perceive you and he are still at odds."

"No, how can you say so?" Elinor watched his retreating form with apprehension. "When he has been so kind to me." She wondered feverishly if his kindness would extend to sheltering a vampiri in his boathouse.

"Hm," said Lady Beresford. "I know you said earlier that James's motive were only kind. But are a man's motives ever pure? He may have just wanted you for himself."

Elinor turned startled eyes towards her. "Excuse me?"

"When he offered for you, you widgeon." The countess waved a finger. "You say he was being noble, or interfering, but has it crossed your mind he was actually being greedy?"

Elinor did not know what to say. She just stared wide-eyed.

"Perhaps you should go for a walk with him," suggested Lady Beresford. "Talk it over. Persuade him to go back to London, instead of making mischief out here."

"Goodness me," Elinor stammered. "Yes, perhaps I will." She had to stop Beresford from reaching the boathouse, and this was a good excuse to chase after him. "Now, you think?"

The countess waved her away, smiling in benediction. If only Lady Beresford knew the truth – that Beresford deeply regretted his 'misguided chivalry'! Elinor swallowed the hope that rose at Lady Beresford's words, and hurried from the room.

Once outside, she broke into something akin to a run. What if Beresford burst in upon Aldreda? Or discovered the gold? With the possibility upon her, she decided it was better Beresford knew nothing of the gold. He would want to lay in wait for the French spy and catch himself some glory. Unlike Aldreda, however, he did not have the advantage of being able to turn into a bat and stay out of sight. He would be caught and probably killed, by the same person who had murdered Harris.

The cream tea lent Elinor's feet wings. Then she saw she need not worry – too much. Beresford had stopped and was in deep conversation with Jaq by the lake.

Elinor was too close to turn back. As she drew nearer, the two men looked up. Jaq's handsome face looked distinctly uneasy, and Beresford's countenance was thunderous.

"What is this I hear about a bat–lady in my boathouse?" he demanded.

Elinor gave Jaq a scathing look. "You told him?"

Jaq became shamefaced.

"Of course he told me," snapped Beresford. "Jaq has a loyalty to me – he owes it to tell me when a bat–lady is using my boat as a bed."

"She is a vampiri, not a bat–lady," said Elinor stiffly.

"Whatever she is, she cannot stay there." Beresford turned and marched towards the jetty.

"No, wait!" said Elinor. "You cannot disturb Miss Zooth. She is a lady, and she is sleeping."

Beresford kept walking. "Then she must wake."

Elinor hurried after him. Jaq followed.

Elinor spoke quickly at Beresford's elbow. "I did not dream you were so ungentlemanly, my lord. You do not understand that a vampiri must sleep during the day. Would you like it if you were woken in the middle of the night?" She debated whether or not to tell him the said vampiri would be stark naked, but she could not quite bring herself to say the words. "Also, Miss Zooth is much averse to the sun. It can do her great harm."

"Is this true?" Beresford threw at Jaq over his shoulder.

"Yes," admitted Jaq. "The lady will suffer greatly if she is exposed to sunlight. That is why I brought her here."

"You're a damn fool," said Beresford.

Elinor felt a vice close over her throat. Why was Beresford so worried about a small bat, or lady, in his boathouse?

By this time they were upon the jetty. Beresford strode up to the door and gripped the handle.

"No, wait!" said Elinor again, a note of desperation in her voice. "Miss Zooth may be – er – unclothed."

Beresford turned to look at her, eyebrows raised. "Pardon me?"

"Her clothes do not survive the transformation from human to bat."

"A *naked* bat–lady?" He paused. "Is she going to eat me for lunch?"

Elinor blinked. "No, my lord. However, she will be discomposed at being disturbed. You have not even been introduced."

"Let me do it," said Jaq. "I have already incurred Miss Zooth's wrath. She is familiar with my visage. She may try to attack you, my lord, purely out of irritability."

"You say this is a *lady*?"

"I would not blame her," said Elinor. "You are disturbing the privacy of her slumbers." Though Elinor doubted it. Surely Aldreda would have heard them talking and would be alerted to their presence. One might hope she was waiting in the ceiling as a bat, ready to swoop into Beresford's face.

"Very well, Jaq," said Beresford, perhaps reading Elinor's thoughts. "You can do the deed, seeing as you put her there in the first place."

He stood aside for Jaq, who sidled by Beresford's broad shoulders nervously. Jaq slipped into the boathouse, leaving Elinor and Beresford staring at each other.

No manly scream met their ears.

Elinor became aware of the blue-green expanse of the lake around them, and Beresford's grey eyes pinned upon her.

"Is this why you go walking about at night?" Beresford asked. "To pursue the acquaintance of a bat–lady?"

"A vampiri lady spinster," said Elinor frigidly. "But yes."

They both listened, to hear a feminine voice raised in ire.

"You wretched sea-dog! You cursed depth-dweller! You dispel my peace again!"

Elinor rather suspected Aldreda relished the opportunity to loosen her tongue upon Jaq's head, with an audience no less.

Jaq's murmured reply was incomprehensible.

"I don't care if the king himself is out there. I am not going with you, you two-faced fishtail."

Elinor raised her brows at Beresford. He had lost his glower and was looking rather entertained. Perhaps he enjoyed the sound of Jaq receiving his comeuppance and did not notice the hints as to Jaq's true nature. Or perhaps he was deliberately ignoring them.

"Perhaps, if I may?" asked Elinor.

"You want to risk it?" Beresford grinned at her, and gestured towards the door. "Be my guest."

Elinor walked past with her head high, and shut the door tightly behind her.

Inside was thick with darkness, so it was hard to see what was occurring. From the direction of Aldreda's curses it sounded as if she was sitting on one of the high beams in the roof.

Elinor spoke cautiously. "Aldreda, we must depart from this less-than-hospitable dwelling. Also, it seems you have run out of rude names."

"Never," asserted Aldreda's voice from above. "That ... pretty boy!"

"You are rather pretty," said Elinor apologetically to

Jaq. Now that her eyes were adjusting to the gloom, she could see his large, dark eyes gleaming at her from a few feet away.

"Not as pretty as you, dear," he replied.

"What is going on in there?" said Beresford loudly from outside. "You should not be alone in the dark with a young man, Miss Avely, pretty or otherwise."

"I have my spinster companion with me," she shouted back.

"A bat–lady does not count."

"A vampiri."

Aldreda interrupted. "I am not going back in that sack."

"I have my reticule here, one that I have double-lined," said Elinor. "I know it is not ideal, but needs must. Besides, I want you at my side, not tucked away in here," she added pointedly.

After a few more choicely worded descriptions of Jaq – ordering him out of the boathouse – Aldreda consented to take up occupancy of the reticule. Elinor drew it tightly shut and went outside again.

Beresford looked up from interrogating Jaq. "Where is she?"

Elinor held up the reticule.

Beresford looked askance at it, but did not demand to see inside. Perhaps he did not want to be faced with feminine nakedness, however miniature. Elinor suddenly regretted she had not in fact left Aldreda hiding in the boathouse. However, Jaq would most likely check the building thoroughly, and would likely not be perturbed by Aldreda's lack of gown.

Elinor became haughty. "You should be more gracious, my lord. Miss Zooth was only trying to stop the jewel thieves from making away with the treasure."

"What's this?" Beresford asked, looking at Jaq.

Jaq shook his head and shrugged.

Elinor explained bitingly. "Mr Delquon rescued Miss Zooth as she was attempting to halt smugglers from making off with the jewels."

"Jaq?"

"It is true men were pulling up a load in the bay," admitted Jaq. "I thought it was just the usual thing. Whiskey and gin. Or lobsters."

Beresford cut a question at Elinor "How do you know they were the jewels?"

Elinor realised she had put herself into a pickle. "Never mind how I know."

"I do mind, if you make wild assertions. Tell me now."

Elinor sighed. "Miss Zooth can sense the presence of jewels. She is most useful in that fashion. Please do not bandy the information around, however."

Beresford looked disbelieving, but not outright dismissive. "She could sense the missing jewels?"

"Yes, and bravely tried to defend them."

"When was this?"

"Before daybreak," said Jaq.

"Which men?" asked Beresford.

Jaq reeled off a few names, one of which was Clodder.

Elinor nodded sagely. "They will be long gone to London by now," she said regretfully. "The jewels have slipped out of our hands."

Beresford shook his head. "I have people watching every road that leaves the county, for those men in particular, as I suspected their involvement. I would have heard if any of them had left for London."

"The jewels were probably hidden in a cartload of

manure," said Elinor. "Or chickens. Your men wouldn't even know it."

Beresford disagreed. "I don't think the smugglers would entrust them to an unknown farmhand. They would deliver it themselves." He paused thoughtfully. "It is possible the jewels are still in Deockley."

Jaq gave a dramatic start. "They will travel under the cover of darkness," he exclaimed. "We could catch them at it."

A steely glint came into Beresford's eye. "Indeed, we will catch them tonight." Suddenly he loomed over Elinor, seeming at least a foot taller. "Miss Avely, I absolutely insist you stay abed this evening."

"I?" She fluttered a hand to her bodice. "Of course. I will be in deep repose."

"I mean it," he threatened.

"So do I," Elinor countered. "Do you really think I want to caper about the countryside at night, looking for jewels, when I could be sleeping?"

"Yes."

"Well, I do not. I have only been partaking in evening strolls for the unexceptionable purpose of cultivating my friendship with Miss Zooth."

Beresford looked, faintly, as if he might believe that. Elinor patted her reticule fondly. "Now, if you don't mind, I shall depart. Good day, gentlemen, and good luck."

As she walked off, she heard Jaq chuckle. Whether or not it was her sixth sense or common sense, she was also certain that Beresford scowled.

20

IN WHICH ELINOR IS DESPONDENT

*E*linor managed to carry herself with dignity back to the house, to say her farewells. Lady Beresford gave her a searching look but, perhaps seeing Elinor was rather wan, did not question her on her 'talk' with Beresford, and allowed her to leave.

Once inside the hired carriage, Elinor slumped against the seat opposite Perry.

Aldreda's voice came muffled from the reticule. "That was entertaining."

Perry jumped. "What was entertaining? Why is Miss Zooth in your reticule? What have you been doing?"

Elinor briefly explained. Perry was horrified, although somewhat reassured when he realised Beresford had not actually seen Aldreda at any point, naked or otherwise.

"Of course not," said Aldreda, from inside the reticule. "I am not completely wanton. I do not display myself to gentlemen."

"You displayed yourself to me!"

"You are not a gentleman. You are a mere boy."

Perry glared at the reticule, speechless.

Elinor was despairing. "Don't you see, Aldreda – Beresford's eagerness to have you gone can only have one meaning." She did not want to mention the gold in front of Perry, in case he leapt to unfavourable conclusions about Beresford. Never mind that she was doing so.

"It merely means Lord Beresford has a dislike of vampiri," replied Aldreda. She inched the drawstrings opening and peered up at Elinor.

Perry grunted meaningfully.

Elinor shook her head. "He is too much of a gentleman to oust you unless he had a very good reason."

"It must be the gold," agreed Aldreda. "He knows it is there."

"What gold?" demanded Perry. "Where?"

With a heavy heart, Elinor explained. "Aldreda found sacks of guineas in one of the boats. We suspect it is going to be smuggled across to France for Napoleon."

"Never by Beresford!"

"No." Elinor gave him a small smile. "Then why did he want Aldreda gone?"

"I could think of several reasons."

"Well, I am glad to be out of there." Aldreda sniffed. "We will just have to change our plans for tonight. Perhaps you, Mr Avely, can watch the boathouse, and Elinor and I can go after the jewels."

Elinor explained to Perry what Aldreda had overheard. He almost jumped out of his seat. "The manor, tonight? Good Gad! I will come with you, Elinor. We'll catch those dastardly fishermen in the act."

"Haven't you thought about the implications?" said Elinor. "The fishermen will be delivering to their leader. We will catch two birds tonight."

"Miss Trent?" asked Perry doubtfully. "Trap her in the act?"

Elinor was thoughtful. "Or the countess," she said slowly. Lady Beresford had sent Elinor to stop Beresford 'making mischief' – and, come to think of it, from going into the boathouse. Perhaps it was the countess's own plans he was in danger of disrupting. "Remember how the marquise heard mention of 'Beresford'? We all assumed she meant the earl, but what if the smugglers were talking about his mother? Why *does* Lady Beresford spend all her time in Devon, when she loves London gossip so much? She is well out of mourning."

Aldreda agreed. "Perhaps the reason she stays here is to collect French heirlooms."

"It is true we don't know whether the estate needs money," Perry mused. "Or how much of an allowance Lady Beresford receives."

Aldreda nodded in her reticule. "Whether it is Miss Trent, or the countess, or that Baron of Reeves, we have a good chance of catching them tonight."

Elinor felt apprehensive. "I don't think we should confront them, whoever it is," she said. "I will simply wait until the fishermen drop off the jewels. I can divine where they are, after all, and whisk them away before anyone comes to pick them up. It is much better, Perry, if you are on the lookout by the boathouse for the French spy. He will be far more dangerous – and it will be a greater service to England if you catch him. Lady Beresford will be easy prey in comparison."

This argument impressed Perry, and he agreed with the plan. Elinor was secretly hopeful that the boathouse would be a scene of quietude that night. Perry's post would keep him from a hot-headed altercation with the jewel smugglers. Unless, of course, the jewel smugglers and the French spy were of the same party, which was a strong possibility. Elinor raised this point with the others, but Aldreda was sanguine.

"Then we will join Perry once we have secured the jewels, and provide additional support," said Aldreda, yawning from within the depths of the reticule. "Now, if you don't mind, I think I will sleep."

"Of course," said Elinor wearily.

She was not so easily reassured. Beresford was clearly implicated. Elinor could think of no other reason why he would be so desperate to protect the sanctity of his boathouse. She slumped miserably against the upholstery, inordinately depressed by this realisation. It was not as if she didn't already find him odious, she thought rather incoherently. Yet spying for the French was so *low*, much lower than flirting with Mademoiselle Laberche, or bragging about plum jam.

Elinor straightened. Beresford might know the gold was there, but that did not mean he was going to sail it across to France and give it to England's enemies.

Perhaps Beresford had already caught the spy, single-handed, when he was hunting for Harris's murderer! That was far more likely, thought Elinor with relief. Furthermore, the spy and the murderer were probably one and the same. In which case, Perry would be safe tonight, and she needn't worry anymore.

Except the jewels were still at large. It was time for Elinor to take a hand in the game – it should be a fairly simple matter of recovering them, with her gift. Then she would have the pleasant task of presenting the missing jewels to the marquise tomorrow – in front of Beresford, of course.

～

ELINOR WAS QUITE prepared to sleep the afternoon away like Aldreda, but soon after lunch Lord Treffler was announced. Mrs Avely had told them he had called that morning while they were away.

"What is he doing in Devon?" Mrs Avely asked. "Why is he not in London?" She paused, then chose her words delicately. "Has he formed a partiality for you, Elinor?"

"I hope not."

"What then?"

Elinor looked at her mother blankly. "I cannot speak for Lord Treffler's motive in visiting Devon," she said finally. "Perhaps he has business here."

Mrs Avely gave her a long, measuring look. "Nonetheless, he is not inclined to snub our company like the rest of London," she said. "You should treat him kindly."

"Yes, Mother."

So it was that Elinor was forced to sit with Lord Treffler, and talk of town, and accept his suggestion they go for a stroll, with Perry acting as chaperone.

Lord Treffler was disposed to be charming in the sitting room, but sharp outside.

"Where were you two this morning?" he asked, as they set off down the path to the village.

"Visiting Beresford Manor," said Elinor coldly.

"Why? I thought you and Lord Beresford were at odds?"

This ungentlemanly reference made Elinor bristle, though it was true. "We escorted our French guests to the manor. They are to stay there for a while."

"You mean the Laberches?"

"Yes, the ones who have lost their jewels."

Lord Treffler turned his attention to Perry. "Have you been looking for the jewels?"

Elinor dared not give any sign to Perry, but hoped he would not betray anything.

"Oh yes," said Perry with aplomb. "All over the demned county. No hide nor hair of the demned things."

"Where have you looked?" asked Lord Treffler. "Surely the field must have been narrowed down by your searches." He looked from one to the other, as if suspecting they were in league against him.

"I doubt it," said Elinor. "There are still the moors inland to consider, and the coast further south. The jewels could be anywhere. I, for one, am weary of looking."

"Faint of heart never won the prize," said Lord Treffler, in determined accents. "I am here now, and we must persevere. Let us try the fields today. We can go for a long walk. I can arrange for provisions."

"I would rather not," protested Elinor.

Lord Treffler turned to look at her. "You would rather not? That doesn't seem like you, Miss Avely. When so much rests upon our search! Your reputation in London! Your acquaintance with my mother! Not to mention the return of jewels to poor, desperate families. I wonder at your lack of eagerness."

Elinor spoke with icy reproof. "You can have nothing to say as to my reputation in London. It is merely that I am too tired to be searching for your precious jewels today."

"Listen here, my lord," interrupted Perry. "There is no use dragging my sister all over the place. The jewels are gone. Just this morning the smugglers pulled them up from the bay and vanished. They are probably halfway across the country by now."

There was a fraught silence. Elinor caught her breath.

"What is this?" demanded Lord Treffler harshly. "How do you know it?"

"Elinor told me to fetch the jewels this morning, and I saw the men at their work," prevaricated Perry, realising too late he had given away too much.

"How did you know they were there?" Lord Treffler turned on Elinor, sharp with anger. "Was this last night, by chance? You deceiving wench!"

"No," lied Elinor. "I went walking early this morning. I sensed them in the bay, so I went back to fetch Peregrine. I did not know where to find you, my lord. By the time Perry returned it was too late."

His lordship scowled at both of them. "Why didn't you say anything of this before?"

"We did not want to disappoint you," said Perry. "We know how much you have set your heart on finding yourself some diamonds."

"I don't believe you," said Lord Treffler slowly. "I think you know the jewels are still in the village, if they were pulled up this morning. The smugglers might wait a day before moving them to London. That means we only have today to find them." He examined them, the cold light in his eye making Elinor repress a shiver. "You are both coming into the village with me. Miss Avely, you are going to find these jewels, and this time you are going to tell me where they are."

Elinor sighed, enacting acquiescence. "Very well, my lord. I suppose you are right – it is our last chance." They must allay his suspicions, as well as exhaust him before the evening. The only problem was that it would also exhaust her.

The three of them continued to the village, with Elinor insisting on silence so she could divine at will. Of course she did no such thing. Aldreda was not around to lessen the effect, and she did not want to become more addle-brained than was needed. Elinor walked on ahead, in a state of abstraction, turning over plans for the evening, while Perry and Lord Treffler trailed behind.

In the village they saw the red-haired fisherman again, who once more followed them for a short time. The fisherman made no attempt to talk to them – perhaps he was made uneasy by the presence of his lordship. Still, the sight of his red beard made Elinor nervous, and she quickened her pace away from the docks.

They saw no one else they knew, not even Beresford. Elinor made a show of stopping and closing her eyes often, but used those moments only to rest, closing her lids against the bright sun and letting her breath slow. She needed to conserve herself for the evening.

After a couple hours of walking, Lord Treffler was prepared to give it a rest.

"Are you certain they are not here?" he demanded.

"I am certain," said Elinor. "What possible reason could I have for keeping them from you?"

"I don't know," admitted his lordship. "I fear you are not being entirely open with me, Miss Avely. Which would be a grave mistake on your part."

"Do not impugn my sister's honesty," said Perry. "If Elinor says she cannot sense the jewels, then we certainly shan't find them here."

Elinor could only admire her brother's cunning. There was a note of utter sincerity in his voice, as he stated this truth, which seemed to have some effect on Lord Treffler.

"Very well," said his lordship. "We will give it up for now. I will watch the village tonight for any suspicious activity. Mr Avely, perhaps you should set up watch near the coast."

"Good idea," said Perry promptly.

"And I?" asked Elinor.

Lord Treffler shrugged. "I would have you in the village with me, Miss Avely, but perhaps it is not the place for a lady. There may be some rough work tonight."

"I thank you for your chivalry, my lord," said Elinor, knowing he wanted her out of the way so he could make off with the prize.

To be fair, she wanted exactly the same thing of him.

IN WHICH THE EARL INTERFERES

*W*ith relief, Elinor came home and found her old room restored. She collapsed onto her bed and slept for a short while, only to be woken by the maid knocking.

"The Earl of Beresford to see you, miss."

"Again? At this time of day?" Elinor peered at the clock; it was close to dinner.

"Your mother said it was best you came down."

Elinor straightened her gown and descended, after first checking that Aldreda was sound asleep. The vampiri, at least, was having a good rest. There were some advantages to being a creature of the night, chief of which was being able to sleep all day.

Elinor saw Samuel prowling on the landing, and shooed him away. She was going to have to install a lock, and convince Aldreda to work her magic on Samuel. Elinor couldn't bear another horrible moment of believing Aldreda had been eaten.

What could Beresford want? Elinor suddenly felt very awake. Had he come to tell her about the venture with the guineas, and how he had bested a French spy? Perhaps he had come to explain, and apologise, for treating Aldreda so cavalierly. Or perhaps simply to apologise to her, Elinor, for being so rude.

Elinor paused at the mirror in the hall, and attempted to arrange her honey-blonde hair into neat ringlets, trying for some semblance of dignity. Unfortunately, her cheeks were still flushed from sleep, and her hair was not behaving itself. She smoothed it down as best she could, then braved the sitting room.

Beresford was sitting with her mother. He was staring at the fireplace, though there was no fire, and his broad shoulders were held rigidly. A conversational lull was holding sway.

He leapt to his feet upon seeing Elinor.

"Miss Avely."

"My lord." She curtsied, glancing at her mother, who remained impassive.

"How do you do?" He did not wait for an answer. "I am afraid this is not a usual call." His grey eyes sharpened on her, intent.

"I assumed as much," she returned, seating herself and waiting in silence for him to elucidate.

He did not sit down but began to pace. "I came to tell your mother about your new acquaintance, as I cannot approve of it. However, I thought it best if you were present."

Elinor's heart sank to her feet, even as anger rose. How dared he expose Aldreda like this?

"My acquaintances are no concern of yours, my lord. You may withdraw your interference."

"Ordinarily, I would agree," said Beresford. "But I cannot stay silent." He turned abruptly to Elinor's mother. "Mrs Avely, I beg of you to curtail your daughter's friendship with Lord Treffler."

Elinor's eyes widened. "Lord Treffler?"

"He is a rogue, and I have good reason to believe he is dangerous."

"Surely not to a lady," said Elinor. Though as she spoke, she remembered Lord Treffler's thinly-veiled threat out in the fields.

"When the lady is engaged in searching for lost jewels, then she may very well be endangered."

"What is this?" asked Mrs Avely sharply. "Elinor, I hope you have not been unwise."

Before she could answer, Beresford spoke for her. "Forgive me, but she has been unwise." Elinor gave him a dagger glance, but he continued. "She has been actively seeking that which Lord Treffler wants to keep hidden, and for that reason I think she is in danger."

"Keep hidden? You are mistaken, my lord. Lord Treffler is eager to recover the jewels, not hide them."

"How can that be, when he is the one who masterminded their disappearance?"

Elinor shook her head. "You have it wrong. He is looking for them – we spent all day looking."

"So you admit it!" said Beresford triumphantly. "You *are* looking for jewels! You cannot help yourself."

Elinor glared at him. "That is beside the point. Why would Lord Treffler be searching for them, if he knows where they are?"

"Perhaps he has been betrayed," said Beresford. "Or perhaps he is making sure that as you look, you do not find."

Elinor closed her lips tightly. She could not tell him of her divining ability, and that Lord Treffler was relying upon it. Or could it really be that Lord Treffler feared her ability, and was trying to keep Elinor under observation? Or that his men had turned on him, and he needed her to find what he had lost?

"I cannot see Lord Treffler as a criminal mastermind," Elinor said instead.

Beresford scowled. "Yet there is someone high up who has organised this jewel venture. Treffler's presence in the district now is indicative of his involvement."

"You are also present in the district," said Elinor coolly. "Are we to take that as an admission of your involvement?"

"Elinor!" exclaimed Mrs Avely. "Apologise at once. His lordship only seeks to protect you, as he has before. My lord, we thank you for your concern and your advice. I agree Elinor should not spend any more time with Lord Treffler."

Elinor began to feel quite cross. "Lord Beresford has no right to intrude upon my life like this. He is no father or brother or husband to me."

"I am well aware of that." Beresford bit out the words. "Yet I have a duty to protect an innocent lady from danger, even if she insists on recklessly seeking it out."

Elinor drew herself up. "The only danger is that I am to be patronised." She turned. "Good evening, my lord. I find I am wearied by this conversation and must retire."

She marched from the room, leaving it silent behind her.

ELINOR ARGUED with her mother after Beresford left. Mrs Avely acknowledged the earl was perhaps overstepping the mark, but asked whether it might be possible he was fond of Elinor? That he still retained an interest in her, after all that had happened?

"No! He is probably trying to punish me for everything."

"Perhaps he is jealous of Lord Treffler."

"Jealous! I think not. He has nothing to be jealous of in Lord Treffler." It occurred to Elinor, however, that she had been seen wandering around Deockley in Lord Treffler's company for hours. The thought made her more irritable.

Mrs Avely raised her brows. "Lord Treffler can be charming."

"Yes, a sight more than Beresford," Elinor fumed, rather contradictorily.

"Hm. Anyway, you should not become involved in jewel hunts, my dear." She paused. "Nor believe everything that people say. Beresford is right to warn you to be cautious. I wish you would remember *vincit prudentia*."

Elinor paid no heed to the family motto. "I am more able than anyone to find those jewels!"

Her mother came over to put a hand on Elinor's arm. "Even if you can find them, that is not to say you must. Especially if there are ruthless men trying to prevent you from doing so. Much better to leave it to Lord Beresford. Or indeed Lord Treffler, if he is as innocent as you say."

Elinor swallowed a bitter retort and nodded rigidly. "Yes, Mother."

So dinner was stiff and silent. Perry burbled on about the Laberches, but soon quietened in the frosty atmosphere. Elinor made her excuses early and left for bed, leaving the window open a crack. She managed to snatch an hour's restless sleep before she felt Aldreda pulling on her ear.

"Wake up, Elinor," came the vampiri's voice, loud and cheery. "The night has begun!"

Aldreda, perched on Elinor's pillow, was dressed in the black silk gown. A sound of claws and hissing came from the door.

"Samuel?" asked Elinor blearily.

"He is not happy," admitted Aldreda. "I offend his sensibilities."

Elinor hauled herself out of bed and dressed, slipping on her cloak and walking boots. "Perhaps you should feed from him? His hostility is very inconvenient."

Aldreda shook her head. "I would rather not, even though he is being so ungentlemanly."

"I don't think any cat is a gentleman," observed Elinor.

"Nor any selkie."

"You are perhaps unfair, Aldreda. Jaq saved you today."

The vampiri folded her arms. "Yes, so he could bargain with. Jaq held my life over my head as a debt. You were not in the boathouse when he tried to make me tell him the whereabouts of the Moria Pearls."

Elinor stopped in the middle of tying her boots. "So he does know of them?"

"He wants them back for his people."

"Back?"

Aldreda looked away. "The pearls are originally from the ocean. That is all."

"Did Henri buy the pearls from the selkies?" demanded Elinor.

"Bargained," admitted Aldreda after a pause.

Elinor raised her brows. "From what you have implied, it was unwise of him to bargain with selkies?"

"Exactly," said Aldreda, smiling her approval. "Even if

Henri perhaps did not fulfil his side to the letter, that does not mean they have a right to the pearls. They are no longer simply an emanation of the sea. They are imbued with Henri's power."

"Do the selkies know that?"

Aldreda shrugged. "I suspect they do. It is why they want them so badly."

Elinor finished tying her boots thoughtfully. "What did you say to Jaq?"

"I told him he was a dastardly excuse for a fish."

"Oh dear."

"He said I was cat bait." Aldreda tossed her black curls.

"Hm."

"I said I would rather Jaq leave me to die, than to betray Henri."

Elinor pursed her lips. "I am sure Jaq took that as a suitable expression of gratitude."

"It is the most he will have from me."

"Do you think he has any clue as to the pearls' whereabouts?"

"No, but we must find them as soon as we have sorted out tonight's venture."

"You are very good to help in this matter." Elinor straightened. "Now to leave without Samuel hurting you."

She lifted Aldreda to her shoulder and, drawing a breath, opened her door. Samuel shot inside, fur bristling. Elinor tutted. He ignored her and hissed at Aldreda.

Elinor hurried past him, but her decorous and secretive descent was somewhat marred by his angry escort. However, they managed to escape without rousing Mrs

Avely, and locked Samuel in the house behind them, much to his outrage.

Elinor carried her largest reticule, containing some bread and water for the adventure. Aldreda drank quickly from Elinor's wrist, while Elinor crunched on an apple.

They made their way to the copse of birch trees, where Perry had promised to be waiting with hired horses. In the dark of the trees the white moonlight showed dappled underfoot, making the shadows seem blacker. Elinor jumped when Perry stepped out from behind a tree.

"Steady, Ellie," he said.

"I am not a horse," she replied irritably. "I'm merely concerned Lord Treffler might suspect us and watch our movements. Did he see you hire these horses?"

"Not he," said Perry. "He is dining in Deockley and then watching the tollgate on the main road."

Perry gave a polite enough greeting to Aldreda, then helped Elinor mount. Aldreda asked to be put on Elinor's lap, and they all discussed the plan as they rode in the direction of the manor.

Elinor began. "Perry, you must find a tree that has a good view of the boathouse. Hide in the branches, where no one will think of looking."

"Oh, I will hide in the boathouse itself," said Perry. "Then I can leap out of the darkness like an avenging demon if anyone comes near the gold."

"They will think you are a bat," pointed out Aldreda.

"Not I," said Perry scornfully.

Elinor shook her head. "Also, Beresford might come for the gold merely to take it back to London." She described her theory that Beresford had already vanquished the French spy.

"Very well," said Perry. "I won't attack if it is Beresford. Anyone else I shall capture first then ask questions later."

"Good plan," said Aldreda approvingly. "Especially if it is Jaq. He is a slippery one. If you see him, detain him at once."

22

IN WHICH PLANS ARE DISRUPTED

"*I* think you should stay out of the boathouse, Perry," argued Elinor. "It is too dangerous."

Of course, this objection was summarily dismissed by her brother. Elinor only hoped she was right that no one would go near the gold tonight.

"Meanwhile, we shall wait in the gardens," said Aldreda. "With my bat vision and Elinor's jewel divining, we shall have a great advantage over any poor smugglers sneaking about."

"Heaven help them," agreed Perry. "Further, if you find yourself in a pickle, you can always appear naked in front of them. That would buy you some time."

Aldreda, who was at that moment demurely dressed in one of Elinor's sombre creations, drew herself up. "I will do no such thing."

"Indeed not," said Elinor, giggling.

They tethered the horses near the river downstream from the manor, where a small strip of forest divided some fields. Ceasing to speak, they followed the river upstream, along a small path, knowing it would take them to the lake and the boathouse.

The lake shimmered in the moonlight. Elinor was uneasy to see everything standing out in stark relief. The pale painted wood of the boathouse would show any figure against it in black silhouette. She pointed this out to Perry, in a last attempt to convince him to stay in a tree. He would have none of it.

"If I go now, I'm sure to be there before anyone else," he whispered. "Good luck!" Before Elinor could protest, he sidled off into the trees along the lake, taking the long way around to the jetty.

"I hope he will be safe," Elinor murmured, watching him melt into the trees.

"If anything happens, we can rescue him," said Aldreda. "And vice versa. Can you sense any jewels yet?"

Elinor reached out with her senses and found nothing by the lake. "Not yet. Are you sure they said the manor?"

"Yes. Let's try near the oak tree."

They made their way up to the house, keeping close to the hedges. More than once Elinor stilled and waited, thinking she heard or saw something. It was useful to have Aldreda on her shoulder, as the vampiri's superior eyesight could reassure Elinor it was only a fox, an owl, or a badger rustling in the dark.

"My nerves are strained," admitted Elinor. "I feel the darkness is teeming with ruthless fishermen, Lord Treffler, an unknown French spy, and perhaps the countess."

"Goodness, I hope not all of those. Just owls. We should be more concerned one may mistake me for a dressed up mouse."

Elinor appreciated Aldreda's effort to divert her, and she laughed. "No one would dare make such an error!"

When they were closer to the house, she did a quick scope for jewels.

"Nothing," she whispered.

They edged their way along the orchard behind the manor, making for the oak tree. The house loomed up beside them. Only one window, in the east wing, showed any light. Elinor stared up but could see no movement.

She spoke quietly to Aldreda. "Perhaps you should determine who is awake at this time of night?"

"Good idea," said Aldreda, rustling on her shoulder. "Time to disrobe."

Soon there was a soft whoosh of bat wings, and Aldreda flitted off into the dark. Elinor lifted the little dress off her shoulder and stuffed it into her reticule.

Elinor watched anxiously as the small, black shape fluttered to the window. It hovered near the sill for a few minutes, and Elinor bit her lip. What if someone should see Aldreda lurking up there? Though they would only see a bat and – one hoped – would not think of any stories of man-eating lady–bats.

Then with uncanny speed, the shape dropped away from the light. Before Elinor knew it, Aldreda was back on her shoulder, and in human form.

"Miss Trent," whispered Aldreda. "She is bent over some sewing."

"Innocuous then."

"I note she was working on an elaborate dress that would not fit her."

"For Lady Beresford, perhaps?" said Elinor. "Maybe that is the only secret she is keeping: a French gown for her mistress."

"Perhaps," agreed Aldreda. "At any rate, she does not seem likely to bother us."

"Do you want your dress back?"

"If you do not mind, I think I will leave it off for the moment," said Aldreda primly.

They crept onward, finally coming within twenty feet of the tree. Elinor knew already the jewels were not within. She could not sense them anywhere. They were on a fool's errand, perhaps. Aldreda must have misheard, or the delivery had already taken place earlier in the day. They were out in the cold and dark on a highly improper adventure, all for nothing.

Elinor didn't like to voice these thoughts to Aldreda, so they waited in silence.

After a while Aldreda moved restlessly on her shoulder. "I will have a look around," she whispered.

Elinor nodded in agreement. Once more the bat brushed past her ear and disappeared into the night.

Elinor stood alone, hugging the edge of the stone wall that divided the rose garden from the orchard. Without Aldreda she felt singularly lonely. She stared at the oak tree, its magnificent branches leaning all the way to the ground. It must be very old, she thought – as old as Aldreda. Was it possible Henri had once hidden things in it? She must mention the idea to Aldreda when she returned. Perhaps this was an opportunity to check for the pearls.

Then she heard something. A faint rattle of stone, as if someone walked nearby. Movement caught Elinor's eye, at some distance from her, by the house. The sound must have been amplified in the quiet of the night. She strained her eyes and ears, trying to make out who or what moved.

A male figure crept furtively along the low wall of the terrace, ducking to keep out of sight. Every now and then his head would show, a black shape bobbing. Elinor caught her breath. She had been so intent on her physical senses she had forgotten to use her inner senses.

Now she could feel the press of jewels upon her mind. The man was carrying them toward the house.

Elinor pursed her lips. They had not planned for this. If he were to take them inside the jewels would be out of their reach. He was supposed to leave them somewhere convenient, like the oak tree: somewhere outside, not indoors. Would Miss Trent be so bold as to have the jewels delivered indoors? It must be the countess who was in charge. Was the man Jaq? It was too dark to tell.

What to do? Aldreda must see what was going on. Even as the thought arose, Elinor saw a small black arrow swoop down on the man, who had almost reached the house.

Elinor took advantage of his distraction, and ran between the trees towards him.

"Ooof," said the man, his gruff voice carrying clearly in the silent night. Not Jaq then. Jaq would never allow such an undignified sound to escape his perfectly shaped lips. Elinor felt slightly relieved. She rather liked Jaq. Another grunt came and she sharpened her ears. It sounded somehow familiar.

She halted by another tree, and waited for Aldreda's next attack. Sure enough it came, and Elinor darted out again. She had a plan.

When she was by the wall she stopped and cleared her throat.

The man was grunting and cursing under Aldreda's onslaught. At the sound of Elinor's throat clearing he whipped his head up.

"Excuse me, good sir," said Elinor, her tone low and disapproving. "Must you make so much noise? You will bring the servants out upon us."

The man was the fisherman from the docks – the tall

and skinny one who communicated by means of grunting. At the present moment he was bent double, clutching something to his chest.

True to form, he grunted at her, and held one hand up expressively against marauding bats and grunted again. This time, Elinor decided, it indicated a question as well as an objection.

"I have been sent by your mistress," she said boldly. "She changed the plans at the last minute. You are to give the goods to me and be gone as fast as you can."

"What of my payment?" His tone was surly, and he added a grunt for good measure.

Elinor paused. She could sense that apart from the cacophony of riches in his hand, there was another jewel humming in his boot.

"You, good sir, have already taken payment. It resides in your boot. That will be enough for you. My mistress says you are welcome to it, but do not try to cross her again."

His eyes widened. "How ... ?"

"Never mind how my mistress knows these things. Take heed and be gone," said Elinor, dropping her voice to a warning cadence.

Suddenly, Aldreda whisked past her face. Elinor felt claws pulling at her hair, and something that – but surely not – felt like a nip on her ear.

A warning.

Elinor began to turn. Then a stunning, exploding pain on the back of her head knocked her to the ground.

She landed face first in the dirt, and a voice spoke above her.

"Your mistress says to tie her up, at once."

Before Elinor could scramble to her feet, the fisherman grabbed her arms and yanked them behind her, pulling her to face her attacker.

"To the boathouse, I think," said the Marquise of Laberche.

23

IN WHICH VILLAINY IS
REVEALED

*T*he marquise had a pistol, which she waved casually towards the lake. "Let us go there now, Miss Avely. You can tell me on the way how it is you know so much."

Elinor struggled against the fisherman, who was strong in spite of his lanky appearance.

"Let me go at once! I don't know anything."

"You knew it was I," said the marquise, prodding Elinor with the gun and gesturing for the fisherman to lead the way. He pushed Elinor in front of him roughly.

"No, I didn't know it was you," protested Elinor. "I was referring to the countess. I thought it was she ... "

"Lady Beresford would not have the acumen or the nerve to carry out such an endeavour," said the marquise. "She sits in her English splendour, with no idea how easy it is to lose it all."

So the marquise had stolen from her own countrymen in their hour of need, to feather her own nest. Elinor dared not say it out loud. Best not to criticise someone holding a gun.

The marquise seemed to hear her thoughts. "You

wonder that I steal from my compatriots? They all abandoned me when my fortunes were low. Now I can return the favour."

"You lost your fortune before the revolution?"

"My stupid husband gambled it away," said the marquise. "We were left destitute, and no one bothered to help us. Now they are fleeing like rabbits. I alone will return to France, triumphant, with something to offer Napoleon. Now tell me, how did you know about the jewel in Clodder's boot? I am most curious."

Clodder. Well, they had been right about something, but too little to save them.

"It was a guess," said Elinor. "Any cut-throat English smuggler would slip a jewel into his boot."

"I think you lie. Now, how could you know such a thing?" The marquise reflected, her footsteps light behind Elinor. "Could it be that you are a Discernor?"

Shock rippled along Elinor's skin. "I do not know what you mean."

The marquise ignored this paltry denial. "If you are Discernor, you are not a very good one. You could not Discern my lies."

"What are you talking about? Are you mad?"

"Yet, I have heard of jewel Discernment. Can you do that, Miss Avely?"

"No."

The marquise stepped forward and tapped Elinor on the arm with the butt of the gun. "A jewel Discernor would be most useful to me."

Elinor shuddered at the impact of metal. "You are talking nonsense. There is no way I can be of use to you."

"Then I will have to be rid of you," said the marquise coolly.

Elinor's breath caught in her chest, making her heart

pound loudly. By this time they had reached the lake. Where was Aldreda? And Perry? He would be waiting in the boathouse, thank goodness, to rescue her. But he would not know the marquise held a gun.

They walked in silence along the jetty. Elinor's wrists were chafing under the tight grip of the fisherman, who appeared to have all his fingers present. Elinor realised, with a sense of shock, that the missing finger had been a fiction, created by the marquise to lead them astray. Mademoiselle Laberche, perhaps, had not lied about the red hair; it was hard to know if she was part of her mother's machinations.

The marquise stepped in front and lifted the latch of the boathouse door. Elinor did not wait for Perry to charge out like the avenging demon he had promised.

"She has a gun," Elinor shouted, though it came out more like a squawk. "The marquise has a gun!"

Silence echoed around them. Nothing stirred within the boathouse.

The marquise turned and hit her again across the face with her weapon. It smashed into Elinor's cheekbone, and she slumped into the fisherman's arms.

When she came back to consciousness, she was in the boathouse. Ropes now smarted on her arms and legs. Turning her head, she saw she was lying trussed on the jetty. A small lantern threw a weak light, fading into the shadows, and the sound of water lapping against the boats seemed overly loud. Elinor strained her eyes, looking for Perry. One of the boats was missing. The boat with the guineas in it.

With Perry in it.

"Awake?" asked the marquise. She sat on a wooden stump of the jetty, the gun still in her hands. Elinor's reticule now hung heavy on her skirts, taken while

Elinor was unconscious, and now carrying a new burden of jewels. Elinor devoutly hoped the marquise had mistaken the miniature dress inside for an ornate handkerchief.

"Now Miss Avely, I think you must be a jewel diviner. I saw you go out last night, walking along the cliffs – what reason would a young lady have to do that?" The marquise shook her head. "It was probably how you found me in that cave, discerning my diamond pendant. I feared you might be out hunting for my treasures, so I asked Clodder here to pick them up and deliver them to me."

Elinor closed her eyes, remembering Samuel's yowl as she and Aldreda left the house last evening. It must have alerted the marquise. In the very act of looking for the jewels, Elinor had warned the thief.

"Yes," said the marquise. "You are a dangerous woman, Miss Avely. I should be rid of you. Yet I have a proposition. You clearly have verve and ambition. You can help me with your talents, and we can make a fortune together in France under Napoleon's rule." She paused. "Or you can die tonight in the dark."

"You cannot just kill me," said Elinor slowly, her voice scratchy with fear. "You will be caught."

"It will be thought that you came back to the boathouse to look for your bats. So fortunate you have a fondness for bats. But so tragic." The marquise smiled. "You slip and fall in the darkness, and drown. It will be very sad."

Elinor swallowed. "Like Harris."

"Yes, indeed. So you know I am capable. He was bigger than you, too – though of course he did not expect me to push him off the cliff. He confronted me, decided he was too virtuous to take from the destitute.

He thought I would accept his reversal!" The marquise shook her head sadly. "Consider wisely, Miss Avely. Perhaps some time in the dark will allow you to see the appeal of a life in France." She turned to the fisherman. "Gag her, Clodder, and put her in that rowboat."

"Wait!" said Elinor. If only she could keep the marquise talking until Aldreda fetched help. "What of the gold? Where have you done with the gold?"

The marquise turned. "What gold?"

Elinor paused, taken aback. "You don't know? The bags of guineas. I thought you must be sending them over to Napoleon."

"Indeed?" said the marquise. "And where are these bags of guineas?"

Elinor bit her lip. Perhaps she had given away something crucial. Or perhaps she had found a card to play. "Untie me, and I will tell you."

The marquise laughed, an odd sound in the gloom. "Tell me, or I will kill you."

That was a rather strong negotiating stance. Elinor thought quickly. "There was gold in one of the boats. The boat is gone now. Not one of your men, I suppose?"

"One of these boats? Ah, Lord Beresford, of course."

"I doubt it," said Elinor haughtily.

"Who then?"

"One of your men," Elinor repeated. "If they are corrupt enough to help you steal, they will not hesitate to help England's enemies. A pity. It was a lot of gold."

"You are a fool," said the marquise. "I know Lord Beresford sails to France regularly. I have heard all sorts of things from my man here. That is where his lordship is going now, no doubt. He is a spy, you stupid girl."

"He is not. He is far too noble for such a thing."

The heat in Elinor's voice appeared to give the

marquise pause. She leaned her chin on the gun, lost in thought. "Who then?"

"I have no idea."

A new voice came from the boathouse door. "I wish I could say it was I."

Elinor's head whipped towards the sound. It was Lord Treffler. Rescue at last. But in the dim light cast by the lantern she could see his lordship was smiling.

"You!" exclaimed the marquise. She lifted the gun. "I will shoot. Begone."

"You cannot leave dead bodies floating about all over the place," said Lord Treffler, smirking. "It is just not done in England, madame."

"I will say you attacked me," the marquise replied. She kept her gun steady. "Everyone will believe a frail, destitute widow over you, my lord. I am sure you have quite the reputation over here, as well as in France."

"Insults!" said Lord Treffler. He took a few steps closer. "My dear marquise, when I am only here to help you!"

He had not even looked at Elinor. She could not tell if he was trying to save her, or simply intent on his own game. She shifted against her bonds but they were tight and unforgiving.

"I don't need your help," sneered the marquise.

"Ah yes, you have the jewels," said Lord Treffler, admiringly. "Mademoiselle Laberche wrote to me from France. She told me all about her mother's little plots. She does not really approve, you know. She trusted me to do something about it. Of course, I was avidly interested to hear there was a priceless collection of heirlooms gathering in Devon."

The marquise shook her head. "Stupid Lucille. I

cannot see why she likes you. You are not worth the sole of her foot."

Lord Treffler sighed. "Your precious daughter is quite lovely, but I hasten to reassure you I am not interested in her. I want the jewels, and the gold. Much more useful than a pretty girl."

"I do not have the gold," said the marquise. "And I am certainly not giving you the jewels."

"Don't you want the gold?" he asked. "It will be two hundred guineas at least. A nice little investment for your new life. I will take half, of course."

The marquise tilted her head. "How do you propose to fetch it?"

"We will stop the boat before it leaves English shores," said Lord Treffler. "Didn't Miss Avely say the guineas were in one of Beresford's boats here? It will be on its way downriver now. If we take horses we can meet it before the bay."

"Oh?" mused the marquise. Not for a moment, though, did she lower her gun. Lord Treffler stayed a cautious distance away, keeping stiff and still. Elinor could see his eyes darting around. It was time, she thought, that she contributed to the conversation.

"May I suggest you hurry up," Elinor said, "if you wish to catch the gold before it leaves England."

Lord Treffler looked at her for the first time. "Miss Avely, good evening. I see you found the jewels after all. Pity you did not tell me. Then you wouldn't be currently so indisposed."

"A shame indeed, my lord," Elinor said politely. "I do not suppose you could assist me?"

Lord Treffler shook his head reprovingly. "Alas, I have other claims on my attention. The Marquise of Laberche requires help in gaining her fortune." He turned his gaze back to the marquise. "We could even commandeer the ship ready in the bay, and gain a passage back to France. Were you not intending to return to your home country soon?"

The marquise wet her lips. "Now?"

"Why not? You have the jewels. Shortly you will have a hundred guineas. All you need is your daughter. You could fetch her now."

"It is a trap."

"Not at all," said Lord Treffler. "You have the jewels, to bargain for my cooperation. As an indication of my eagerness to help, let me tell you I have found two horses waiting a little downstream. Belonging, I believe, to the Avelys. Perfect to transport you and Mademoiselle Laberche to the bay."

Elinor felt a little of her hope die within her.

"Very well," said the marquise. "This gold is tempting. But if you cross me, your life will be forfeit."

"I expect nothing less." Lord Treffler bowed. "I would much rather gain half the loot. Of course, if *you* cross *me,* your daughter will be forfeit. I shall greatly enjoy ruining her reputation. If you stay in England, you can guarantee that tomorrow everyone will know you as a jewel thief. Or if that fails, I have other ways to compromise a lady."

The marquise glared at him, but she stood. "Put Miss Avely in the boat," she said. "You can help, my lord, if you are so eager to manhandle pretty young ladies. Gag her first, and do it properly, Clodder."

Rage and fear swelled in Elinor as she was roughly gagged. Lord Treffler stepped forward and helped Clodder haul her into one of the rowboats. Elinor had hoped, desperately, his lordship would at last make his move to free her. Instead he heaved her into the boat with careless hands.

"Deepest apologies, Miss Avely," he said. "Needs must."

She shot him a look of scorn. He had the grace to look a trifle ashamed.

"Hurry up," said the marquise. She turned her gun on Clodder. "Off with your boots, my man."

"Yes, madame." He shook his left boot off and reached inside. "I am sorry, madame. Just a little insurance for a poor fisherman." He held out a small object, which glinted even in the gloom. Elinor felt sure it was a diamond ring.

The marquise took it and slipped it on her finger. "Never again, or you shall end up lame or dead. Lead the way out, please. Good evening, Miss Avely. I will be back for you shortly, once I ready my daughter for the journey. I hope you will join us. Consider well. I am sure you would not like to die tonight, when you could live a wealthy life in France."

Elinor made no reply, as she could not. The cloth in her mouth was stale with the taste of fish, making it exceedingly unpleasant even to breathe. The marquise gestured with her gun for Lord Treffler to follow Clodder. His lordship bowed, and vanished through the door. The marquise blew out the lantern and followed. The door creaked shut on the moonlight.

Only thin slithers of white trickled onto the wooden beams. The rest was pitch-black. Elinor strained her senses in the dark. Long moments passed before she finally felt the whisper of bat wings past her cheek.

Still there was silence, as Aldreda effected her change into human form. Wisely, the vampiri waited until the others were far away before murmuring in Elinor's ear.

"Sorry, my dear. Didn't warn you in time."

Elinor shook her head slightly.

"Perry has gone with the boat," Aldreda continued. "I flew ahead, to tell him of your arrival, and saw him wrestling with a burly red-haired fellow while they were afloat on the lake. I fear Perry was overcome."

Elinor shook her head again, this time in despair. Both Avelys defeated. Probably Perry was also trussed up like a chicken.

Aldreda's other words sank in. Red-haired fellow. Not Beresford then. Relief coursed through Elinor. Of course it was not Beresford, in spite of the marquise's ideas. Who, then, did the red-haired fellow work for? And what would he do to Perry? With renewed worry, Elinor remembered the fisherman's warning in the village and his intimations about cliff-tops.

"Never fear," said Aldreda. "We will rescue Perry."

Elinor tried to indicate a wry laugh, but it was difficult with a gag. Not to mention her own fear clogging her throat.

Aldreda was wrestling with the gag. Her tiny fingers could not loosen the knot, but with a great heave she managed to pull it down from Elinor's mouth.

Elinor drew in a long, shaky breath, relieved to smell the dank air of the boathouse after the stench of fish. "Thank you. And my bonds?"

These, it turned out, were beyond Aldreda's powers. The sturdy rope was securely tied, and her little fingers could do nothing with them. She tried her sharp teeth, but these were even smaller and ineffectual against the rope.

Aldreda grimaced, her naked body gleaming palely in the dim light. "Do you think Lord Treffler will come back to rescue you?"

Elinor shook her head. "I fear not. I don't think we should wait to find out. What about a knife? Could you fetch a knife, and cut the ropes? I fear you are too small for that."

Aldreda sat dejectedly on Elinor's ankles. Her small white shoulders drooped.

"I wish I could dress," she sighed. "It is difficult to be heroic without your clothes on." Then she looked up, with renewed determination. "If I cannot untie you, I must at least rescue you from this boathouse. Before that monstrous woman returns."

"How will you do that?" enquired Elinor calmly.

Aldreda was already at the rope that tethered the boat to the jetty. With a huge effort she pushed it up and up, until it toppled off the mooring. It fell with a faint splash into the water.

"I will take the boat out into the lake," she announced.

Elinor watched, helpless, as Aldreda once again turned into a bat and flew to the door that opened onto the lake, at the other end of the boathouse. After some struggle, the bat managed to open it. Moonlight poured in like a beacon of hope.

Meanwhile the boat slowly drifted away from the jetty. However, it was moving in the opposite direction of the open door.

Aldreda flew back, swooped down, and grabbed the tether rope with her little claws. Then, straining every fibre of her being, she tugged on the boat.

It was slow, torturous work, inching the boat towards freedom. Elinor waited in taut silence, expecting any moment to see the marquise once more silhouetted at the jetty door. She kept still, not wanting to disturb Aldreda's efforts.

Tension vibrated along Elinor's body, and she tried to expel it, knowing she needed to keep her nerve. The boat rocked gently on the water, and she closed her eyes, feeling the rhythmic movement. The darkness lay above and below her. What had she done, to put herself in this pickle? Her pride, her foolish pride, had laid her low. She should have asked for Beresford's help. If she had not been so eager to prove she could gain the jewels herself – if she was not so entranced with her own precious gift – she would not be tied up in a damp rowboat, relying on a bat to drag her to freedom.

Elinor lifted her head, murmuring an encouragement to the valiant Aldreda, then dropped it back on the wood, despondent. She was no better than the marquise, putting all else aside for the sake of seeking trinkets.

After a few long minutes, she felt a slight change in the rocking. Looking up, she saw moonlight now bathed the wood and her body. She was in the path of the door. The water flowed slightly stronger against the boat, but Aldreda, with her impossible strength, was slowly urging the vessel forward.

At last the boat edged out the door. The sound of the water lapped stronger. Elinor, eyes wide, looked up into a moonlit sky sprinkled with stars. Night birds called, their eerie voices carrying clear across the lake.

"Well done, Aldreda!" she whispered. "Onwards!"

The little bat kept straining against the weight of the boat. Slowly, slowly, she tugged it out into the expanse of the lake.

Relief gradually spread through Elinor, even though she was still bound. Out here the marquise would find it hard to reach her. Surely someone would see the boat drifting and fetch it ashore. Even if Elinor had to lie here all night, perhaps Beresford would pull her to safety in the morning.

Except Perry was in danger.

Fear gripped her again. How was she to save him, tied up like a drunken sailor?

Suddenly, they heard the faint creak of the boathouse door carrying over the lake. Aldreda flew back over the rowboat, dropped the rope, and landed to hang from the prow. They both froze. The boat continued to drift slowly in the dark.

A short while later they heard a voice raised in anger. Elinor felt sure it was the marquise. Elinor lifted her head to peek over the rim of the boat.

"There!" said the marquise, her voice carrying sharply over the water. "The boat is out there!"

Elinor could make out four figures on the edge of the lake. The marquise, Clodder, Lord Treffler, and a slighter silhouette, cloaked, that must be Mademoiselle Laberche.

There were the sounds of a muffled discussion, and a few raised words. Then the group appeared to decide the gold was more important. As one they turned, abandoning Elinor to her drifting, and hurried along the path. They were heading off downstream to the horses. Only Mademoiselle Laberche seemed to pause and stare out at the moonlit lake for a moment.

Elinor let her head drop back down in relief. "They are leaving us."

Aldreda gave a faint squeak in agreement.

"Thank goodness," said Elinor. "Now we just have to catch up with them. Perhaps we should try to direct this boat towards the river."

Aldreda swung up into the air with the rope once more in her claws, and changed course a little. She kept batting her little wings, pulling, pulling, through the endless black water.

Elinor hauled herself to sitting. She scanned the

shore, hoping to see signs of Perry, even though she knew in her heart he was already travelling downstream with the gold.

Eventually Aldreda stopped flying, letting the rope fall with a splash into the lake. She fluttered back and flopped onto Elinor's lap, exhausted. She remained a bat, too tired to change form.

The boat was still moving, even without Aldreda's help. The vampiri had not abandoned her quest. The current was taking them towards the river.

"Well done!" Elinor said. "Now we just need to gain on Perry and stop the gold before it leaves for France. And catch the marquise and the jewels. Somehow."

Aldreda was unresponsive. With a flash of worry, Elinor besought her to feed from her arm above the rope. The bat crawled across and drank long and deeply. When she was done she turned back into human form.

"Thank you. I feel much better," Aldreda said. "Now, the gold must be going to that sailing ship we saw on the coast. If we don't stop the jolly boat, we could try to stop the ship. But how?"

They were silent a long time. The rowboat was approaching the mouth of the river, the currents drawing it inexorably on. The progress, however, was rather stately.

"This is too slow," wailed Elinor. "And I'm tied up."

"It is a problem," agreed Aldreda.

They both jumped a foot when something lurched out of the water next to the boat. A head popped over the rim and grinned at them. It was a handsome head, with wet black hair clinging to the finely shaped skull.

"May I be of assistance?" asked Jaq.

24

IN WHICH A CHAPERONE PLAYS
HER PART

"*Y*ou seal pup!" shouted Aldreda. She dove under Elinor's dress. "You made me jump!"

"Apologies, ladies. I heard you needed assistance."

"Avert your gaze, Elinor!"

With a blush, Elinor realised Jaq was not wearing any clothes. His white muscled arms held onto the boat, water glistening in droplets and hanging off his long eyelashes.

Elinor tried to keep to the important matter. "Jaq, we need to stop some gold leaving for France. Can you untie me?"

"Ah, which gold would that be?"

Aldreda spoke sharply. "Those bags of guineas, as you very well know, you blunderbuss."

Jaq blushed.

Elinor stared at him. "You do know of it! Are you the French spy?"

"Oh, no. But I am afraid I cannot let you interfere with the gold."

"Why on earth not?" snapped Aldreda, from the folds of Elinor's skirts. "That is English gold."

"What do I care for these national conflicts?" said Jaq. "I am from the oceans."

"Then why are you trying to stop us?" demanded Elinor.

"I owe a loyalty," said Jaq. "A personal one."

"To Beresford," said Aldreda, with finality. "It is Beresford's gold."

To Elinor's shock, she saw a look of annoyance cross Jaq's face.

"*Beresford's* gold?" she said. "I don't believe it."

"So what if it is Beresford's gold?" said Jaq defensively. "It is not your concern."

Elinor stared at him, her world shifting and righting around her. The initial sick lurch of her stomach gave way to a new certainty.

"He is a spy," she said slowly. "An English spy. He is taking the gold across as a front."

Aldreda nodded. "So he can gather information in return."

"I don't know what you're talking about," said Jaq. The boat rocked a little as he gave a jerky movement of denial.

"When does Beresford leave?" demanded Elinor. "We must warn him."

"I don't know what you mean," repeated Jaq. "Regardless, I cannot let you interrupt Lord Beresford's plans. Your brother has already caused enough trouble."

"Perry?" asked Elinor, urgently. "Is he harmed?"

Jaq was glad of this distraction. "Mr Avely is currently occupying a state similar to yours."

"Do you mean he is tied up?" Elinor sighed. "The Avelys are making a poor show of it today."

"He tried to commandeer one of Beresford's boats, in a rather reckless fashion. Rusty had to take measures."

"You mean the red-haired fisherman? Beresford's man, I suppose?" Elinor thought crossly of Rusty's warning to her – no doubt on instruction from the earl.

Jaq nodded. "Perry said something about you, Miss Avely, and I thought I had better investigate upstream before I joined the crew. And here I discover you have taken possession of Beresford's rowboat. Why all these attempts upon his boats, if I may ask, my dear?"

"Perry was trying to stop the gold going to France."

Jaq shook his head. "It is all part of his lordship's arrangements. Don't you worry your heads too much about it. Now, perhaps I should escort you home."

"Don't patronise me, young man," said Elinor. "Beresford is in danger. We must go after him."

Her grim voice had some effect.

"How is he in danger?" asked Jaq.

"The Marquise of Laberche and Lord Treffler are set upon gaining the gold. They are heading towards Beresford's ship as we speak."

"What do they know of the *Crescent*?"

"Too much. They are both villains, and she has the jewels," said Elinor. "Now untie me at once. We have to hurry."

Jaq chewed his full bottom lip. Then he nodded. "But you must close your eyes. I'm afraid I am not dressed as a gentleman."

Elinor screwed her eyes tightly shut. "I swear not to look."

"You too, Miss Zooth," said Jaq pointedly.

"I plan to leave the vicinity entirely," said Aldreda.

Elinor protested. "You can't do that, you're my chaperone!"

"True," agreed Aldreda. "Yet what good is a chaperone who has to close her eyes?"

"Oh, look all you like," said Jaq. "I have nothing of which to be ashamed. I will lean over the boat, so you won't be exposed to my admirable lower regions."

Elinor heard Aldreda give an outraged sniff, and she giggled in spite of herself. The boat heaved as Jaq hauled himself higher and leaned over the rim. Water dripped onto Elinor's wrists and hands as he grappled with her ropes. Soon she felt them slip off. Jaq then splashed over to the other end of the boat and made quick work of the ropes binding her feet. Elinor tried not to think about the impropriety of a naked gentleman inspecting her ankles.

"Thank you," she said, as the rope loosened.

"It is nothing, my lady." The boat rocked, and a splash announced that Jaq was once more modestly covered by water. Elinor dared to open her eyes.

Jaq grinned from the river. Aldreda frowned disapprovingly, wrapped up tightly in Elinor's skirt pocket.

"What a relief." Elinor stretched out her arms and legs and pulled the ghastly gag over her head and threw it into the water. "Now, the plan. I think we must first attempt to gain on the boat of guineas before Treffler and the marquise. We must go downriver as fast as possible – we have a quicker route than they will have on horses. Do you know when Beresford plans to leave?"

"At daybreak," replied Jaq. "I was to meet him there, after he scoured the county for the jewels. You say the marquise has them?"

"Indeed. We need to reach the ship before she does. I don't suppose you could pull us, Mr Delquon? Miss Zooth has brought us thus far, but she is wearied."

"I can do so as a seal," he said.

"Good. Please hurry."

Jaq's dark head disappeared. The water churned and a few moments later he reappeared in a new guise. It gave Elinor quite a shock to see the evidence of what, up to now, had only been hearsay. A large, sleek seal, in dark chocolate-brown, now bumped the side of the boat. Jaq was completely transformed, with long whiskers, and a soft flat nose. But the same black eyes with long lashes gleamed up at her.

"Still very handsome," she observed. Jaq winked.

Aldreda tutted. "The boat, if you please."

With barely a splash, Jaq managed to hook the rope over his head. Then he began to swim, strong and steady, pulling the boat behind him. The vessel rocked, gaining speed.

Elinor grasped the seat. Now would not be a good time to fall out.

"Jaq must be in servitude to Beresford," observed Aldreda, over the churn of the water.

"Servitude? What do you mean?"

"It is the only thing that can explain his behaviour. Normally selkies avoid humans. Secretive lot. They only spend time ashore briefly, unless they have been caught and enslaved. Beresford must have managed to catch him by stealing his seal star."

"What is that?"

"It holds a selkie's freedom, given to them on coming of age. They usually have it on their person. I have not seen Jaq's, though he may have hidden it to keep it safe."

"Beresford would never take it!"

"He might if he needed help in his ocean ventures."

"Jaq wouldn't allow him to take it," objected Elinor.

"If Jaq were under the influence of mermaid tears, he might not even know what had happened."

"Is that a strong drink?"

"Worse, a drug."

"Oh." Elinor remembered how Jaq's eyes had been strangely dilated when she found him by the oak tree. "Oh dear."

"I hope he has not partaken of it recently."

"He seems quite chipper," remarked Elinor.

"Mmm."

Elinor watched the strong, sleek body plough through the water. The fields and hedges along the river were now passing by rapidly. She wondered if they were travelling faster than the horses, who had a more circuitous route. "How far ahead is Perry, I wonder? I suppose we can't sink the boat if he is tied up in it."

They travelled on in silence, until the dim shape of a bridge showed up ahead. As they passed under, Aldreda stiffened. "Oh no," she said, staring ahead through the dark. "I think we are too late."

Elinor's head turned sharply to follow Aldreda's gaze. On the bank of the river a body lay, half in the water. For a heart-sickening moment Elinor thought it was Perry. Then she saw the figure was too large. Also, it was not dead, for one hand began slapping the water feverishly.

"Jaq!" she cried. "Stop."

Elinor realised suddenly the man was Rusty, the large red-haired man who had accosted Perry and her in the village. It seemed he was trying to signal Jaq. The seal slowed and swam over to him, the boat skidding behind.

Rusty's pale face was washed out with moonlight and loss of blood. He had been shot in the shoulder. Blood pooled into the water, showing dark slicks on the surface.

"Jaq," he said, his voice gravelly. "We were hijacked. A party of villains attacked me from the bridge."

"What of Perry?" demanded Elinor. "Is he safe?"

"I told thee to stay out of it." Rusty glared at her. "Your stupid brother is hostage. Tied up ready in the boat. They are planning to use him as barter to gain entry to the *Crescent*."

"You shouldn't have tied him up!" snapped Elinor, tense with worry.

"He shouldn't have been in my boat!" growled Rusty.

Jaq slipped the rope and transformed back into his human form. "When was this?" he asked, flicking long black hair out of his eyes.

"About ten minutes ago," replied Rusty. "And with I out of action and thee escorting a lady, that leaves the captain with only one other man aboard the ship."

"The marquise has a gun," said Elinor. "We must rescue Beresford. Can you climb aboard, Rusty?"

"No time for that," said Rusty, gritting his teeth in pain. "Thee must hurry to warn the captain. I will be an impediment."

"We cannot leave you here!" exclaimed Elinor.

"Thee can. It's not as bad as it looks."

"It looks fairly bad," said Jaq. He swam forward and heaved Rusty further up the bank. Aldreda and Elinor averted their eyes from Jaq's muscled, naked back, but not before Elinor had noted his nether regions *were* rather admirable.

Aldreda spoke softly. "The marquise will not harm Perry, if she is using him as hostage."

"Until she has what she wants," pointed out Elinor shakily.

"Which is the gold and the *Crescent*. I can fly ahead if you like. Though I note that sunrise is not far off." Aldreda peered into the horizon, a crease between her brows.

"Do you need to fly home?" asked Elinor. "We do not have the reticule anymore. That cursed marquise took it."

They heard the sound of Jaq ripping fabric, fashioning a bandage for Rusty. Elinor glanced over and felt ill at the sight of the wound. God forbid Perry suffer anything like that.

Aldreda shook her head. "I won't fly home. If we can reach Beresford's ship I could sleep in the cabin."

"Very well then. How long do you think we have?"

"One hour, perhaps."

Elinor tried not to think about what would happen if they did not reach the ship in time. Beresford would be a sitting duck for Lord Treffler and the marquise, Perry would die, and Aldreda would be reduced to a shrivel. And it was arguably all Elinor's fault.

Jaq finished helping Rusty out of the water before recovering his modesty. The fisherman grunted his thanks, probably for both circumstances. "I will drag myself to the vicarage," said Rusty. "The vicar will take me in."

"I must swim ahead," Jaq turned to Elinor. "I will be faster alone."

"Wait!" said Elinor. "Take us with you. We can help. We can distract them while you gain the ship."

"No." It was one, uncommunicative syllable, a stark contrast to Jaq's usual flowery manner of speech.

Elinor leaned desperately over the edge of the boat. "The marquise wants to take me to France with her. I can bargain with her, while you climb the ship and warn Beresford." When Jaq still looked sceptical, she added, "Surely we are not so heavy we will slow you down too much. And I have a plan."

She leaned forward and outlined her idea. Aldreda raised her brows and nodded reluctantly in support.

"It's crazy," said Rusty, listening from the riverbank. "It might just work."

"Please, Mr Delquon," said Elinor. "We are more likely to succeed with three of us than one of you."

Jaq heaved a sigh and dove underwater. When he emerged he was a seal again, and hooked the rope around himself.

He set off downriver with renewed speed. The rowboat lurched behind him. Elinor clutched the side, feeling a bit sick.

"God speed," called Rusty. "And good luck!"

25

IN WHICH ROLES ARE REVERSED

*A*ll depended on the speed of a handsome seal.

Fortunately, this was quite fast. The river was becoming wider and flowing stronger. Elinor could smell the sharp, briny scent of the sea, and Aldreda said she could hear the crash of waves. Soon the water broadened out before them, with small waves cresting against the boat. Jaq's dark head still bobbed in and out of the water, though the passage was becoming rougher for his cargo. The moon had disappeared now, but Elinor could still see in the murky twilight of the summer night.

"Look!" cried Elinor. "The jolly boat! And the ship!"

Much farther out, the sailing ship lay in the bay, its graceful figure still in the faint, predawn light. Elinor was glad to see its sails were still furled, though a lantern glowed on the decks. Tracking towards it was the jolly boat, oars flashing in and out of the water. It was moving slowly, weighed down by its numerous passengers. Elinor strained her eyes to count four, but she could not see Perry among them. He must be tied and stowed in the bow.

"Hurry, Jaq!" Elinor called, though she doubted he could hear.

Their passage became turbulent. The waves surging into the bay buffeted against the rowboat. It tipped its nose up into the air, arcing and diving in a most unsettling fashion. Elinor only kept her balance with difficulty, becoming more wet and cold by the moment as the spray soaked her gown. One particularly big wave almost overturned them entirely.

Jaq slowed, tilting an inquisitive head back. Elinor waved him forward. But he did not resume his former speed, and swam more carefully, at a diagonal.

"Too slow!" she cried.

"Better than ending up in the water," said Aldreda.

"What do I care for that?"

Elinor kept her eyes pinned to the *Crescent*, and soon saw what she feared – the jolly boat had gained the side of it. She watched, holding her breath.

A figure leaned over the side of the schooner, gesticulating with sharp movements. Even at this distance Elinor could tell it was Beresford. Suddenly he straightened and lifted his arms, still staring down at the jolly boat.

Perry was now apparent, held at an awkward angle against Lord Treffler, who shouted something. After a tense moment, Beresford threw a rope ladder down, his movements rough. Elinor watched as Clodder scaled the ladder, followed by the marquise and Mademoiselle Laberche at slower paces. Finally Perry was pulled up while the marquise pointed something at Beresford. Her gun.

Elinor felt frenzied with impatience. Was she to watch here while the marquise shot them both? Jaq still pulled their boat diagonally against the waves, and progress was slow. Grimly Elinor watched as the sacks of gold were hauled up. Finally Lord Treffler vaulted onto the ship.

Elinor hoped Beresford might use the opportunity to vanquish the marquise. Instead he stood by, his hands still raised. Clearly Beresford did not feel he could risk it, with the marquise's gun now trained on Perry.

It was time to adjust the plan.

"Jaq! Jaq! We have to hurry!"

His seal head popped out of the water. The boat careened towards him, nearly knocking him on the ear. He widened his eyes in question.

"We won't catch them like this! We'll be too late!"

The seal pursed his lips.

"You can go faster carrying me," said Elinor. "You can tow me, instead of the whole boat. Aldreda can fly."

The seal shook his head vehemently.

"It is the only way." Elinor was already undoing the ties on her dress. "You can't leave me out here adrift in the waves. Beresford will have your hide if you do that. We have to reach the ship as fast as possible, to carry out our plan. We'll simply have to do it without the rowboat. You must pull me along in the water."

The big black eyes looked very apprehensive.

"Don't worry, I will tell him it was my idea," Elinor said, and kicked off her boots.

She wriggled out of the overdress, which was heavy with spray. Standing up in her shift, she took a gulp of cold air, feeling a fresh breeze prickle her skin. Grey waves lurched in all directions around her.

"I'll see you aboard," she said to Aldreda. Then Elinor jumped into the icy water.

It struck her flesh like a physical blow. She went under,

gasping with the cold, and flailing to keep abreast. Then with relief she felt the warm body of a seal come up under her, pushing her to the surface. She swung her arms wildly around until she had them fast around his neck.

His fur was silky and a bit slippery. Grasping her own hand to make a loop, Elinor held on tightly.

Jaq began to swim.

It was an odd sensation, being dragged along the surface of the sea, with the powerful body of a seal underneath her. All Elinor's attention was occupied with gasping for air, as the water kept slamming into her face. Soon Jaq must have gathered her difficulty, because he changed his technique, doing a dive over the waves every minute or so, and swimming below the water in between. Before each submersion Elinor took a mouthful of air and clung tightly, holding her breath for the rapid underwater swim.

With each surfacing, she saw they were gaining on the ship. Its sails were starting to unfurl now, and her heart tightened. They were so close!

Even as the sails extended, Jaq gained on their object. Elinor kicked her legs at each rising, to attract attention as much as to assist the selkie. Finally she heard a shout carry on the wind. They had been seen.

Two figures leaned over the ship rail, peering at them. Jaq slowed as he approached the vessel. Holding Elinor afloat – a white ballooning shape – he towed her forward more gently.

Elinor tried to blink the water from her eyes. She knew she must make a spectacle, her white shift soaked through, her hair bedraggled, and her method of transport a seal.

She gathered her resolve and looked up.

Beresford's stormy visage stared down at her. Next to him was the marquise, looking astonished and angry.

"By heavens," said the marquise. "It is the Avely girl. How on earth did she arrive here?"

Clodder peered over the edge and grunted.

"I rode a seal," shouted Elinor. "One of my many talents." She thought the marquise needed a reminder Elinor was particularly gifted. "Please, madame, let me aboard. I come to bargain with you."

Jaq chose this moment to slip away out from under Elinor. He slapped his tail on the water and swam off ostentatiously. To all appearances he was off to frolic in the waves somewhere, but Elinor knew he would swim around to the other side of the boat, where he had a special entrance to the ship.

Elinor made a show of struggling in the water. "Please help me. I have something to say, but I cannot say it here."

Beresford growled. "Do not allow her on board. My ship is overburdened enough."

The marquise looked from him to Elinor. Beresford's obvious desire to keep Elinor away seemed to sway the Frenchwoman in the other direction. "I should mention, Miss Avely, I have your brother and the earl here in difficult positions." The marquise waved her gun at Beresford. "Any misbehaviour from you and they will suffer for it."

"Yes, madame." Elinor floundered a little more. "Only please let me up soon, or I shall be no good to anyone. How will I help you in France if I am drowned?"

"Throw a rope down," said the marquise brusquely.

Beresford stood like a stone. "No."

Clodder grunted and did it for him. Elinor grasped at it and found herself being hauled through the air. The rope burned her palms and it seemed to take forever, swinging in the air above the waves like a marionette. Then suddenly she was tumbling onto the deck in a wet puddle at the centre of a circle of interested spectators.

"Ooof," came the sound of Perry's voice, through a gag. "Eoof, oof, oof."

Elinor took this as Perry reciting *vincit prudentia* as best he could.

She stood up, flicked the hair out of her face and took in the scene. Perry was sitting on a barrel, tied up and leaning against the mast. Lord Treffler stood next to him with a gun to his head. Mademoiselle Laberche stood aghast against the cabin on the quarterdeck, her eyes glued to Perry and Lord Treffler. Beresford stood against the far rail, with the marquise and Clodder on either side of him. Another man, unknown to Elinor, but presumably the other one of Beresford's crew, lay face down on the deck. She could not tell if he was conscious or not.

The trim deck gleamed in the light of the lantern, the white sails elegant and filling with wind. A small black creature fluttered onto the rigging.

It was time for Elinor to play her part.

"Lord Beresford!" she cried. She threw herself at his feet, careless of the sight she made in her dripping wet shift and bare feet. "Let them take the gold! Do not betray England like this!"

Beresford stared down at her. She cast a glance up at him from under her lashes, to see his face still and stern.

The marquise sneered. "I told you his lordship was a spy. We will take the gold from the earl, don't you fear. Have you decided to come to France with us, Miss Avely?"

Elinor turned her head. "I will do anything, as long as

you do not hand him in. I beg of you, madame. I will die of shame if my fiancé is tried for treason."

The marquise raised a brow. "Fiancé?"

"Yes," declared Elinor, clasping her hands to her breast, even as she knelt on the deck. It was time to return a favour, in the same manner Beresford had done her once. "We are betrothed."

She glanced up. Beresford's eyes widened slightly, and his lips pressed together. Then he spoke, his voice rough. "Miss Avely. It is kind of you to try to protect me, but I cannot have it. You need not bargain for my safety."

"It is my duty to protect my future husband," Elinor cried, and for good measure she tossed her head about wildly. Might as well do the thing properly, and she hoped it would distract the marquise from Beresford's recalcitrant attitude.

"I am not betrothed to you." Beresford's noble denial was undercut by his next words, directed at the marquise. "Would I betroth myself to this wild woman?"

"Oh, my lord," Elinor murmured brokenly, bowing her head. "How can you say so? I beg you to remember we are indeed affianced.'

"I am not." He denied it firmly, just as Elinor had done once. She shot him another look from under her lashes. His grey eyes met hers, and she found herself indeed transfixed, a strange thrill running through her as their gazes locked.

Lord Treffler snorted. "Make up your mind, you two." He looked from one to the other, from Elinor's arrested expression to Beresford's unreadable face. "I think the earl is lying, madame, trying to save her. Beresford is prone to that kind of thing."

"It is irrelevant," said the marquise brusquely. "As soon as we are out to sea, we will throw him overboard.

However, we will save him a traitor's death, Miss Avely. That is, if you can guarantee your cooperation."

Elinor clung to Beresford's feet and sobbed gustily. Even though her head was bent in apparent grief, she could sense the bag of jewels still hanging at the marquise's waist. With a sinking feeling she also became aware of a faint lightening of the sky.

Sunrise was near. They did not have much time.

"Anything to save him!" she cried. "I will do anything."

At that moment, Perry uttered a startled noise through his gag. All eyes turned to him. A small black bat had landed to swing from the rope around Perry's middle. His eyes widened in horror, and he tried to shake it off. Elinor thought he realised what was about to happen before anyone else. After all, he was the one who had suggested it.

Aldreda transformed. Before everyone's gaze she shimmered into her human state and fell onto Perry's lap, as pure as the day she was born. She stood, her white figure shining in the starlight, unmistakably female. With her long, black hair flowing over her shoulders, she looked like a miniature Venus.

Lord Treffler gasped, his finger slackening on the gun. At that moment, the cabin door burst open and Jaq strode out. He was dripping wet and stark naked. He came to a halt on the quarterdeck and struck a pose.

If Aldreda was Venus, Jaq was Adonis.

It was quite a sight.

Mademoiselle Laberche gasped and fell back. The marquise's jaw dropped. Lord Treffler turned, confused, pointing his gun at this new threat.

"Halt!" declaimed Jaq. "Beresford is mine! Do not harm him!"

There was a stunned silence.

Elinor lunged.

She went for the jewels, grasping the reticule with both hands and pulling it roughly from the marquise. Clutching the heavy bag to her chest, Elinor rolled out of the way as the marquise flailed to defend herself.

Elinor strode quickly to the edge of the ship and held the jewels out over the water.

"Stop! Or I drop the jewels!"

The marquise froze. She looked ludicrously startled. Her eyes darted from the dangling reticule to the wet figure of Jaq to the tiny shape of Aldreda standing on Perry's lap.

Beresford moved fast. He swung an efficient punch at Clodder, and closed the gap between him and Lord Treffler, who still held a shaky arm aloft, pointing the gun at Jaq.

Beresford spoke coolly. "Don't shoot an unarmed, naked man, your lordship. It isn't the act of a gentleman."

Lord Treffler kept his gun trained on Jaq. "Whatever gave you the idea that I am a gentleman? I will not hesitate to kill your lover, Beresford."

"He is not my lover," snapped Beresford.

Jaq shook his head mournfully, still dripping onto the deck. "How can you say that, magnificent one?" He put his chin in the air, and his hands on his hips, so as to cast a finer picture of outraged dignity.

Aldreda tutted.

"You cannot talk, Miss Zooth," said Jaq. "Look at you."

Lord Treffler's eyes darted to Aldreda, just to check that it was indeed as he first saw: a beautiful, miniature, naked woman on Perry's lap.

Beresford took advantage of his distraction. He knocked Lord Treffler's hand, quick and hard.

Lord Treffler's gun fired, the report sounding loud in the predawn stillness. At the same time as Beresford moved, Jaq dropped to the ground, as if they had rehearsed it. The shot sailed above his head. Beresford swung a punch, and Lord Treffler dropped like a rock to the deck. The gun clattered to the floor.

Beresford turned to glare at Jaq, who was prostrate on the quarterdeck. "Put some clothes on." He turned in a circle. "That goes for all of you."

26

IN WHICH OBLIGATIONS ARE
RELEASED

First, they tied up the marquise. Elinor didn't trust her for a minute, though she herself still held the jewels hostage over the ocean. Only when the marquise's wrists were bound together did Elinor bring the reticule back in.

Beresford was busy tying up Clodder and Lord Treffler, with Jaq's help. Perry grunted in frustration, still bound. Elinor was too preoccupied to help him. The sky was a faint pink.

"Quick, to the cabin!" she said. Aldreda turned into a bat, which at least relieved Perry's discomfort somewhat. She flew after Elinor, who clambered up onto the quarterdeck and through the open door of the cabin.

The cabin was surprisingly spacious, panelled in brown wood with a maroon rug on the floor. Elinor shut the door and quickly pulled all the curtains shut. She found a small cupboard and emptied its contents – bottles of some drink – to clear a space for Aldreda.

"In you go," said Elinor. Aldreda fluttered past her. "Thank you so much, my dear Aldreda. I know that was difficult for you." Elinor rifled in the bag of jewels and pulled out Aldreda's dress triumphantly.

Aldreda turned into a naked woman once more and held out her hand for the gown. "Actually, it was quite enjoyable. I don't think I have caused such a stir for a hundred years."

"You should have seen the expression on Perry's face," said Elinor. She suddenly dissolved into giggles. "And the marquise's face when she saw Jaq!"

"Hmph," said Aldreda. "Jaq enjoyed it far too much."

Elinor wiped her eyes and looked up. "What of the pearls?" she asked. "I'm sorry we haven't had a chance to look for them yet."

"They can wait another day," said Aldreda. "I think we have accomplished enough for the moment."

Elinor heard Beresford clear his throat from behind her. She swung the cupboard door shut to conceal Aldreda and turned to face him nervously. She was conscious that she was still wet, bedraggled and under-dressed. Yet she also hoped that the example of Aldreda – her supposed chaperone – cast Elinor's own state in a good light.

"Elinor." Beresford looked her over as if to make sure she was unharmed. "What were you thinking?"

She felt a rush of pleasure at the sound of her given name on his lips. "I was saving you."

He crossed the room and stood right before her. "Don't do it again." His broad shoulders blocked her way, as if he would not let her pass until she promised. His grey eyes pinned her to the spot.

"Typically autocratic, my lord," she replied. "Don't land in trouble again, and I will see if I can oblige you."

"I am quite capable of looking after myself."

"You were merely waiting for the right moment?"

"Indeed. And the next time you rescue me, at least try to leave your clothes on." A reluctant smile tugged at his mouth. "I have had quite enough of unclad rescuers for a while. And you must be freezing." Beresford's tone softened, and he shrugged off his jacket, placing it over Elinor's shoulders.

She smiled up at him. His hands paused, surprisingly gentle, holding her arms.

"I release you of your obligation to marry me," he said. "I understand now why you were so angry with me. It is not pleasant to be betrothed for the sake of necessity."

Elinor couldn't say it was not an obligation. She couldn't say: please marry me, out of a different necessity. Instead, she held her breath.

Beresford leaned forward slightly, his fingers tightening on her arms.

Then he kissed her.

It was slow and tender. Elinor felt something like bliss loosening her limbs. She found she had to lean into him to keep her balance. His kiss deepened, becoming more demanding.

Perry's voice floated in from outside the cabin.

"Elinor, keep your bat–lady in line next time!"

Beresford let go of Elinor and stepped backwards. His expression flashed a mixture of frustration and guilt, then became its usual inscrutable mask.

Perry pushed open the cabin door and paused at the threshold. "I have never been so mortified in my life!"

Elinor turned on Perry crossly. "How can you say that? Miss Zooth saved you!"

Aldreda popped her head out of her cupboard, her black curls tumbling around her face. "Ungrateful boy."

"I am not a boy," said Perry. "When I said take your

clothes off, I didn't mean in front of me. Egad," he added, "what are all those bottles? Are you bosky now? Or perhaps you were already drunk?"

Aldreda stuck her chin in the air, glaring at Perry. "I was not drunk. I was rescuing you, little though you deserved it."

"Well, thank you, I suppose," said Perry reluctantly. He looked around. "You're popular today, Beresford."

"It was all an act, as I'm sure you're aware," Beresford replied.

"Yes, my sister has a hitherto unsuspected theatrical streak," observed Perry. "At least she kept *some* clothes on, unlike Miss Zooth here."

Jaq came inside the cabin. "Miss Zooth has nothing of which to be ashamed," he said. A blanket was wrapped over his shoulders. His wet feet and muscled calves were still visible, leaving footprints on the wooden floor. "Unless you say *I* should be ashamed."

"Of course you should," said Beresford sharply. "Bringing Elinor into this mess."

"Jaq saved me," said Elinor, hoping to mitigate Jaq's sins with this information. "He found me in the rowboat. It was my idea for him to bring me here. You cannot blame him."

"I can and I will," said Beresford. "It is most unseemly for you to be travelling by seal."

"As to that," said Elinor, "I do not see why you are so rude about my vampiri companion when you have a seal."

"What's this?" said Perry. "What seal?"

Elinor blinked. She supposed she ought not reveal Jaq's secret. "Beresford has a tame seal."

Jaq cleared his throat. "I would rather say a *wild* seal." He grinned at Elinor.

Aldreda tutted and withdrew her head, closing her cupboard door with a pointed snap.

Perry looked confused. "A seal who follows the ship?"

"Something like that," said Beresford shortly. "How did you end up in the rowboat, if I may ask, Miss Avely?"

Elinor mourned the return to formal address. She hoped it was not a sign Beresford regretted their kiss, but she answered his question. "The marquise and Lord Treffler tied me up in it. You should thank Jaq for untying me."

"You were tied up?" Beresford's voice went icy. "Traitors' deaths are too good for them."

"What will you do?" asked Perry. "If we take it to the law, all our names will be dragged through the mud."

"Could we send them back to France?" asked Elinor. "That is where they want to go."

"I suppose so," said Beresford, though Elinor could see he was reluctant. "They believe I am a French spy. If they inform against me to England, my superiors will play along with it."

Mademoiselle Laberche's voice came from the door. "Please do not send me with them."

Everyone turned to stare at her. There was no doubt she had just heard what Beresford had said. She smiled weakly. "I would much rather stay in England with you all. I promise not to betray you. I couldn't bear to go back to France with my mother."

"Of course," said Perry quickly. "You must stay in England." He went over to stand next to her, glaring at everyone as if they might object.

There was a long silence, but eventually everyone nodded. Indeed, thought Elinor, they had no choice. They could not send Mademoiselle Laberche back into the French troubles with her monstrous matriarch.

However, Elinor rather thought she would keep a close eye on the young woman.

"Very well, Mademoiselle Laberche," she said. "Perhaps you can help us return these heirlooms to their rightful owners."

Elinor drew open the reticule and poured the contents onto the cabin table. The pile of jewels gleamed dully in the dim light, the colours still apparent: ruby red, sapphire blue, and the white glint of diamonds. Mademoiselle Laberche nodded, her eyes wide.

"Thank you so much, Miss Avely," she said. "Even my own diamond earrings are in there, taken by my mother. And the rest of my compatriots will be so glad to see their treasures again."

"Think nothing of it," said Elinor. "I would not have been able to do it without certain unashamed assistance. Now – I need some dry clothes. Then we all need tea. I don't suppose you have any Beresford jam and chudleighs on board, my lord?"

Beresford heaved a sigh. "I suppose I cannot send you home."

"Not by seal," said Perry. "Not the thing."

"There is the rowboat," said the earl. "However, I do in fact have some jam. Useful for bargaining with the French, among others."

"Oh good," said Perry. "Let's have some. Even I admit your jam is good in this instance. I'm starving."

Jaq had disappeared behind a partition to dress. He reappeared still doing up the buttons on his white shirt.

"I say, Jaq," said Perry, amiable on all fronts. "Thank you for rescuing my sister."

"My pleasure," said Jaq, grinning. "Sorry I didn't rescue *you* earlier. Did you like my performance?"

Perry blushed, and Elinor was surprised to hear him mumble something about a dashed fine effort.

Elinor stood, still dripping, the strength suddenly draining out of her. Now everything was resolved she found her legs were rather weak. She looked around for a chair and collapsed upon it.

Beresford turned and began rifling through a chest. He held out some linen. "These will have to do, Miss Avely." He gave her a rueful grin.

Her eyes widened. He was holding out his own clothes: a shirt, breeches, and a jacket.

So it was that as the sun rose, Elinor poured tea for a misfit crew while dressed as a boy. Aldreda, exhausted, slept in the cupboard. The white sails of the schooner caught the apricot light, fluttering in the wind. Beresford's man (returned to consciousness) pulled them to half mast, and kept watch over the prisoners. They all munched on bread and jam, and drank cups of scalding hot tea while the blue sea stretched out beyond.

Eventually Beresford murmured something in Jaq's ear. The selkie took Perry's arm and offered to show him and Mademoiselle Laberche around the ship. They eagerly agreed, leaving Elinor and Beresford alone on the quarterdeck.

Elinor took a last reluctant sip of her tea. "Thank you for your clothes."

"You look charming."

She turned to look at him, surprised. He could not be serious – her hair was still damp and wild, and she was dressed as a boy.

Beresford smiled at her. "Very beautiful, in fact." There was a quirk to his mouth and a warm glow in his eyes that she had seen too little of late. She smiled back, her heart lightening.

"You are a brave woman," he said. "Riding Jaq out here. I am sure you received a mouthful of water for your pains."

"I'm sure what you mean to say is that I am a foolish one." She put down her cup. "I owe you an apology, my lord."

"Oh? What for this time?" He grinned at her.

She rejoiced in his sudden levity, and shot him a mischievous look. Then she continued with more seriousness. "You were right about Lord Treffler. He is a dangerous man and left me to my fate. I should have heeded your warning."

Beresford quirked his eyebrows. "Yes. And I must apologise for my officious behaviour."

"Bossy, you mean."

"Protective." He looked down at her, something tender in his eyes.

Elinor blushed. "Towards Jaq too, I observe." She hesitated, curious. "What is your relationship?"

"Nothing like that!" Suddenly Beresford did not look so amiable. "Why do you want to know?"

"Miss Zooth suggested Jaq only does your bidding because he is ... enslaved."

Beresford's shoulders relaxed. "I did not enslave him. His mother gave him into my care."

It was not what Elinor was expecting. "His *mother*?"

"Queen Glowdon. Jaq is the selkie Queen's oldest son. His wealth and status allow him access to all sorts of mischief in the deep seas."

Elinor took a moment to absorb this. Jaq was a young prince – of course he was. She remembered what Aldreda had said about his libations. "Ah, you mean his experiments with coral cutthroat and mermaid tears?"

Beresford looked surprised. "You are very well

informed. It is true that Jaq was a bit injudicious in his reckless youth. His mother was desperate to sober him up and give a safe direction for his energies. Jaq, however, was reluctant to agree. So the Queen took the unprecedented step of willingly giving me his seal star, to give me some authority over him."

"Jaq must have resisted," observed Elinor. "I can't imagine a spoiled young prince taking kindly to such intervention."

"Initially he was rather sulky," agreed Beresford. "But we have come to an understanding. He is very useful in spy work. He enjoys it."

Elinor let out a sigh, glad Beresford had not captured Jaq for his own gain. But Aldreda would be unimpressed to learn that Jaq was royalty.

Perry bounded across the lower deck to stand below them, the sea brightening behind him. "What of the gold, Lord Beresford? Must you really take it across to France?"

Beresford nodded. "I must sail within twenty-four hours. It is vital I keep my rendezvous."

"Will you steal it back?" Perry's eyes were bright with curiosity and admiration.

"Of course," put in Jaq, behind him. "With my help. Here, I will show you my secret entry to the ship." He dragged Perry off to the portside of the cabin, where Mademoiselle Laberche was admiring the view.

Elinor did not like the sound of Beresford's plan, but he did not give her time to object. "You must all go ashore soon. Chaperonage on this ship is completely insufficient, and you are being horrendously compromised." He leaned over the railing, and turned to look at her, the sun slanting across his face. "However, I will not marry you just to save your reputation." He smiled. "You will have to wait for another proposal."

The waves sparkled around them and the ship creaked underfoot. Elinor smiled back.

"Likewise you, my lord."

~

THE END

AUTHOR'S NOTE

Thank you for reading *The Lady Jewel Diviner*! If you enjoyed it, I'd really appreciate it if you took the time to write a a review. Reviews help other readers find the book, and they give me the encouragement to write more with these characters.

If you would like to know What Happened in London at the notorious garden party, you can read the prequel novella, *A Pendant for Trouble*, free and exclusive when you sign up to my newsletter: https://rosalieoaks.com/newsletter.

Book 2 in the Lady Diviner series, *The Moria Pearls* releases on 1 February 2021! Join Elinor and Aldreda for another mystery with plenty of tea, magic, and romance.

And please connect with me on Goodreads, Facebook and Twitter, I would love to hear from my readers!

Happy book devouring,

Rosalie

ROSALIE'S NEWSLETTER

Join my newsletter for your free copy of *A Pendant for Trouble*, the prequel novella to the Lady Diviner series: https://rosalieoaks.com/newsletter.

What *did* happen between Elinor and Beresford in London?

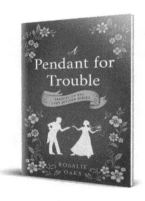

A PENDANT FOR TROUBLE

A mysterious pendant, a distracting earl, an unfolding scandal...

Miss Elinor Avely can't resist the call of a large jewel mysteriously concealed at a ducal garden party. After all, if the Earl of Beresford isn't attending, what else is Elinor to do with herself? Her talent for divining jewels can be an intriguing distraction for once, instead of a carefully guarded family secret.

Of course, her hunt for the jewel leads her straight into a mystery – and worse, an undignified encounter with Beresford. Yet when Elinor's quest goes from unseemly to scandalous, he is the one who tries to save her.

A Pendant for Trouble **is the prequel novella to the Lady Diviner series, where the magic, mystery, and romance all begins.**

Sign up for your free copy here: https://rosalieoaks.com/newsletter.

NEXT IN THE SERIES...

The Moria Pearls

A missing necklace, a murder, and an extra helping of plum pie...

The magical Moria Pearls are hidden somewhere in Devon, and Miss Elinor Avely and the tiny vampire Miss Zooth are on the case – but a certain washed-up selkie prince is determined to find the powerful necklace before they do.

Pearls aren't diamonds, curse it, so Elinor's secret gift for divining jewels cannot help this time. And the bossy Lord Beresford would rather she stay out of trouble. His opinion holds some weight, given that Elinor is hoping he might kiss her again soon.

When a selkie's murder disrupts the Devonwide hunt, however, Elinor is backed into a troubling corner. She might be able to find both the Moria Pearls and the killer... but everyone still believes that Miss Zooth is the diviner. Somehow, Elinor and her vampiric chaperone must maintain the façade, extend Elinor's divining gift, and find the pearls before the murderer does ... or risk forfeiting their lives.

Who poisoned the selkie? Where are the pearls? And just why *does* that plum jam taste so good?

Rosalie Oaks serves up the second novel in the Lady Diviner mystery series, full of magic, manners, and romance.

ALSO BY ROSALIE OAKS

The Lady Diviner series

A Pendant for Trouble (a prequel novella, free when you sign up
to Rosalie's newsletter)

The Lady Jewel Diviner (Book 1)

The Moria Pearls (Book 2)

The Sapphire Library (Book 3)

And don't miss out on *The Selkie Scandal,* another prequel
novella to the series, telling how Beresford and Jaq came to be
linked. Out in March 2021!

www.rosalieoaks.com

ABOUT THE AUTHOR

Rosalie Oaks writes magic, mystery, and romance into Regency England, with side servings of jam, jewels, and the occasional naked shapeshifter.

As a child, Rosalie loved conducting home-made theatre productions with her three younger brothers. Now she directs her characters instead, but like her brothers, they don't always do what she says.

Rosalie wants to live in a world where scones are good for you, cream is slimming, and she can make the perfect jam. While writing, however, she contents herself with vast quantities of tea and chocolate.

Join Rosalie's newsletter for bonus scenes, book gossip, and your free copy of *A Pendant for Trouble*: https://rosalieoaks.com/newsletter